SUICIDE OR MURDER?

"You don't believe it was suicide, do you?" Perlman asked.

"No," Hanson said.

"I read the whole chart. Looked at the way she was living her life. She had every high-risk behavior I could imagine, short of skydiving without a chute. Picking up strangers, unprotected sex, IV drug use. What am I forgetting?"

"Okay, she had borderline personality disorder. It's like blaming someone with a cold for sneezing. She was getting better."

"She was getting more paranoid. Which you know is normal for people with BPD under stress. Maybe she had decided to tell you less."

He frowned.

"Listen, Brian, in case you can't tell, I'm concerned. You're one of my best. I don't like what I'm seeing."

"You ever heard the story about Freud? He had a client, Jewish, who was nervous early on about the rise of the Nazi Party in Austria. Freud psychoanalyzed him, convinced him the anxiety was unresolved father issues, so the guy stayed put, wound up in the gas chamber at Auschwitz."

"Don't even get me started on Freud," she said. "What's your point?"

"Even paranoids can have real enemies...."

MARK SCHORR

BORDERLINE

LEISURE BOOKS   NEW YORK CITY

To Sima, my wife and in-house editor

A LEISURE BOOK®

August 2007

Published by

Dorchester Publishing Co., Inc.
200 Madison Avenue
New York, NY 10016

ISBN-10: 0-8439-5979-7
ISBN-13: 978-0-8439-5979-6

Printed in the United States of America.

Visit us on the web at www.dorchesterpub.com.

BORDERLINE

PROLOGUE

Henry "AK" Dekalb had earned his nickname two decades earlier, when he was thirteen years old and sprayed a rival gang member's car with an AK-47. Since then he'd been a suspect in a dozen killings involving disputes over drugs and territory. He was a striking figure, with a small gold star in a front tooth that he bared in a predatory smile. Weight lifting during frequent prison stints had given him Popeye-esque forearms. The hedonistic life when not imprisoned had resulted in a generous potbelly.

AK had moved to Portland in 1989 when his independent crack-dealing operation in Oakland was facing police scrutiny and, more scarily, intrusions by both Crips and Bloods. In Oregon, being unaffiliated was not a problem. He built his network and hired enough independent muscle to enforce his operations. His sloppy hits were characterized by gunmen wreaking havoc with Tec-9s, Uzis, or MAC 10s. In his most recent execution, a seven-year-old girl in the house next door to his target had been killed.

Wolf knew his violent history as he followed AK through the Lloyd Center, Oregon's biggest mall, with four major anchor stores, close to two hundred smaller businesses, and an ice-skating rink that had briefly hosted Tonya Harding. Walking a quarter-mile-long promenade was running the gauntlet of franchised America—Gap, Victoria's Secret, RadioShack, Lady Foot Locker, and on and on.

AK sauntered through a half dozen mall stores, a young woman on either arm, taking great pleasure in buying them clothing and accessories. The women had tight skirts and bare midriffs, looking a bit flashier than the typical mall rats.

Even with the women hanging on to him, AK took the time to flirt and banter with numerous other girls in the mall. He also had whispered conversations with several tough-looking young men. Some walked with him for a while, then dropped off and began talking into their cell phones.

Wolf watched the transactions from less than a dozen yards away. AK was a merchant king doing business with no sense of shame or fear of legal retribution. The mall was crowded with shoppers who scarcely noticed; the few who did more than glance in his direction were quickly intimidated into looking away.

Wolf carried a Sears shopping bag that made him look like just another happy shopper. He had a wool cap pulled low, hiding his hair and ears, with Gap clothes that made him look like a middle-aged guy trying to be cool.

Wolf had initially planned a quick hit-and-run with

a stolen car. But during a week of following AK, the gangster was never alone. There were bodyguards, bimbos, family members, or part of the large posse that clung to him like remoras on a shark.

AK led his entourage to the third-floor food court. At McDonald's he paid for fifty dollars' worth of Big Macs, McNuggets, and assorted side orders and beverages for the two women and three beefy young men who had joined him. At one point, AK threw pieces of food down from the balcony on the ice skaters below. His followers laughed and the girls fed him french fries.

After about a half hour he strutted, by himself, down the corridor to the men's room. Inside the bathroom, a couple of teenage dudes preened in front of the mirror. Wolf entered and used the urinal next to AK. Wolf nodded to him; AK gave his gold-toothed smile. "If you a fag, better go look elsewhere or I'll kick your motherfucking ass," AK said. "This ain't the showers at San Quentin."

The preening teens left. Wolf looked away, seemingly embarrassed. He reached into his pocket and took out a thumb-sized black aerosol container labeled "Security Pepper Spray."

AK deliberately bumped into Wolf and said, "Get outta my way."

"Sorry," Wolf said, driving a quick palm heel strike to AK's forehead. While the dealer was momentarily stunned, Wolf grabbed him in a headlock and sprayed the aerosol up his nose. The synthesized crack, four times a recreational dose, overstimulated AK's heart. The dealer's eyes grew wide and he reached to grab Wolf but crashed to the floor.

Wolf dragged AK's thrashing body into a stall. The drug dealer was still conscious, his saliva-frothing mouth pressed against the toilet.

"Didn't think it would end like this, did you, pretty boy?" Wolf whispered. Using toilet paper, Wolf pulled a dime bag of crack from his pocket and dropped it on the floor, half open.

As Wolf stepped out of the stall, a couple of young men were coming in. Their casual chatter about the movie they'd just seen stopped instantly when they saw AK's legs sprawled across the floor.

"Call security!" Wolf said. "This guy just OD'd."

The young men exchanged looks as if trying to decide what to do. Finally, they nodded their heads and hurried out.

They rushed to one of the food counters, trying to get the attention of a young cashier who was more interested in serving McFlurries. Eventually, she made the call to security.

Wolf left as attention focused on the men's room. The posse, seeming to realize their king was dead, abandoned the table to race toward the bathroom. Mall security rent-a-cops tried to establish a perimeter and keep the crowd back.

As he passed by the table, Wolf picked up an unopened Big Mac, fries, and a Coke, and headed to the parking lot.

CHAPTER ONE

Brian Hanson held the phone six inches away from his ear as Tammy LaFleur screamed on the other end. He could predict what her barely intelligible words would be.

"I tried to come in, really. But they were outside my apartment again, those men. They're watching me. They're probably listening in on this call right now." Her voice rose a notch in pitch and volume. "I don't care, you bastards, hear me?" Her voice lowered to a harsh whisper. "I know they're spreading rumors about me and I'm gonna get them. They think they got me, but they don't know who they're fucking with. I know about their tampering with my mail. Yeah, you bet I do. But anyway, that's why I couldn't come in."

If Brian charted that she had missed another appointment, her PO would revoke the twenty-eight-year-old's parole. Coming in for every-other-week counseling sessions was part of Tammy's plan to clean up charges of possession with intent to distribute, prostitution, and resisting arrest.

Layers of makeup did little to conceal the damage done during her ten years of methamphetamine use. She had gone from fashionably lean to gaunt, with strangely protruding silicone breasts. Her bleached blond hair looked brittle. Her nose, broken by an abusive boyfriend, listed slightly to the left. Her teeth would cost as much as a Lexus to restore to presentable.

In her early sessions with Hanson, she'd brought in five-year-old Glamour Shots. While carefully maintaining boundaries, he'd agreed how beautiful she had been. She had set goals of getting back that glow and recognized that she'd have to stay clean and sober, attend Narcotics Anonymous and an anger-management group, and keep counseling appointments.

The first few months she had been treatment compliant. Hanson had gotten optimistic, not that she'd be a beauty queen, but that she could swim out of the hopeless whirlpool she was in. Stop dating exploitative boyfriends. Maybe get her son back from child protective services custody. Resume community college classes to become a veterinary assistant.

Brian knew he'd changed in measuring success from when he'd first started in the mental health field, nearly twenty-five years earlier. Using veteran's benefits to get a master's in counseling after going through his own turmoil, he'd been convinced he could change the world. Don Quixote with a couch.

Her diatribe broke into his thoughts. "Why do I even bother calling in? You don't give a damn. No one cares. You're part of the whole fucking moneymaking system. Telling me what to do, not really helping. Making things worse. I'm better off without all of you stuck-up bloodsucking bastards."

God, what a schmuck I've been, he thought, as Tammy continued to spew her anger. It was a struggle most days to convey hope to his clients when he had little himself. For too many years he had seen people at their worst, vicariously absorbing jolts of their pain. On top of his own.

Tammy had missed two appointments already. With some clients, like those with ADHD or dissociative problems, Hanson would allow them to exceed the clinic's three-strikes rule. With those who had substance abuse or personality disorders, limits and consequences even-handedly enforced were vital to the therapeutic process.

His small office was near the waiting room and he could hear Mr. Edgars—an African American man in his sixties who was most at peace when he was in the waiting room of the Rose Community Mental Health and Addictions Agency—wailing and railing against the demons that haunted him. When on the streets his paranoia would cause him to waylay citizens, get picked up by police, and wind up in the psych ward. Mr. Edgars was harmless, but only those who knew him could tell. The wailing was louder than usual.

Tammy was talking about the conspiracy. "They know I've got proof. I'm involved with big names. You'd know 'em right off the bat. The newspapers would love it too. They don't know who they're messing around with. I'm gonna make those bastards pay and then go down to L.A. I got a cousin who's been an extra in a bunch of movies."

Tammy's delusions didn't have the obvious break with reality that Mr. Edgars's did. There were no aliens or CIA satellites beaming messages. Her beliefs were not plausible, but they were possible. Her paranoia could be coming from meth relapse or be part of her personality disorder. Still, Hanson wondered if she was experiencing a first major psychotic break and showing signs of schizophrenia. Usually it hit earlier, though the illness could have an insidious onset. Like most of the clients in the clinic, LaFleur already had several serious diagnoses.

"What do you want from me?" Hanson asked, trying to keep the weariness out of his voice. Phone crisis work was particularly difficult. There were no visual cues to assess, and he needed to find nonvisual ways to show the client that he was attentive.

"I gotta come in and see you. I don't want my PO giving me a hard time."

Hanson was about to wonder out loud how the PO would feel about her leaving the area with money she had extorted from the conspiracy that was persecuting her.

"I know you don't believe me," she said. "Maybe that's why I trust you. You're not trying to sweet-talk me. I might tell you a little. Guarantee it will rock your world. The conspiracy is bigger than you think. I've seen people at your center I know are involved."

There was more noise from the waiting room. A thump. Unintelligible sounds.

Because of his history and his being bigger and stronger than the largely female staff, Hanson was the de facto security guard. There had been talk at one point of having a real guard, but the majority of the staff felt that would "create an oppressive atmosphere." Instead, it was just added to his responsibilities.

"Okay, Tammy, I've got an opening at four p.m.," he said quickly. "If you don't make it in, I will notify your PO and close your chart for ninety days. Do you understand?"

"Thanks, Brian. Listen, I appreciate the slack you've cut me. I know you don't believe that I'm clean, but you know my UAs have been good."

It was not the time to talk about the fifty creative ways clients could beat a urinalysis. "Yes. Just be here at four."

"I will. I been thinking, maybe, like as an insurance thing, I should tell you my proof. You have to keep it confidential, right?"

"Unless there is a threat of imminent danger to yourself, someone else, or abuse of a child, senior, or developmentally disabled person." He had said it so many times during intakes that the exceptions spilled out like a menu recited by a bored waiter.

Another loud thump. The receptionist yelled, "Stop it! Stop it!"

"Tammy, I gotta go," Hanson said, hanging up and hurrying to the nearby waiting room.

Several clients had backed away. A few stared, wide-eyed. One woman didn't look up from the three-year-old *Ladies' Home Journal* she was reading. Mr. Edgars sang a hymn. Roxanne, a three-hundred-pound Caucasian woman, was as silent as Mr. Edgars was noisy. She sat in her usual corner, glowering at anyone who came in, her four shopping bags spread out around her. A couple contained food clearly past the expiration date.

A man and a woman thrashed around on the floor. They slapped at each other, more concerned with getting attention than actually doing damage.

Ginger, the always-emotional receptionist and file clerk, had climbed on top of the front counter and was screaming, "Stop it! Stop it, Fred!"

It had taken Hanson a fraction of a second to take in the scene. The door behind him opened and his supervisor, Betty Pearlman, barreled through. She was a stout woman with close-cropped gray hair and a no-nonsense manner. They'd worked together for more than ten years, had never had any contact outside of the office, but had a powerful camaraderie on the job.

She nodded to him and they went into action. Hanson grabbed the man's belt and yanked, his other arm dislodging the woman. Pearlman hustled the woman into an interview room in the back. Hanson easily ducked under the man's theatrical punch and grabbed his wrist, tugging the man forward. With his left arm he pushed up under the elbow, folding the man over. His movements were smooth, conveying the complete confidence of someone who had several years' inpatient experience as a psych tech.

"I'd like to talk with you," Hanson said. "If I let you stand upright, can we walk into the back without any trouble?"

"Okay," the balding thirty-year-old said docilely.

Another clinician who wasn't in session came into the waiting room to calm the other clients. And the receptionist.

Sitting in the six-by-ten cinder-block-walled treatment room, Hanson resisted the urge to give his sore shoulder a rub. He secured Fred's basic demographic information and was assured that the man wasn't suicidal or homicidal. "Okay, Fred, what's going on?"

The man wanted to complain about his wife. Hanson redirected him repeatedly, trying to get enough information to see if he was appropriate and eligible for treatment. Fred finally explained that police had dumped the couple at the center after responding to a half dozen domestic-disturbance calls at their apartment over the past week. The couple had been arguing about having a kid. He wanted to, she didn't. Hanson made a mental note that that would be his entrée into working with Fred. Hanson continued his assessment, drawing out that Fred had no prior treatment, drank "a few beers" every weekend and reported no substance abuse, had an uncle who had bipolar disorder but no other mental illness in the family. "Other than my wife, who's fucking nuts!"

Even though structured by Hanson's directed questioning, the conversation had helped the man de-escalate. It took a little more than forty-five minutes to gather the basic information, a tribute to Hanson's skill and Fred's willingness to talk.

"Well, I think there are issues we could work on."

"How nuts women are? Are you married?"

Hanson nodded, thought momentarily of his own marriage, then rapidly shifted his attention back to Fred. "I see you've got strong conflicts with your wife."

"Wouldn't you? I mean, she's—"

"We only have a few minutes left. I want you to know what we can help with and what we can't help with."

Fred nodded.

"Okay, you've got conflicts. In my experience, there's usually energy coming from both partners." Fred started to speak and Hanson cut him off. "Not always fifty-fifty. It may even be ninety-ten, but there are always some issues both partners can address."

Fred nodded.

"You want to have a child with her. I presume that means you want to stay together?"

Fred murmured, "Yes."

"You want your kid to grow up in a house where his parents are acting like they're part of the World Wrestling Federation?"

Fred almost smiled. "No."

"Fine. We can work on that." Hanson's words were gruff but his eye contact and warm facial expression were welcoming, a professional balance. "I'm going to talk with my supervisor, who's with your wife now, and see if we can develop a treatment plan for you two."

"That woman is your boss? You see, they're running everything."

"Do you want to try treatment with us or not?"

"I'll give it a shot."

"Go to the receptionist, complete the paperwork she gives you, and set an appointment for a week from today." They shook hands and Fred ambled out. His wife was exiting at the same time. They hugged, then locked in a passionate embrace in the waiting room. Only when Roxanne and Mr. Edgars began applauding did they break their openmouthed kiss and head out.

In the chart room, Hanson made a few brief notes while his memory was fresh. Pearlman came in and began writing as well. The steel-shelf-lined chart room, walls packed with binders filled with tales of sorrow, was like Rick's American Café in *Casablanca*. Somehow, everyone ended up there.

"Think they'll be back?" Pearlman asked.

"Probably not until the next time they need an audience for their drama."

Pearlman raised an eyebrow. "My, my, you're sounding more cynical than usual. That's pretty hard to do."

"Think I'm burning out?"

"What do you think?" she asked.

"Spoken like a good therapist."

She stared at him patiently, attentively.

"Therapeutic silence," he said. In their supervision sessions they could be like two veteran chess masters who knew each other's moves, yet could improve only by playing against each other. Hanson and Pearlman had about the same number of years of experience. At one point, before she had been hired, he'd been offered the clinical director position. He had declined, saying he preferred direct service work, even though it would have meant a five-thousand-dollar-a-year pay hike. Pearlman was now the chief clinical officer for the agency, which had seventy-five case managers and counselors.

"Yeah, I think I'm burning out," Hanson admitted. "I mean, I can take joy in handling Fred smoothly, but I've got little hope of seeing him change."

"Maybe," she said. The word was one of their ways of mutual acknowledgment. They both enjoyed the old Chinese story of the farmer who marries a beautiful girl and gets congratulations from everyone. When villagers say how great it is, he replies, "Maybe." Then she dies giving birth to their son. Everyone says how terrible that is, and he says, "Maybe." Then he inherits her family's large farm, and the villagers say how great that is. "Maybe." But the locusts come, and etc., etc.

"Maybe," he repeated.

During the course of the day the police brought in a man prone to suicidal gestures, whom they had once again talked down off the bridge. Initially officers had taken him to the hospital. Now they dropped him at the center.

Then Hanson met with a middle-aged Native American man with schizophrenia who had first been brought in by the police a year earlier, babbling an incoherent string of letters. While everyone else had been confused by the babbling, Hanson had recognized the "word salad" and its ingredients: Prick 25, Rough and Puffs, Bloop Gun, Oodles, Law, White Mice, REMF, Victor Charles.

Vietnam. The Salish Indian's first psychotic break had occurred while in combat and hadn't been noticed for three months. Hanson had worked with him for two years, gotten him to be aware of his symptoms, take his medications, connect with his family and tribe, and maintain his own apartment. Major achievements, and they had begun to talk about cutting back service to a quarterly check-in by phone.

Hanson's three o'clock appointment was with a girl who had been sexually abused starting at age eight. She was now sixteen and probably going to be in the system for life. She had made a suicide attempt after her thirty-five-year-old boyfriend forced her to get an abortion. He was now in jail for statutory rape. The girl was beginning to show glimmers of realizing that the rape was not her fault.

This is my city, Hanson thought, ironically amused that it had been named by *Money* magazine as one of the five best places to live in the United States. Property values were solid and reasonably priced compared to similarly sized cities. Employment rates had been steadily growing the past few years, while the crime rate had dropped precipitously. Portland had a temperate climate, minimal air pollution, a slew of great restaurants, the best bookstore in the U.S., and an award-winning mass transit system. The Cascade Mountains, the central Oregon desert, numerous rivers, and the Pacific Ocean were within easy driving distance.

By 4:15 p.m., he knew Tammy wouldn't show. Which was fine, since it allowed him to clean up the inescapable pile of paperwork. Including closing her chart.

CHAPTER TWO

It was a little past noon, and Johnny D's snores echoed through the shabbily furnished house. He was sleeping deeply after a long meth run. The last batch he had brewed was primo stuff, and he had sampled it. Then spent days sampling more.

Wolf knew that during the week Johnny D had also raped two women during late-night prowls. Meth made him horny, unable to sleep, and aggressive. He was skull-eyed, as twitchy as a raw nerve ending.

Johnny D had moved to the city from Los Angeles after running his deals and assaults for years. Six months in Portland, and he was building his networks, getting to know the neighborhoods and backyards. Johnny D prided himself on being a professional criminal.

His MO was always the same, going through back-yards until he found an unlocked rear window. He had learned tricks in prison, like to improvise at the scene and never to carry a weapon in case the cops stopped him.

Wolf, noting the irony that Johnny D's own rear window had been unlocked, padded toward the snores coming from the bedroom. Johnny D had been identified on many cases because of his poor hygiene. Rotting teeth and an aversion to showers earned him the nickname "the Stinky Rapist." Detectives checking street names had noticed "Johnny D" and gathered enough evidence to make an arrest. The case fell apart under a legal attack from the high-priced defense attorney he paid with meth money. Johnny D was a suspect in more than a hundred rapes in other cities and a dozen in town. Victims ranged from fourteen to seventy-two years old. Wolf knew that there was a meth lab in the garage and how much his meth sold for in pill, powder, or chunk form.

Johnny D snorted and Wolf tensed, ready to slit his throat with the foot-long K-bar knife he carried. When Johnny D settled down, Wolf grabbed the cigarette pack and matches from the cheap wooden dresser. He moved silently to the interior garage door, just off the living room of the ranch-style house. Wolf wore shoes one size too large and disposable latex gloves.

He found the organic solvents in big drums and chose one labeled ETHER. He spilled a rug-size puddle of ether on the floor, then uncapped the other cans. The air rapidly reeked of volatile chemicals.

Wolf returned to Johnny D, still deep asleep. Just to be sure, he grabbed the dealer in a powerful stranglehold. After a few semiconscious gasps, Johnny D breathed rhythmically. Wolf didn't worry about leaving marks—there wouldn't be much soft tissue left.

He dragged the dealer-rapist from the bed and set him in the garage next to the puddle. Then he went back to the bedroom and made the bed look like it hadn't been slept in. As soon as the firefighters saw the lab, they would call the hazardous-materials team. By the time the firefighters, the hazmat team, and the cops were done trampling things, they would find out a meth chef had died while brewing his poison. It would not be a high-priority investigation.

Wolf lit a cigarette, the most dangerous time in the whole operation. There was already a fair amount of flammable chemicals in the air. But he had calculated correctly, and nothing flared. He puffed until the cigarette was burning, then tucked it in the matchbook, tilted slightly up, at the edge of the puddle.

Knowing he had less than four minutes, Wolf moved briskly. Out the back door, through the backyard, around a hedge, and onto the street. Gray skies, light drizzle, few pedestrians. He had a wool cap pulled down on his head, covering his hair and ears. Probably unnecessary, but he wore a bushy glued-on mustache, the kind an eyewitness would remember, and he could toss as soon as he was safely away from the scene.

Two blocks from Johnny D's house, he got into his gray 2001 Honda Accord, as nondescript as a black shirt at a Goth gathering. It had plates he had borrowed from another Honda Accord he had found a dozen blocks from his house. He would switch plates back that night.

He started his car, tuning the radio to the light rock station. The music came on, and he slowly pulled away from the curb, checking his mirrors and diligently observing traffic laws. As he glanced at the digital clock on his dashboard, he heard a muffled *whump*. Within seconds, there was another explosion, then fire burst out of Johnny D's house. Wolf watched as pleased as a Cub Scout at his first campfire.

Brian Hanson stood in the doorway looking into his son's room. The bed was made, the night table clear. Shelves of books lay undusted. Fading posters for Smash Mouth and Barenaked Ladies were still stapled to the wall. Hanson had first felt like a parent and an old fogy when he'd had to order his son to "turn that music down." With his son gone, the house was too big, too quiet.

Jeff was a bright kid, an A student, popular, good-looking, a demon on the soccer field. Often when he had watched his son, Brian had wondered how someone as flawed as himself could have been part of something so wonderful. Always independent, Jeff had moved on to the University of Michigan. He maintained frequent e-mail contact but was already pretty much out of his parents' life.

Forcing himself to turn away, Hanson moved deeper into his West Hills home. Propped on stilts, the redwood deck that surrounded the house offered an exquisite view of the west side. The house was much more than he could have afforded on his salary alone. His wife's inheritance, and salary, made it possible. Four bedrooms, three baths, two fireplaces, sunken living room, finished basement. For many years, he'd had the habit of sitting in the hot tub on the deck, listening to sixties music, watching the sun go down. Often with his wife cuddled against him.

Jeanie now wanted to move to a smaller place in a fancier neighborhood. She raved about the Pearl District, the gentrified downtown, an area of half-million-dollar lofts, art galleries, and chichi restaurants. Many times she'd wanted to clear Jeff's room out, but Brian resisted.

In the months before Jeff's departure, Brian had seen her as a mother hawk, eager to push her baby out of the nest. Jeanie and Brian had been married for more than twenty years, but emotionally they were further apart than ever.

Jeanie wasn't in, of course. She'd left a message on his voice mail that she was working late. It was an unusual day when she'd get off at five.

He padded into the kitchen, grabbed a fried chicken TV dinner, and popped it in the microwave. The spacious kitchen was a study in gleaming stainless steel, highlighted by matching Jenn-Air stove, dishwasher, and refrigerator. The room was seldom used. Jeanie was a "Let's eat out" kind of cook. With access to a generous expense account, she was known by name at most of the better restaurants in town.

He wasn't hungry but ate, leaning on the counter. He heard the rain tapping at the aluminum porch awning. A soothing sound, though it reminded him of Vietnam. On good days, that was a time he almost believed hadn't happened. It had taken him so long to accept what he had seen and done. How much pain was there still to work through? It was hard to believe that he had been the same age as his son was now. When he had been a kid and had seen interviews with World War II veterans, and they'd cried over lost comrades and bloody battles, he'd thought they were so lame. With his youthful innocence and arrogance, he'd thought, That was more than twenty years ago— get over it. He'd since learned that some experiences once burned in would never go away.

Hanson sat in the bedroom that had been converted into the home office/den. A large desk was dominated by Jeanie's computer and stacks of papers she brought home from work. One wall was a floor-to-ceiling bookcase with two clear themes. The lower half, Jeanie's, held books on banking, accounting, investing, real estate law. The top half held his books on Vietnam, from classics like Michael Herr's *Dispatches* and William Broyles's *Brothers in Arms* to numerous volumes by lesser known and less talented writers. He had books that were long on detail and short on emotion, and others that screamed like an open wound. He had photo books that he never opened, since the images were never as powerful, but yet too close, to those he held within him.

Jeanie came in at nine. They no longer bothered to tell each other about their workdays. He found what she did hard to understand. Sometimes her decisions— like to foreclose on mortgages or not extend a non-profit's line of credit—offended him. She found his tales of the poor mentally ill and addicted to be sleazy and depressing. He was absorbed in his world, she in hers. They had negotiated a bored détente.

They watched TV and were in bed by eleven. She fell asleep within minutes. Whenever he closed his eyes, he flashed back to images of Vietnam. Waves of grief, remorse, and anger swept through him with tsunamilike power.

The first person he killed, a slender teen at close range. Probably a year or two younger than Hanson. The scarlet burst of the M16 5.56 mm round hitting a thin chest at a couple thousand feet per second. The retelling with his buddies, the macho boasting, not mentioning the throwing up, gasping-for-air feelings of horror, guilt, and "What if he'd shot first?" After his best buddy was killed by a sniper, the second killing was easier.

Juiced up on adrenaline and testosterone, then smoking marijuana and later heroin, as his personal body count climbed. He remembered the hard-eyed old guys, in their mid-twenties, offering tips. Use all your senses, you can smell 'em before you see 'em at night. No smoking, no bullshitting, no time off on patrol, noise discipline. Learning the implications of dozens of different shades of green in the triple-canopied tropical foliage. The telltale disturbance patterns of a *pungi*-stick pit in the rich loam. Differentiating the low of an alarmed water buffalo from the usual sounds. How to booby-trap a claymore so that when the VC went to disarm it, the claymore would explode. Learning to look slightly off side to maximize night vision.

His coworkers knew he had been in the war. But not the details. Many of them hadn't even been born. The Vietnam conflict was just a sour stain in their history books, not even a declared war. They could never understand. He couldn't understand it himself. He had come back from the war with his body unscarred and his mind a troubled mess. Heroin was too expensive in the States and he kicked it with surprising ease. Not so alcohol and pot, which helped control the nightmares and tremors. Then there was the anger, the fights, the nightlong wandering the streets looking for something he didn't know.

Bill McFarlane was only three years older, a cop, also a Vietnam combat veteran. One night when Hanson had been picked up drunk and disorderly, McFarlane had driven him to the outskirts of the city. Fear kicked in. Hanson sobered immediately.

"What's going on?" Hanson demanded from the back of the squad car.

They parked on a dark road at the edge of the Columbia Gorge. Douglas firs blocked out the moonless sky. McFarlane, with thinning, prematurely gray hair and a dangerous stare, took him out of the car and uncuffed him. The Mace, nightstick, flashlight, long-barreled .38 Smith & Wesson, spare ammo, and handcuff case hanging from McFarlane's Sam Browne belt rattled as he moved, making Hanson aware of how silent the isolated spot was.

"Scared, huh?"

"No," Hanson snapped.

"Bullshit. You're scared all the time. Not of fucking up, scared of what you've done, what you've become."

Hanson said nothing, breathing in the cool night air, not sure what was going to happen.

"I can take you in, feed you into the system. Six months from now, you'll be another scumbag vet hanging out on the street panhandling for cheap liquor. Or worse."

Hanson had seen a couple of guys he knew doing just that. The image haunted him.

"In a lot of ways, the VA sucks," McFarlane said, handing Hanson a card with a name and number on it. "But this guy is okay, runs a support group. Helped me get my shit together. If you go there with an open mind, who knows."

The two men stood by the squad car. Hanson nodded, McFarlane indicated he should get into the car, and they drove back into the city. Hanson still occasionally wondered what would have happened if he'd refused.

Later, McFarlane would be his sponsor as he worked his way through Narcotics Anonymous. He knew McFarlane had saved his life. The anger that made him a good soldier didn't dissipate when he was dumped back in the civilian world. It wasn't until he got to his eighth step, and started making amends, that the pressure within him started to abate. He'd gone into a Vietnamese restaurant and apologized to the owner for what he had done in his country. The owner turned out to be a former ARVN captain. They had talked long into the night about the extremes that young men endured and were warped by. Deep down, Hanson wondered whether it was ever possible to truly make amends for past misdeeds. But if not, how could he honestly talk with clients in therapy about forgiving others, and themselves, to be able to move on?

What had triggered his memories so vividly tonight? He decided it was having to grab Fred. It had been a while since he'd been in a scuffle. But something else was bothering him, bubbling up in his subconscious. In Vietnam, he had joked about his "spider sense," based on the then new comic-book hero who felt a strange tingling before trouble. Young soldiers would get comic books mailed from the World. *The Fantastic Four*. Look out, creeps, it's clobberin' time. *The Amazing Spider-Man*. *Sgt. Fury and His Howlin' Commandos*. The comics would be passed around until they fell apart in the tropical humidity. Almost, but not quite, as popular as *Playboy*.

Hanson now knew the spider sense was probably what mental health professionals labeled "hypervigilance." In trauma survivors, it was the on-the-edge feeling that could warn of a blow before the attacker completed the thought. In part, the sensitivity was what made him an effective therapist.

He focused on his breathing, trying to relax. It was a long time before he finally fell asleep.

Louis Parker had ten years clean and sober but still went to an AA meeting a day. The seventy-year-old lived alone in a downtown single-room-occupancy hotel. He had a dignified presence, wanted little social service support, and always seemed to be on the verge of disclosing a big secret. At first Hanson didn't believe his stories. But the sharp-eyed Parker, who had the battered face of the bantamweight boxer he had once been, was intriguing enough that Hanson had visited the newspaper office and verified several of his tales in their archives.

Parker had been a private investigator, the buddy of a lawyer who became the mayor in the seventies. It had been a heady time of growth and corruption, and Parker had been right in the midst of it. The mayor had been wiretapped by the feds and caught taking money, and had turned on everyone around him, including his buddy. Parker served three years at the minimum-security prison in Sheridan, Oregon. Being a convicted felon with a swiftly growing alcohol problem had kept Parker from ever holding another high-paying job.

Hanson allowed himself a few lower-acuity clients at the clinic, and Parker was one who wasn't in extremis. Parker set goals and met them, sort of. Not suicidal, homicidal, or indulging in high-risk behaviors. When questioned, he'd get vague and segue into an anecdote about bringing prostitutes into city hall for a council meeting, or tell a story about "tailing some moke." He often sounded like a character out of a hard-boiled detective novel but seldom took himself seriously. Hanson liked the feisty Parker and let himself be distracted. Their appointments might not be therapy, but they were therapeutic. Enhancing the aging ex–city aide's self-esteem, he rationalized. And elderly white men did have some of the highest suicide rates.

"Yeah, I remember when this town had a personality. Hey, Doc, you know where the words 'skid row' came from?" Parker liked to sprinkle his conversations with factoids, delivered in a self-amused staccato.

"No." Hanson had told him several times he was neither a Ph.D. nor an M.D., but the older man was more comfortable addressing him as "Doc."

"They used to let the lumber skid down to the harbor to load on ships. Muddy, sloping, dangerous streets by the waterfront. Who'd wanna be there but bums? Never thought I'd wind up there."

"That reminds me, did you set an appointment with the housing specialist from Senior and Disabled Services?"

"It's two months out. I wouldn't be surprised if they screw with me," Parker said with a sneer that was more endearing than menacing. Parker repeated a story Hanson had heard a couple times before, about when the bantamweight had gone toe-to-toe with a corrupt bar owner. "You know, Doc, I got enemies in this town."

His words reminded Hanson of LaFleur. The counselor wondered what excuse she would use when she called in. Would he allow her back sooner if she admitted a relapse and agreed to treatment? He made a mental note to call her parole officer.

Hanson turned his attention back to Parker and nodded along. Funny that his mind was drifting—usually he stayed focused in session. Even if a story was repeated, there was a detail or nuance that would make listening worthwhile. People repeated themselves until they felt heard.

Tammy LaFleur lurked in his thoughts. Was it because she was seductive and his marriage was stalled? Or that his desire to rescue was overcoming his common sense? He should talk with Pearlman about it.

"Yeah, I oughta do a book. I ain't told you even half the stories."

"We've talked about your journaling."

"Yeah, the stuff I could tell you. Maybe you could write it down."

"It's more therapeutic for you to do it."

"Ah, I never liked writing. Fieldwork was my thing.

Still keep my police scanner going. Hey, Doc, that reminds me, I heard bad news about one of your clients."

"You know I can't confirm if someone is my client or not."

"You don't have to be coy with me, Doc. She and me spent some time in the waiting room together. Plus we were in that symptom-management group together. Her name was Tammy, a flashy blonde."

"Tammy?"

"They found her yesterday. Shot in the face. Saying it was suicide, which don't sound kosher to me. A pretty babe like that, she'd put on a fancy dress, do it up with pills, lay herself out on the bed like a movie star. 'Cause it's always possible she might've just blown her head off. We're all nuts here, right?"

"You seem pretty blasé about it," Hanson said, stunned and trying to sound composed.

"What do you expect me to do, break down bawling?" Parker shrugged. "It's a pity. She was a nice girl. Well put together, in a high-maintenance kinda way. But she was cuckoo for Cocoa Puffs, if you know what I mean. Started asking if I wanted to do bodyguard work for her. Coming on flirty. Like if she needed a bodyguard, I'd really be able to do much. And if she didn't, well, then she was nuts. Twenty years ago, I would've probably fallen for it." Parker switched to a high-pitched voice, "'I bet a big strong man like you could keep me safe.' You wanna know a benefit of getting old? You're not led around by your schlong so easily. Hey, you look pale."

"I'm okay. A bit of a surprise."

"It's nice seeing you get upset," Parker said with a

grin. "Tammy and me, we're numbers in the system. You think John Q. Citizen would give a flying fuck if we turned up dead? Less of a drain on the taxpayers. Nice to see you give a damn."

Hanson was silent, still absorbing the news.

"Don't feel so bad. She was a big girl, she made choices. Like, I've got a niece and a nephew. Both of them were sweet kids and visited me when I was in prison. My nephew wound up a biker in San Francisco, got killed a couple years back. My niece is a hotshot FBI agent. Sometimes it's bad luck, sometimes bad choices. Mainly a mix of both." Parker looked at his watch. "Well, as you usually say now, 'Our time is about up.' See you in two weeks, at this time?"

"Sure."

Hanson had ten minutes before his next appointment, with phone calls to return to a couple of welfare workers, a Child Protective Services worker, a parole officer, and a Social Security hearing officer. Plus a few from clients.

But he sat and focused on his breathing. The small room was stuffy, a couple of cheap, brightly colored lithographs on the wall, the well-worn furniture looking like hand-me-downs from a seedy motel lobby. He could hear the ineffective ventilation wheezing stale air. The smells of body odor, cigarette smoke clinging to clothing, beery breath in the morning. Too many people with too many problems in too small a space.

Tammy LaFleur was dead. He had lost clients before, of course. Working with Portland's most troubled, it was inevitable. How much of his concern was caring about her, how much of it was a feeling of failure? The catcher in the rye, missing the kids as they went over the cliff.

If she had been an open client he would be responsible for notifying the state so it could investigate. Deaths of mental health clients that might be related to their symptoms were supposed to be investigated, to make sure there was no abuse or neglect. Did her death occur when her chart was still open?

He checked the "In/Out" board. Pearlman was attending a meeting at one of the other sites. The mental health agency had eight clinics around the county. Hanson was stationed at the largest, in the downtown area, with the most intense clients. He could have used his seniority to be transferred to a quieter site. His wife urged him to so he would have more energy for a private practice or to go back to school and earn a Ph.D. By staying downtown, he got to work with the hardcore, those who had been kicked hardest by Lady Luck, those who had made the worst decisions, those whom society wanted least.

There wasn't any staffer around he felt he could talk to. He provided clinical supervision for half the counselors and liked his role as the "wise old man," the person that others went to. Half of them were just out of grad school—who else would take such a low-paying, high-stress job?

After a few minutes of relaxation breathing, he was composed enough for his next appointment, Brittany, a teenage girl who had cut on her arms and thighs. Small neat slices which had alarmed her parents.

"People cut on themselves for lots of different reasons," he began his session with the slender girl with long red hair and dark makeup.

Brittany regarded him with adolescent distrust. "Like what?"

"Some people do it because they dissociate, zone out, and the cutting helps them stay grounded. Others cut because it helps them zone out. Some like to see the blood, to make internal pain visible. Some feel it is a good way to punish themselves, others are seeking attention. A few hope to scar their bodies in certain ways. Peer pressure when a bunch of girls are doing it. Maybe something you read about. And some want to kill themselves. I leave anything out?"

She pouted, then smiled. "You've worked with people who cut? I'm not nuts?"

"More than a few people, mainly girls, do try it. A very small percentage actually kill themselves. I had one girl, an artist, damaged her tendons and weakened her hands, very sad." He paused. "But most recognize cutting isn't a good idea."

"Tell me about it," Brittany said, bobbing her head. "I took a shower and they stung like a son of a bitch." She smiled, curled up into the chair, and played with her brightly colored sneaker laces.

As they talked, he saw her as a young Tammy LaFleur, and he was aware of his own countertransference, thoughts about the dead woman. He forced himself to refocus on Brittany, and the session went well. Afterward he hurried to where the charts to be closed were stacked. Perennially understaffed in clerical as well as clinical areas, there was often a week-long backlog before paperwork was done.

What was hard about accepting her death? Client death was an occupational hazard for community mental health. Suicide, getting killed by an ex-partner, police, angry drug dealer, hepatitis, HIV, car accident, overdose. Not what would be boasted about on the chamber of commerce's posters for "the Largest Small Town in America."

"Is everything okay?" Michelle Benjamin asked. She was a dark-brown-eyed social worker, fresh out of grad school and full of enthusiasm. Hanson had the feeling she would take most of the clients home, like a little girl taking in errant puppies. He had known counselors who actually had taken clients home and usually found everything they owned, and the client, gone. He'd seen dewy-eyed do-gooders become cynics and change careers.

"Yeah, sure."

She stared at him as he rooted through the "Terminated" charts in a big, blue Rubbermaid bin.

"Really?"

His urgent movements made his words a transparent lie, but he didn't want to tell her his true concerns. He was the wise old man, after all. "I had a client suicide," he admitted. "I had discharged her recently."

"I'm sorry," she said.

"Thanks."

She nodded respectfully. "I appreciate you sharing that. It's good for me to know that even someone as experienced as you can have that happen."

He gazed into her concerned, idealistic face.

"Do you want help looking?" she asked.

"I bet you've got a client scheduled."

She nodded.

"I can handle it."

She squeezed his shoulder supportively before hurrying away. He dug into the stack of charts, finding LaFleur's after a few moments. He took it to his office and shut the door. Most clinicians shared a large, open bullpen, walls plastered with crisis alert sheets and notices of concerts for worthwhile causes. As a supervisor he had his own office, with a window. By corporate standards it was a couple notches up from a janitor's closet; by community mental health standards, it was the corner office with a private executive bathroom. About eight by twelve feet, it looked out on a busy street where he could watch the police bust an occasional drug transaction or roust a drunk from the dingy doorway of the Somewhat Honest Bob's Pawn Shoppe. The sleazy businesses—tattoo parlors, pawnshops, shabby hotels, and raunchy bars—had been crammed into a few-block area downtown, and that included the main social service agency offices.

What was he looking for? Closure or proof he had done right? Paperwork oversights or justification? Was the answer to his distress somewhere in the chart?

He skimmed the demographic and financial-eligibility information, as well as her signature on the informed-consent forms that laid out treatment expectations. He jumped to recent progress notes, where she had sounded more upbeat. He knew that suicidal clients sometimes appeared happier once they had made up their minds that death was the best way to solve their problems. But there was none of that feeling with Tammy. Despite her evident paranoia, she seemed to look forward to her future. No disconcerting giving away of belongings or declining to make plans.

She spoke of her father as "neglectful or bullying" and her mother as "passive" and "more concerned about appearances than anything else." She had refused to identify her parents, but vague references to vacations and living in West Slope made it clear that they were upper-middle-class. She graduated high school, took a year of community college toward becoming a veterinary assistant, then was licensed as a cosmetologist. She became an "exotic dancer," and had her first arrest for prostitution at age eighteen.

There were hints of grandiosity, or maybe her stories had been true. "Dates" with two visiting basketball players, an aging rock star on tour, three nationally known politicos at a convention. Reminded of her Glamour Shot, he thought it might be possible. Young, pretty, wild, available, exploitable.

Over the next four years, two arrests for drugs and another for prostitution, birth of a son, with six men the possible father. Taken away when he was three by Child Protective Services for her involvement with a guy who ran a sleazy bar. Then she seemed to have quieted down. Maybe she had gotten old enough to realize she wasn't immortal.

The knock at the door jolted him. "C'mon in," he said, hastily closing the chart.

It was Pearlman. "Michelle said you were upset. Had a client die."

At times the center felt like a family, with a similar level of support and intrusiveness.

"I'm okay." How many times had clients told him that, meaning, "I'm miserable"? But was it an opening to probe or a way of saying, "Back off"?

"Which client?" she asked, and he held up the chart.

"Tammy LaFleur," she said, reading the label. "We talked about her in supervision a few weeks ago, didn't we? Had been stable, with increasing paranoia?"

He nodded, impressed as usual with her memory.

"She was closed?"

"Maybe. Not sure if she killed herself before I did the paperwork or not. And the closure certainly hasn't been entered into the computer system."

"Your call?"

He understood what she was saying. If the client was open, they would have to do a critical-incident review and forward their conclusions to the state. If she was closed for any substantial period, there was a quick in-house review, and a one-sheet follow-up was added to her chart.

"I'd like to do a full critical-incident review."

She sighed. "I knew you would."

It meant more paperwork, more staff time away from direct service. But it would help give him closure. A bureaucratic funeral. Which reminded him of a real funeral. He looked at the emergency contact number. Pat Grundig. The name was vaguely familiar. It didn't specify the relationship, and he presumed the police had notified related parties. He had had to do it enough times, brought in as the mental health professional who should do better at breaking terrible news, even though there was no good way to tell people that they would never be seeing a loved one again.

"You'll set it up?" Pearlman asked, referring to the review.

He nodded.

"If you want to talk, you know where to find me," she said.

Hanson rescheduled a couple of clients who could bear canceling and put off two clinical supervision sessions in the afternoon. He left a voice mail for the agency medical director to arrange a time for the critical-incident review. He also left voice mails for a case manager involved in Tammy's treatment, as well as the leader of the coping skills group she had been in. Once he set a possible time, he'd notify Pearlman, and they could complete the review in a half hour.

He called the police and tried to get information about the death. "What's your relationship to her?" the clerk at the other end of the line asked.

The right to confidentiality survived death unless there was strong evidence that disclosure would be to the benefit of the client. Which was hard to argue when the client was dead. Confidentiality could also be broken if it could be shown that it would help catch the killer. But when the victim was the killer . . .

"I'm her brother."

"When's her birthday?" the clerk asked.

"February 25, 1978," Hanson said, reading from the chart.

"I can release basic information over the phone. Your sister died from an apparent gunshot wound to the face. She died at roughly four o'clock p.m.," the woman said, stiffly reading from a form. "Official cause of death will be determined by an autopsy which is scheduled for later today. If you wish additional information, you need to go in person to the medical examiner's office with photo identification. Do you want that address?"

"No."

"I'm sorry for your sister."

"What?"

"I'm sorry. I've had my share of tragedies. I know how hard it is."

"Thank you."

"God bless," she said, and hung up.

He allowed himself a few minutes to contemplate the sorrow. Tammy's, the clerk's, his own. The thought of numbing out with a drug came sudden and strong. Heroin was best—it had gotten him through Vietnam. Marijuana was a close second, liquor a distant third. No matter how many years had passed, the craving crouched in the darkness like a hungry tiger. He knew he would never relapse, but how many addicts said the same thing as they called their dealers?

He dialed a number.

CHAPTER THREE

As her white garage door went up, Jeanie Hanson saw her husband's parked 1989 gray Volvo sedan. Strange, since it looked like the lights in the house were off. She carefully pulled her red 2004 Acura coupe into the cluttered two-car garage. She was home early, for her, a little after 7 p.m.

She stretched as she got out of the car, wishing it were with catlike grace, but more with the body of a tired, middle-aged woman. She did yoga and Pilates, and exercised at least four times a week. She ate right, took vitamins, and hadn't smoked in twenty years. Still, just like Brian's car needed more maintenance than hers, she knew she was valiantly fighting a losing battle. With her hair dyed a light brown, artfully applied makeup, and the right lighting, Jeanie could pass for a dozen years younger than her forty-five, and most days she felt like a thirty-something. Last night, however, Brian had been restless, waking her with a nightmare he wouldn't discuss. Anyone would be fatigued after a night like that, she told herself.

She felt most youthful with the joy of closing a deal, that final handshake, the papers signed, the smiles. Or the frowns of the opposition. The spirit was in her blood. Her father had been one of the town's most successful real estate lawyers. She had put the jugular instinct aside, married a decent man, stayed at home to raise their child. By the time Jeff was entering middle school, she was halfway to her MBA, working through the state university external degree correspondence program. The day he started high school, she'd mailed out résumés and begun networking. Jeanie had thrown herself into work like a Doberman unleashed, rising to become a vice president for operations at Pacific Northwest Bank. It was her father's name that got her initial interviews. But it was her skill, personality, and determination that made her the fastest-rising female executive within the company.

She dropped her thin, burgundy leather Vuitton briefcase in the usual spot and kicked off her matching shoes. While Brian favored Reeboks, she had thousands invested in Ferragamos and Pradas. Where he was content with a Timex, she insisted on a Swiss twenty-one-jewel Movado. For him, Eddie Bauer was fancy shopping, where she would be embarrassed to be seen anywhere less than Saks or Nordstrom. Despite numerous lectures on the importance of dressing for success, which he called "dress to impress," they could never agree.

"Brian? Brian?"

The lights were off. He was sitting in the maroon

Barcalounger that faced the picture window to their small backyard. Staring straight ahead. The view was pleasant, but not spectacular. Layers of rhododendrons and camellias, the blooms long gone, coupled with a few spindly rosebushes. She was scared, then angry. She'd seen him sink into dark moods before.

"What is it, honey?" she asked. "Bad day?"

He grunted assent.

"Let me slip out of this and we can talk."

He didn't respond.

In the bedroom upstairs, she undid the strand of Mikimoto cultured pearls from around her neck, then eased off her gray wool, knee-length Armani skirt and matching jacket, silk slip, and nylons. She gazed at herself in the floor-to-ceiling mirror, knowing the demise of their romance wasn't due to her physical appearance. She slipped on a puffed red terry-cloth robe with nothing underneath it.

How long had it been since they had been intimate? Several months, at least. Jeanie still found him attractive, though he was a lot hairier and a bit chunkier than when they first met. His moods could go several different ways. Depression, which would last a couple weeks. Angry outburst, which was brief but could lead to a week of bruised feelings. On rare occasions, she could talk and soothe him out of it. But first she had to get over her own frustration with him.

Gliding down the stairs, she remembered how mad her father had been when she brought home a psych tech, "a goon from the state hospital" he had said, after she made the mistake of asking what he thought of Brian. That had only made Brian more desirable to her. He was a combat veteran with deep-set, brooding eyes, a couple of years drug-free, and the desire to save the world. Oh, the passion he'd had, for school, for work, for her. Now he was an okay guy, but nowhere near as sophisticated as the men she spent her days with.

She knew better than to approach him too quietly. He startled easily and once, on awakening from a nightmare, had grabbed her by the throat. He had let go instantly, but she'd had to to wear high turtlenecks for two weeks while the bruises healed.

"Would you like to talk?" she asked, moving closer to him. She sat on the arm of the chair and ran her hand through his hair. Her robe gapped open artfully.

After a long silence, he said, "Just work stuff."

"You want to tell me?" She began massaging the tight muscles of his trapezius.

"You really want to hear about it?"

"Sure."

"This client killed herself. She had promise. I thought she was turning her life around. It hit me harder than I thought it would. I had a killer craving."

"What did you do?"

"Called my sponsor, McFarlane. He agreed to ask his cop buddies a few questions about the death and meet with me tomorrow."

"He's still a policeman?"

"Detective sergeant now. Used to be in homicide and still has friends there. He agreed it was weird that my client had shot herself in the face."

"You think it wasn't suicide?"

"I don't know. Women prefer pills. That's why women attempt suicide three times more often than men, but men succeed twice as often."

"Charming," she said.

"Almost no one shoots themselves in the face. More than three-quarters of the time in the temples, another twenty percent or so in the mouth, the remaining right in the heart."

"Ecch. Maybe she put it in her mouth, decided not to, then jerked it out but accidentally pulled the trigger."

"Possible, not probable."

"You're sure you're not trying to find a reason where there is none? I mean, you'd feel better if it was murder, right?"

He didn't answer.

"It's too bad, honey. But you know how it is with those people you work with," she said, rubbing his neck. "What about trying private practice?"

"You don't understand. I gave her short shrift in my last contact with her. I was distracted, dismissive. She . . ."

"I know how dedicated you are. For what?" She struggled to control the pressure to speak.

"She deserved more," he said. "She deserved better."

"You spend every day wallowing in the sewer of the city. There's a nicer world out there. Normal people with normal problems."

"Normal," he said with a snort.

"We've had this discussion before."

"Right. You'll be telling me how I could get a doctorate, I'll tell you it doesn't pay at my age. You'll ask where my ambition went, I'll ask where your greed came from. You'll talk about the promise I had, I'll point out that ultimately what I do contributes to humanity, while you profiteer in fancy clothes."

She pulled her robe tight around her. "Why don't

we save some time?" she asked through clenched teeth. "It's a big house. We can stay apart and avoid talking altogether." She marched away.

He opened his mouth, about to speak, but ultimately didn't suggest alternatives.

The next morning in the gym, she used her leftover anger to push herself to new limits. The Metro Gym was the one of the city's premier places to work out. That applied to muscles, as well as dating, making business contacts, or being seen in the right spot. High-ceilinged, inside a renovated warehouse from the 1920s, Metro had the trendiest machines and the best personal trainers. Even in the locker room there were no funky odors, as if the rich and powerful members didn't sweat.

After a few stretches she punched in her usual program, electronically tilting the treadmill to a ten-degree angle. A video of a country road played before her, and with arms swinging she strode briskly, soon feeling her pulse climbing. She didn't need to check the computer to know she was above her target rate.

He was a couple of machines over, listening to headphones, working hard. Jeanie had seen him before, many times. She had asked at the desk, telling them he looked familiar, which was true. She had found out he was deputy mayor Tony Dorsey. Then she'd seen him at a couple of zoning board meetings, quiet, in the background, watching. Rumor was that the mayor wouldn't floss his teeth without checking with Dorsey. He was handsome, a Russell Crowe type, smugly self-confident. Well muscled, with an intense gaze, he was probably a few years younger than she.

She moved to the free weights and followed her routine, dreading the flappy, flabby triceps look. After thirty minutes, she finished with a half hour on a recumbent bicycle. Five minutes into her closing routine, Dorsey began pedaling on the bike next to her.

"Not that crowded today," she said, telling herself it was an innocuous comment. And even if she got to know him, it would help the bank, she rationalized.

The deputy mayor smiled, simultaneously neutral and predatory. "Yeah." He had headphones on and was listening to a silver, ultracompact sports MD Walkman. He wore a gray spandex outfit with a black stripe that highlighted his muscles.

They pedaled a couple more minutes. He glanced over again with an all-knowing smile. She enjoyed flirting, particularly with good-looking, powerful men who could help her career. She had never gone further than flirting—the gentle pat on a senior banker's thigh when he told a risqué joke, the slightly extended gaze into a real estate attorney's eye when he boasted of closing a deal, the subtle wiggle in her walk when she knew the owner of a mall was watching her behind.

She had seen the change in her mother after her parents divorced. Her mother had gone from being a put-upon hausfrau to a pseudo-socialite. Jeanie recalled the many nights she was left home alone, and heard her mother coming in with a new vulture, eager to peck at her reputation and clear out her dwindling cash.

It was during those long early conversations with Brian that she was able to get perspective. He had been helpful back then, reassuring that he wouldn't abandon her. Now his leaving probably would be doing her a favor, she mused.

"What're you listening to?" she asked.

"Seven Habits of Highly Effective People," he said. "I review it every six months or so."

She nodded approval. "Stewardship, moral compass, listen to be heard, and all of that."

He nodded back. They discussed Peter Drucker, Peter Senge, and Tom Peters, theories of knowledge workers, learning organizations and systems, and adaptability. They scoffed at pop business books like *Who Moved My Cheese?* while acknowledging that Ken Blanchard had a lot of wisdom in his thin books.

She got up with a slow sinuousness that she saw he noticed. She moistened her lips ever so slightly, saying, "Boy that juice bar is tempting."

"Agreed," he said, as if she had been overtly inviting him.

Sipping overpriced, vitamin-fortified fruit drinks at a small round glass table in the corner, they chatted about mutual acquaintances, acknowledged they had seen each other before at the gym and at meetings. "I'm surprised you remembered I was there," she said.

"You're a strikingly attractive woman," he said, making it sound more like a pleasant observation than a come-on.

She felt a deep warmth that she knew didn't come from exercise. His cool gray eyes locked on hers, his lips in a relaxed half smile. "Quite a workout today," she said, taking a few slow breaths.

"Uh-huh," he said, nodding slowly. "You know, it's lucky we met."

The heavy beat of the aerobics-class music thumped through the floor, filling the silence between them. She waited for him to speak, noticing how fine his eyelashes were. His strong jaw bristled with five o'clock shadow, and she wondered how rough it would be against her soft skin. He seemed to be taking his time, enjoying letting her study him.

"That urban growth boundary extension for the Springfield mall, it's important for the city." She eagerly rushed into talking business, realizing how gawky their flirting had made her feel. "There've been some missed deadlines, procedural hang-ups. It's a major project. Will mean lots of jobs, will expand the tax base by—"

He waved his hand, cutting her off. "I'm off duty now. How about we discuss it over lunch, say, this Friday?"

"Uh, I don't know."

"Okay. I'll have my assistant prepare a statement of our concerns. You can bet I've gotten a stack of them from environmentalists and some of the old farm families out there. I'll just fax it over to your office and you can prepare your rebuttal."

The flirtatious warmth was gone. She recognized the tactic, had seen her father do the same thing during negotiations, go from Mr. Softie to cold-eyed killer when he wasn't getting his way. The message was clear—lunch, or she was just any old constituent with a concern.

"Of course the EIR hasn't come in yet, and—"

She boldly interrupted him. "You're right. We shouldn't be talking about environmental impact reports when we're supposed to be in cool-down mode. I wanted to say I have to check my calendar. I would much rather discuss it over a nice lunch than fire memos back and forth. Unless *you* would prefer that?"

He smiled. "A chance for a nice lunch and conversation with a beautiful woman, or sitting in my office making notes on the computer. Tough choice." He stood up and gently squeezed her shoulder. "I better go take a cold shower." He paused, making the words rich with innuendo. She could feel the power in his hands and almost expected him to lean over and kiss her. "Call my assistant and set an appointment."

She sipped her drink until the glass was dry. That would be some lunch. He'd pick the place. Different restaurants had different reputations, nothing to do with the cuisine they served. Power lunch, high visibility versus romantic quiet chat. A place to be seen, or a place to whisper. It would be interesting to see which he would pick.

The deputy mayor sauntered into his office with even more bounce than usual. His assistant, Edith, who had worked for him for a half dozen years, noticed and grinned. "Satisfying workout at the gym?"

"Definitely, Edith my dear." A few years from retirement, she was a career civil servant who knew the best gossip. Efficient and as tightly wound as her bun of gray hair, Edith was his loyal and protective gatekeeper.

Dorsey's office was dark red wood, and it would have been coffin-like except for the huge windows. He kept the thick blue velvet drapes pulled back most of the time, enjoying both the view of the greenery around City Hall Park and any chance at sunlight. He missed the warm climate, but that was another life.

He had eight voice mails and twenty-seven e-mails. Mayor Robinson had a press conference at 1 p.m. on an appointee to the school board getting charged with drunk driving. Dorsey would meet with the press secretary in an hour and prepare the response, then brief Mayor Robinson. Dorsey insisted that the mayor needed to make a statement rather than issue it through his press secretary, to show his concern on this hot-button issue. Robinson had potential. He was known to be tough on crime, and the city's plunging crime stats had been the subject of national media attention. There had been rumblings of a Senate race.

Edith buzzed him: "Chief Forester—he already called once. Do you want me to take a message?"

"Put him through. . . . Hey, Chief."

"How did it go?"

"I got my pulse rate up to one eighty, did twenty minutes on the StairMaster, and bench-pressed three hundred."

"You know that's not what I mean. With her?"

"I got the first piece of the pipeline in place. With any luck, before long I'll be laying some pipe."

"Don't let your dick do the thinking."

"I thought you were a God-fearing man. I'm shocked hearing that sort of language from you so early in the morning."

"Dorsey, I know about your habits."

"What, you wish I was like your son? Not interested in girls?"

There was a long silence, and the deputy mayor could imagine the chief's face reddening. His son was openly gay, and the Fundamentalist Christian police chief struggled to maintain control whenever the subject was brought up.

"Listen, Chief, I'll do what needs to be done with

her. I've got my priorities right. Which reminds me, what the hell was your guy thinking when he pulled over the mayor's latest appointee to the school board? Are you a team player or what?"

"Your boy was weaving all over the road. A couple people called 911. There were witnesses when he just about fell out of the car. Blood alcohol was .28. My officers recognized him and tried to smooth it out, but there was a news team monitoring the scanners. They were there within five minutes."

Dorsey sighed. "Okay. I'll keep you posted on my progress with Jeanie Hanson. You want the juicy details?"

"No. This was supposed to be a reconnaissance."

"Well, it could turn into a deeper probe if I'm lucky," Dorsey chuckled. "And I'm usually lucky."

"We've got an important thing going on here," Forester said. "We're taking back the streets, seeing what effective policing can do."

"Yeah, right," Dorsey said cynically. "You know what's driving the change. I got a better idea for you— why not set up a surveillance camera and Jeanie Hanson and I could do a movie like Tommy Lee and Pamela Anderson, or Paris Hilton and that guy. Sell it on the Internet to balance the budget. Would you buy a copy?"

Forester hung up. Dorsey set the phone down, grinning. He put his feet up on his desk and gazed at the city flag, the state flag, and the American flag, poking from a heavy brass stand in the corner. Who would have thought a dozen years ago he would be where he was today?

Pissing off the police chief was almost as much fun

as seducing another man's wife. It was one of the few pleasures he allowed himself. The late-night club-hopping, speeding around Third World capitals in a Land Rover, the drugs, multiple combinations of flashy female partners, the decadent pleasures of his younger life, were gone. Now he was tied down with a wife, three kids, and a well-maintained house in a better part of town.

He thought about the drunk-driving charge. Some flaw could be introduced into the arrest. It sounded like the police had more than probable cause, but maybe the Breathalyzer was defective. Still, there were the witnesses to the erratic driving. Maybe the appointee could have been having an allergic reaction to medication or a bee sting. There might be problems with the subsequent search or the way he was advised of his rights. But having the police look bad on this high-publicity case would have worse ramifications.

Ultimately, Dorsey decided the appointee would resign. Maybe get another chance at the office in a year, after completing treatment. He came from a family that was one of the larger contributors to Robinson's campaign. The family liked the respectability it gave them, since they had made their money in construction work and most hadn't completed high school.

The deputy mayor buzzed his assistant. "Edith, I'm going to be getting a call from a Jeanie Hanson. When she gives you a date, book us for lunch at Antoinette's."

"Got it." Edith chuckled. Antoinette's was in a gabled, renovated house on the outskirts of downtown, a romantic French restaurant known for private booths for secret business deals or errant lovers. Her boss was such a naughty boy.

CHAPTER FOUR

On the phone, Hanson hadn't detailed his connection with Tammy LaFleur, but as he walked into the block-square park in downtown, he presumed McFarlane had figured it out. Hanson sat on a bench and people-watched, trying not to anticipate what he might hear. He kept the large bag he carried close to him, knowing what the detective was expecting.

As his wife had so cuttingly asked, would he feel much better if he knew Tammy had been murdered? Did that mean it was okay, that he had done his job? Not really, but death by homicide was less of a treatment failure. What could he have done differently? What had he missed?

He thought about how distant Jeanie was. They had had good weeks, months, together. On an intellectual level, he could understand her drive. For him, being economically stable with basic needs met was enough. She had been raised upper class; he had come from a lower-middle-class background. For her, there always needed to be more. Maybe he'd try and reconcile when he got answers on Tammy.

He spotted McFarlane ambling into the park with a cop's combination of "I own this ground" and alertness to threat. McFarlane was a trim six-footer who carried himself with a linebacker's athletic grace. He had aged little since they first met, though Hanson knew the detective sergeant had been involved in two shoot-outs, and one arrest where the suspect pulled a knife and had slashed his shoulder. Even dressed in a dark blue tapered Brioni suit and five-hundred-dollar shoes, with his graying hair slicked back, his eyes in a perennial questioning squint, McFarlane could be more obviously a cop only if he had a siren and revolving red cherry light on his head.

He dropped his bulk on the bench and reached for the bag. "The usual?"

"A little different this time," Hanson said.

McFarlane squinted and pulled the bag to him. He opened it and peered in.

"Cheddar cheese popcorn," Hanson said. Meeting, with enough popcorn for the two of them and the inevitable pigeons, was a decade-long tradition.

McFarlane took a handful. "You've become a wild man in your old age."

"The clerk said this was their best." Hanson took a handful.

They filled their mouths at about the same time and chewed.

"Not bad," the detective sergeant said. "How've you been with the urges?"

Hanson was more eager to talk about LaFleur's

death than his own cravings, but he knew McFarlane wouldn't open up until he had an answer. "One day at a time, sometimes an hour at a time."

"Working your program?"

"Pretty much. No meetings, but looking at the Big Book. Reviewing the steps."

"We could catch a meeting tonight. There's one I like in Northeast."

"I'm comfortable in my recovery," Hanson said, raising his hand to interrupt McFarlane before he could speak. "And I know denial is a river. I've been clean and sober all these years, admit I'm an addict, and recognize my triggers."

"So what are your triggers right now?"

"Part of it was a scuffle at work—it's been a while since I was involved in anything physical."

"But the main thing was the girl's death. She was a client, right?"

"I can't say."

"You know why the first step is the first step? The addict's desire to control everything. And the serenity prayer. God grant me the serenity to accept what I can't change, the strength to change what I can, and the—"

"Wisdom to know the difference between the two," Hanson interrupted. "I do know all of that. I also know you won't bullshit me. If the Tammy LaFleur suicide is righteous, tell me so, and I'll be on my way. I'll even go to a couple meetings over the next few weeks."

McFarlane took another big handful of popcorn and tossed most of it to the birds. A couple dozen pecked and cooed around the men. "Flying rats," the cop said. "Nothing definite, but they've got Quimby on it. He's the chief's cleanup guy. I tried asking around and got shot down. Even by people who usually like to chat. I'm not really surprised. You know who her father was?"

"No."

"Did you think LaFleur was her real name?" McFarlane asked.

"Not really. But my job isn't to investigate. Who's her father?"

McFarlane milked his anticipation, tossing a few more kernels to the birds. "Does the name Grundig ring a bell?" They were both looking at the birds. It was easier for them to talk not making eye contact.

"I saw a Pat Grundig as her emergency number."

"That's her sister, who's a lieutenant in the sheriff's department. Her father was deputy chief of police until he retired a couple years ago. There's about a half-dozen Grundigs in law enforcement around town. A couple more off working for various federal agencies. Tammy was the black sheep of a cop royalty family. The case will be quickly shitcanned."

"But if she didn't kill herself, she was murdered."

"Right."

"Don't they want the killer brought to justice?"

"Brought to justice, yes. Taken to court, no."

"What do you mean?"

"Brian, you wanted to know in my professional opinion whether it was suicide or homicide. From the little I know, I would guess, and that is *guess*, homicide. The Grundigs won't want publicity about Tammy. They'd rather see the death fade from memory. They will find out who killed her, and that person

54

will wind up fertilizing a patch way back in the Mount Hood National Forest."

"Could one of the Grundigs have killed her? Maybe she was getting too embarrassing for them."

"That's the kind of talk that could get you in *big* trouble," McFarlane said sincerely. "And honestly, I doubt it. Cop families can be more dysfunctional than most. I'm talking heavy-duty drinking, drugging, domestic violence, abuse. It's a rare meeting I go to that I don't see a couple guys I know from on the job. But when the shit comes down, they pull together. It's very impressive in a truly screwed-up way."

Hanson fed a few more pigeons, throwing toward the back of the pecking flock, hoping to feed the less aggressive birds. "You got any theories about Tammy's death? Any leads that can be followed up?"

McFarlane turned and faced him, his weary blue eyes locking in with a force that Hanson remembered from past confrontations. "My advice is forget about it. Do some meetings. Work your program. This is not something you want to get involved in."

"That's not your usual 'listen to your higher power' talk."

McFarlane stood. "Like you said, I've always been straight with you. Always had your best interests at heart. Don't get involved." The cop strode away without saying good-bye.

At work, thoughts of Tammy LaFleur kept intruding. What could he have done differently? What was going on with her? What were her last moments like? Could she really have been so desperate, so disconnected, that she killed herself? In all his years, he'd had only two other clients kill themselves. One was early on in his career, when a woman was having her kids taken away by Child Protective Services. The other was an HIV-positive man who had just progressed to AIDS. The first still haunted him occasionally. The second he had suspected was coming, and the client had had a posthumous note sent to him, thanking him for the comfort he had given.

As he thought of his last conversation with Tammy, he had a sense of failure, a feeling that somehow he had missed a key clue if she had indeed killed herself. She had sounded optimistic, future-oriented, he reassured himself. But he felt he was not without self-blame, even if she was murdered, since it would mean that the paranoia he had dismissed had been justified.

Tammy's critical-incident review meeting didn't change anything. They met in the medical director's office, a room larger than anyone else's except for the agency's CEO. The psychiatrist, who took pride in his world travels, had furnished his twelve-by-eighteen-foot sanctuary with masks from around the world—Indonesian frog faces, brightly colored Sri Lankan demons, big-nosed Japanese tengu, Zulu war masks. He saw clients in a nearby treatment room—many of the psychotic clients would have decomped to the hospital immediately after seeing his eerie office display.

The doctor presided over the review and was joined by Hanson, Pearlman, Tammy's case manager, a skills trainer who had had her in a couple of groups, and the quality-assurance manager.

The psychiatrist, who was close to seventy, could have made twice as much with a private practice but remained dedicated to community mental health. A

Grateful Dead fan who bore a more than passing re-
semblance to Jerry Garcia, his greatest joy was playing Santa at the Christmas party for clients and their
children.

He peered through his glasses at the chart while
Pearlman spoke. "I've reviewed the records and it ap-
pears appropriate precautions were taken." All but
Hanson nodded along, their minds already on their
next appointments.

"Looks complete to me, Brian," the medical director said. "It's hard to lose a client. The timing on closing her is awkward, but it's clear there were no
indicators of suicidality or even depression. Your sessions are well documented, contacts with collateral
agencies and releases up-to-date. You had a solid therapeutic relationship."

"But she's dead nevertheless."

"Even when I worked inpatient, we'd lose someone
every now and then. That's in a locked ward where we
had control of access to weapons. If someone is determined to kill herself, she's going to be able to do it.
Particularly in an outpatient setting."

"What if she didn't kill herself? What if she was
murdered?"

"The police and medical examiner say it was suicide," Pearlman said. "You mentioned her paranoid
ideation. Had she discussed her concerns with the
police?'

"If she did, I'm sure it would have been covered
up," Hanson said tersely.

The psychiatrist mused, "I remember I had a client
who had convinced me the FBI had her under surveillance. I actually started talking with her about getting

an attorney and the Freedom of Information Act files. She hit my old lefty buttons. A month later, when she told me about the aliens in the UFO, I got suspicious."

Everyone but Hanson chuckled, and Pearlman asked, "Any conclusions or recommendations?"

Hanson sighed as they reached a foregone conclusion, signed off on the paperwork, and filed out of the office. Walking down the narrow hallway, Pearlman patted his back. "You're taking this personally."

"You think I shouldn't?"

"There's that fine line of caring about clients but not caring too much. You've been in the business long enough to know where it is."

"Maybe I should take a couple days off."

"That would be good. Don't even bother filling out a vacation request. I can have support staff call your clients to reschedule."

"I can handle that myself. They've got enough to do. I've got an intake scheduled for tomorrow at eleven, and then one at three p.m."

"We'll cover it. Do you need to fill out crisis alerts on anyone?"

He hesitated. "I don't think so. Then again, I didn't think Tammy needed an alert."

"You don't believe it was suicide, do you?"

"No."

"I read the whole chart. Looked at the way she was living her life. She had every high-risk behavior I could imagine, short of skydiving without a chute. Picking up strangers, unprotected sex, IV drug use. What am I forgetting?"

"Okay, she had borderline personality disorder. It's

58

like blaming someone with a cold for sneezing. She was getting better."

"She was getting more paranoid. Which you know is normal for people with BPD under stress. Maybe she had decided to tell you less. Go home. Take a hot bath. Read a trashy novel. Cuddle with your wife. Practice that healthy self-care stuff we tell our clients to practice."

He frowned.

"Listen, Brian, in case you can't tell, I'm concerned. You're one of my best. I don't like what I'm seeing."

"You ever heard the story about Freud? He had a client, Jewish, who was nervous early on about the rise of the Nazi Party in Austria. Freud psychoanalyzed him, convinced him the anxiety was unresolved father issues, so the guy stayed put, wound up in the gas chamber at Auschwitz."

"Don't get me started on Freud," she said. "What's your point?"

"Even paranoids can have real enemies."

Police Chief Harold Forester paced his office. He tugged at his nose, ran his hand through his thinning hair, and looked out the window. The view from the eighteenth floor included the two rivers that flowed through the city and helped it prosper, the six crowded bridges over the rivers, the freeways, and the business towers in the commercial district on the east side. On the horizon were the snowcapped Cascade Mountains.

Home to courts and the police, adorned with highly praised cream-colored limestone columns and stained-glass works, the Justice Center building was hailed as a triumph of postmodern design. The police bureau controlled the upper floors, the peak of one of the taller buildings in town. Forester enjoyed that the sheriff and the district attorney, his rivals in law enforcement power, were both in less touted buildings with less commanding views. Of course the higher he was, the further to fall. Portland police chiefs had a long history of spectacular flameout, consumed by scandals, politics, or a mixture of both.

That bastard Tony Dorsey would love to see him ousted. The Old Testament was unforgiving of sinners. The New Testament tempered that, but with restrictions, depending on which of the Gospels you believed. Was it sinful to question the origin of the scriptures, to wonder about the human hand as it tried to capture the words of the Lord?

He thought of immersing himself in the Bible he kept in his desk. The huge desk, a rich mahogany piece that had belonged to the city's police chiefs for several decades, was as much a symbol of his power as the badge and gun.

Instead he paced, wondering if he could find peace in the Twenty-third Psalm or by humming "Amazing Grace." Basics, but they usually helped. He had a small ivory statue of Jesus he took from his desk drawer. It was weathered, losing its identity from all the times he had clenched it with sweaty hands.

Tammy Grundig. He'd known her as a girl, sweet, friendly, a six-year-old cutie climbing onto his lap at police barbecues. What had she turned into? Let he who is without sin cast the first stone, he thought, as his own son came to mind. Forgive him, O Lord. The tale of Job, a righteous man, afflicted, a test of faith.

Forester had dedicated his life to the law as set down in the Bible and the more secular provisions of city government. He had gradually compromised as he rose higher, learning what it meant to be a "team player." He recognized the irony, having, to some extent, reached his lifelong goal, yet being unhappier than he had ever been before.

If the mayor followed what seemed to be a natural trajectory, Forester might become head of a national law enforcement agency. If he broke free of the mayor—and Dorsey, his more dangerous and conniving toady—Forester could move up only a notch. Police chief of Seattle, or maybe San Diego. He had been a featured speaker at the International Association of Chiefs of Police conference a few months earlier. Then the press had quoted him extensively, describing him as a candidate for president of the IACP.

The more he gained in power and influence, the better he could spread the Lord's word. But maybe he was deceiving himself, and his ambition really masked pride, one of the seven deadly sins. He wished he didn't feel like he had sold his soul to the devil.

Before leaving the office, Hanson tracked down Tammy LaFleur's chart. It had to pass through a couple of departments, including Billing and Quality Assurance, before it could be officially closed, put in a folder, and sent to archives. The chart was a confidential medical-legal document, subject to federal HIPAA regulations that could result in a fine or even jail if grossly misused.

"I thought you were done," the officious but perennially overworked office manager said.

"Ah, you know how it is, Mary. The paperwork is never done."

"I'm not sure if I can find—"

"If anyone can, you can," he said with his most charming smile.

Mary came back in five minutes with the chart and a lecture about how he was making her job more difficult, how she wasn't paid enough, and how no one appreciated her.

"Would a box of See's candies show how I feel?"

"Do doctors have bad handwriting?"

Hanson took the chart back to his office and spent fifteen minutes taking notes on LaFleur's addresses, demographic information including Social Security number, and the names of anyone she had mentioned. He felt strangely guilty, violating the privacy of a dead person, particularly when he slipped the Glamour Shot into his pocket. Before her death, he would have been the primary clinician, who "owned" the chart, responsible for annual reviews, release of records, treatment-plan updates, follow-up-care inquiries. Now, he was snooping.

He drove out to the last address she had in the records. A neighborhood of small two-bedroom houses, apartments, and a few shabby larger homes that had been subdivided into individual rental units. It's nickname, Felony Flats, came from the jail that had been built in the late 1950s. Wives of prisoners had settled there, to be near their loved ones. The area was divided by Broadway—on one side whites and Asians, on the other side African Americans and Latinos.

Everyone was at or below the poverty line. No one lived in Felony Flats if he could find better housing.

Her last address was a garden apartment complex. Surly dogs barked a deep-throated warning as he approached the building. Pink stucco walls, a broken metal gate at the entrance, rusted wrought-iron railings, a leaky fountain in the center of the courtyard. Early on as a caseworker, he'd visited dozens of places like this. He'd had to be careful as a male stranger, wary of overstepping boundaries, dealing with jealous boyfriends, agitated drug dealers, mothers fearful he was there to take away their children, minorities convinced he was symptomatic of systemic prejudice.

The old cautions emerged as he entered the complex and found Tammy's apartment number. Would the crime scene be sealed? Did he dare sneak in? What would the licensing board think if they knew he was visiting?

There was no crime scene seal on the door. He knocked. Expecting no answer, he tried the doorknob. Locked. He was startled when a young woman opened the door.

"Who are you?" She was not much past twenty, but with hard eyes and a cold smile. Her dyed black hair was pulled back in a tight bun. She was dressed in a black leather bustier, red panties, long black leather gloves, and knee-high black boots with three-inch heels.

Hanson was surprised by anyone answering, and then stunned by her appearance. "Uh, my name's Brian."

"Can I help you?" she asked, clearly used to flummoxed men.

"I, I knew Tammy." He thought of the verb "to know" in the biblical sense as the young woman sized him up. "Not as a prostitute or anything."

"Yeah, right, you knew her from a book club?"

"No."

She waited for him to clarify, but he didn't. And legally couldn't.

"Wanna come in?" she asked, and he nodded.

She stepped aside, slightly, so that he had to brush against her to get in. The apartment was dimly lit by red bulbs, decorated with heavy red velour curtains, and a dark red couch and love seat set. Helmut Newton posters on the wall depicted couples in sado-masochistic poses. She saw him glancing at them and smirked. "You're new to the scene?"

"Uh, very new. Like not really part of it."

"Let me guess. You're here doing research for a term paper or a friend told you about it and you're just not sure?"

"No. I knew Tammy and can't believe she killed herself." The words were blunt but necessary to ground him. He felt overwhelmed by the young woman and the apartment, and the bullwhip lying on the coffee table next to a stack of pornographic magazines. There was a funky, goaty smell, with an overlay of perfume. And something else, faint, which brought back memories. Cordite and blood. Battlefield smells.

His stomach rolled. She sensed his weakness and moved closer. "You want a drink?" she suggested with slightly slurred speech, and he realized that she was drugged. A central nervous system depressant, maybe alcohol, a benzo, or even heroin. "I was expecting a customer. I mean, a friend. I'm Trixie. Are you looking for a date?"

"No. I was trying to understand what happened with Tammy. Were you the one who found her body?"

She glanced at her watch. "I guess he's not gonna show. The wuss is probably afraid the cops will be back. Or maybe the place is haunted." She strode to a shelf and poured herself a scotch, added ice, then made it a double. "You want a shot? No charge." She went to the CD player and put in Creedence Clearwater Revival's *Greatest Hits*.

Hanson moved to the love seat and turned to face the couch. She rejected the hint and sat next to him on the love seat.

He asked, "You and Tammy were roommates?"

"Yeah. Plus we did an occasional scene together. T and T. Get it?" She squeezed his thigh for emphasis but didn't wait for an answer. "Man, what happened to her really sucks."

"It sounds like you think someone did something," he prompted.

"I don't know. Maybe she flipped out. I think the cops are covering up."

Creedence filled the air with the praises of "Proud Mary" while Trixie sipped. He sensed she was deciding whether she wanted to open up or stay in her professional character.

"I know who you are. Her counselor."

He said nothing.

"She described you, thought you were cute for an older guy."

65

"You found her?" he asked, avoiding distraction as she adjusted one of her breasts that nearly escaped the enhancing embrace of her Wonderbra.

She nodded, shivered. "Maybe it would help to talk to you. Like going to a priest."

Was it a conflict of interest, a blur of his role, investigating? He was trying to decide how to answer when she began talking. "I came home, didn't expect her here. The place smelled funny, you know, like fireworks on the Fourth of July. I yelled for her. No answer." Trixie closed her eyes and swayed, reliving the moment. "I'm thinking she had burned weird incense. Then I saw her lying in the bedroom. Looked like she had one of those Indian things in the middle of her forehead, you know, a red dot. But the dot was huge. Then I thought maybe it was like a burn. Then I saw her eyes." She shivered. "Wide open. Scared. Not seeing anything no more. I didn't scream, just called 911. I did that even though I've had trouble with the cops in the past." She looked to him for praise.

"It was the right thing to do," Hanson said reassuringly. "Did you see a note?"

She shook her head. "Her two eyes open, and that red one, like a three-eyed monster. I had a nightmare about it, like the same thing happening over again. Only this time she sat up in bed and said, 'Watch out, Ellie.' That's my real name, Eleanor. She never called me Trixie. You want to call me Ellie?"

"Whichever you'd prefer."

"Ellie. I mean, who'd believe a name like Trixie anyway?"

"You didn't go into the room?" he asked to get her back on track.

"I watch *CSI. Law & Order* too," she said proudly. "I know about fingerprints and like that. Though the cops were sure right from the start she committed suicide. Which was weird, wasn't it?"

He nodded. "You think it was something else?"

She had finished her drink and held up the empty glass. "You want?"

He shook his head.

"Would you be a nice boy and get me one?"

He stood and took the glass. Pouring, he noticed a slight shake in his hand. He gave her a single, with lots of ice. He hesitated, eyeing the bottle. Would it really hurt to have a shot? He set the bottle down. One minute at a time.

"Tell me more about what you think about it," he said, sitting on the couch. She moved from the love seat and sidled in next to him without hesitation. She crooked a finger for him to lean close. "I think there's a serial killer," she whispered. He could smell her whiskey breath. It repulsed and attracted him, fragments of memories of alcoholic carousing.

"What makes you say that?" he asked gently.

She lowered her voice, even softer, and he barely heard her slurred words.

"I've known other girls who've disshappeared," she said. "Copsh don't know or care."

"But Tammy didn't disappear," he said.

"There have been other deaths," she said, wide-eyed, like a kid telling a horror story around a camp-fire. "And disappearances. Unexshplained. Maybe you can keep me safe." Her hand had flopped onto his thigh and crawled around on his lap.

She had long, artificial glitter green fingernails. He

moved her pale, slender hand, then held it down near his knee. "Is there anything else that makes you suspicious?"

"She wasn't even living here," Trixie said, beginning to sniffle. "She was kind of moved out. I only seen her a coupla times in the pasht month." There were long pauses between her words as she struggled to compose her thoughts. Then she began to cry. "Life sucks. Tammy was nice to me."

"Where did she move to?" he asked awkwardly. He was used to asking feelings questions, and Trixie was awash in them. His usual work didn't involve sitting on a couch in a prostitute's apartment while she draped across him in full leather regalia.

"Eagleton."

"Are you sure?"

Eagleton was a posh riverside condo development, a bastion of successful yuppies, a place where most who worked in community mental health couldn't afford to live. There were more than a hundred luxury condo apartments in the development, all with a waterfront view and lots of amenities.

"She told me about it," Trixie said, speaking slower and slower, with more effort. "Had this great view of the river."

"Which apartment?"

Trixie swayed and leaned on him.

"Do you know her apartment number?"

She belched, opened her mouth to speak, and dozed off with a smile.

"Trixie? Trixie?"

She snored as he lifted her off him and set her down on the couch. He found a blanket in the bedroom, covered her, then returned to the bedroom. During his early crisis-outreach work, he had been a visitor to crime scenes. He knew the chaos that followed after a police invasion. Here there was no fingerprint powder clinging to surfaces, no furniture moved aside. Had someone done a great job cleaning up or was the initial investigation skimpy?

Reassuring himself that Trixie remained asleep, he rummaged through the big wooden dresser drawers, unsure what he was looking for. He found enough gawdy underwear to outfit a Frederick's of Hollywood franchise. There was a crack pipe that looked like it hadn't been used in a while and a bag with a half gram of marijuana. He felt the urge to roll the buds between his fingers, sniff the sweet oily residue. He knew if he did, he'd quickly be filling a pipe full. He dropped the bag in the drawer and slammed it. Not without considerable regret. Sitting on top of the dresser was a worn, fuzzy brown teddy bear with sad black button eyes. How much of it was Tammy's, how much was Trixie's, and how much was a prop for tricks?

LaFleur had been dead for a day and Trixie was ready to do business in the bed she had been found in. Trixie snored contentedly on the couch as Hanson slipped out.

It was close to 7 p.m. and dark out. The high-intensity streetlight was broken, and he crunched broken glass underfoot as he walked to his car.

Tapping the black ergonomic keyboard on the Dell computer in her home office, Jeanie Hanson's Google search on Tony Dorsey produced more than one hundred thousand hits. She refined the search by adding Portland, then deputy mayor, narrowing it down to twenty-three entries. Her best information came from a three-year-old newspaper article.

Dorsey was forty, married with three children, had a law degree from an unnamed university but had never actually practiced law, and considered himself a moderate Republican. He enjoyed cross-country skiing, had a summer home at the coast that he described as a cabin though it had a couple thousand square feet, and lived in the trendiest suburb. She smiled when she read the reporter's description of him as "cruelly handsome, like a young Sean Connery."

She could flirt and dicker with Dorsey. Jeanie was thinking about putting together an outfit that was both professional and sexy when she heard Brian come in. "Where've you been?" she asked, quickly exiting the article she had been reading.

"Cleaning up paperwork," he said tersely.

They had been married for two decades, so Jeanie Hanson knew something was wrong. She guessed he was brooding over the client who had killed herself, and she didn't have the patience to discuss that.

Didn't he get that he was immersed in his dirty little low-life section of the town while she was working to build a world-class city? Negotiating with a Japanese bank for a new twenty-five-story downtown high-rise. Renovating and developing the industrial inner east side. Expanding the urban growth boundaries with the mall development. Why couldn't Brian grow up?

She didn't want to talk about her interest in the deputy mayor and plans for lunch. Although she could justify it to anyone who might ask, deep down she felt squirmy. But more excited than she had been in several years.

While Brian Hanson spent decades trying to flee Vietnam memories, for the man known as Wolf, Vietnam was glorious. Raw talents he had evidenced as a youth were honed and polished with the SEALs. The Army Green Berets got the publicity, a hokey song, a bad John Wayne movie. They were force multipliers, the leaders in securing the hearts and minds of the local people. The SEALs, coming out of the Navy's underwater demolition teams and known to the Vietnamese as the Greenfaces because of their scary camo makeup, were more of a killing force. Infiltrate by land, sea, or air, execute or blow up, then exfiltrate. Though he worked with the Green Beanies as part of the Military Assistance Command Vietnam—Studies and Observation Group, Wolf saw anyone but a SEAL as an action wannabe. When the war ended, he found that his skills were in even more demand. He briefly engaged in counterterrorism and floated as a quasi mercenary.

Standing at the pay phone outside the 7-Eleven, in a minimall about fifteen minutes from downtown, he was the essence of nondescript. He wore clear glass spectacles and had a well-worn baseball cap for the Seahawks pulled tight on his head, with loose-fitting dark clothing hiding his large frame. He dialed a number and it was picked up after two rings.

Wolf said, "Speak."

"The target's name is Jorge Gonzalez. He lives at

2100 Oak Street in Gresham, a one-story light blue clapboard house." His tone made it clear he was used to having commands respected.

"I don't like to do a job without a picture," Wolf said. "This is pretty quick on my last piece of work."

"I know," the man with the commanding voice said. "It will be easiest tonight. He's alone. Beat up his girlfriend. She'll probably go back to him in a couple days."

"Got a description? It would be annoying to kill his visiting cousin."

"He's about five eight, brown hair and eyes."

"That narrows it down. Let me guess, dark complexion?"

Neither man was used to back talk, and despite their working relationship of several years, there was as much tension as collaboration.

"He's got tattoos of three tears next to his right eye and prison-made tattoos on his arms. A snake with JG. Think you can identify him?"

"Why the rush, other than his girlfriend being away?"

"He's done an armed robbery a week for the past couple months. Pistol-whipped clerks a couple of times. Seems to be escalating."

Wolf grunted. He liked to get the information, then check it independently. Make sure the target was truly deserving of his attention. The reports had always been accurate, but his visits were irreversible.

"Just so you know how dangerous he is. Suspect in two homicides. Word is he plans on killing a witness to one of his robberies in the next few days."

"How do you want him?" Wolf asked.

The man at the other end of the line knew what he meant—should the target disappear, seem to die from natural causes, or die a violent death?

"I understand that Jorge likes to go fishing."

"Sometimes you get the fish, sometimes the fish gets you," Wolf said, as he hung up the phone.

CHAPTER FIVE

"You look particularly nice today," Hanson said the next morning, trying to connect with his wife. Jeanie nodded, gave him a polite peck on the cheek, and hurried out. Sitting with his coffee, in the silence of their home, Hanson thought about his therapy sessions with Louis Parker, and what the old private investigator had told him about digging up information.

"Maybe one-quarter of my time I did surveillances, meeting with witnesses, the kind of stuff you read about in those PI books," Parker had said. "Truth is, the bulk of the time I spent at the county courthouse, city hall, hall of administration. Real adventures, like when the microfiche machine breaks or they find a file out of alphabetical order. Of course sometimes you had to get out to the scene, do a canvass, look for the pieces the cops had missed. Or tried to hide."

Hanson had the advantage of already having Tammy's basics—real name, alias, Social Security

number, birth date, address. Parker had claimed that
with name and birth date, any investigator should be
able to put together a twenty-page report without
beating, bribing, or sleeping with a single source.

Hanson strolled along the waterfront, wondering
how Parker would find where Tammy lived, knowing
only the development, Eagleton. On this sunny fall
day, during the break between the bouts of clouds
and rain, the walkway was crowded with Rollerbladers, bicyclists, kids on scooters, skateboarders,
and pedestrians. Many of the wooden benches were
occupied by people reading, gazing at the boats on
the slow-moving river, or lost in conversation. An elderly couple held hands sweetly. Hanson came to the
Eagleton complex and stared at the hundred redbrick
three-story units, daunted by the size and his lack of
information.

He visited the rental office and pretended to be interested in a condo. A perky middle-aged woman told
him there were fewer than a half dozen units available, that a studio started at $250,000. The most ex-
pensive was a $1.2 million three-bedroom.

"Breathtaking harbor views, convenient docking,
fully equipped gym with . . ." His mind wandered as
she continued her sales pitch. "And how did you hear
about us?" the saleswoman was asking.

It was the entrée he'd been waiting for. "A friend of
mine, Tammy LaFleur, lives here. She raves about it."

"All of our tenants do."

"I'd like to stop by and talk with her. You wouldn't
happen to know her apartment offhand? I left my address book at home."

"I'm afraid I couldn't divulge that even if I knew. We honor our tenants' privacy."

"She'll be disappointed. She had pretty much sold me on getting a place here."

The saleswoman hesitated, then dug a list out of her pocketbook. "Tammy?"

"LaFleur. Though it might be under her maiden name, Grundig."

"I don't see those names on my list."

"Can I take a look?"

The saleswoman shook her head and tucked the list back in her pocketbook. "I only checked because you have such honest eyes. Do you want to see a luxury condo?"

He toured, feigning attentiveness and wondering what it would be like to live there. He had told the woman he was recently divorced and she boasted of the exciting social scene. After a polite half hour, he accepted her card, ambled to a park bench by the river, and pondered his next step.

Jeanie Hanson pulled on her reading glasses and studied the papers. "You've got quite a negative variance here," she said.

"But if you look at the AR—," the nonprofit's comptroller began.

"Your accounts receivable doesn't impress me," Jeanie said. "I see from your last few years how much you had to write off."

"Our projected revenue from Medicare billings means—," the nonprofit's chief financial officer started.

"Look, let's not waste each other's time," Hanson said, setting the papers down on her large black wrought-iron and glass-topped desk. She kept the surface free of knickknacks, no family photos, reinforcing the cold and clear look she liked to present.

There were two plaques on the off-white walls, awards from banking associations she had received with suitable pomp and circumstance at annual dinners. Brian had been dragged along, suffering and muttering like Jesse Jackson at a Klan rally. She thought about him and what his reaction would be at this meeting. He would find a way to bail out the nonprofit, extend its line of credit, allow them to inflate the value of their assets that they could borrow against. That would be fine for the nonprofit, which served developmentally disabled clients. Short-term kindhearted but ultimately blocking the city's progress. She had tried to explain to her husband many times that increasing the city's tax base meant more funding for social services, which would help the disabled more. As well as all the other citizens.

"There are a few donors who have come through in the past," the CFO said.

Jeanie Hanson glanced at the sheet, though she knew the numbers by heart. "They've been tapped out for this year. And your largest donor has shifted priorities." What she didn't say was that one of the bank's influential board members had spoken to the largest donor, suggesting that money be given to another worthwhile cause. Jeanie didn't feel bad, because it wasn't like they were shutting the charity down, just helping it to make the best decision.

"What do you propose?" the CFO asked.

"In reviewing your inventory of assets, I noted that four-bedroom home on Northwest Twenty-fourth near Lovejoy. Has that been appraised recently?"

"That was our founder's first RCF. It's been run by the foundation for nearly fifty years."

"You can be sentimental about a run-down residential care facility, or you can be practical. Because of the location, you can sell that, probably for close to a million. Put one-third into reserves, one-third into buying a facility out of the downtown core, and then one-third to fix it up."

"I don't know," the comptroller said. "The family that runs this is pretty attached to that property."

Jeanie looked at her watch. "That's fine. You bring them the proposal, have them think about it, and give me a call."

"What about our line of credit?"

Jeanie shrugged. "We're not the only bank in town. You know what we're suggesting. If you can find anyone else who would give you a better deal, go for it."

There were polite, terse good-byes. As Jeanie shut the door, she allowed herself a broad grin. She guessed they would accede within forty-eight hours. It was basically a good deal, and these nonprofit types didn't have the spirit for hardball.

She had a half hour to get to Antoinette's. She spent fifteen minutes in the executive bathroom, playing with her hair, plucking at her eyebrows, adjusting her makeup. She realized she hadn't primped like this since she was a teenager. Brian never seemed to care how she looked. Both a blessing and a curse.

Sitting on the park bench, Brian Hanson twitched with unchanneled energy. He thought back to Vietnam-era braggadocio, locked and loaded, ready to rock and roll. The trite little phrases that had become part of his vocabulary. Spray and pray, for indiscriminate firing into the brush; shoot and scoot, lock and cock; tag and bag, for the good-byes to comrades. Most of all there was the mantra he had repeated to himself incessantly, when he saw a water buffalo shredded by an M60 on a soldier's whim, or a buddy gut shot and leaking intestines, or a grenade tossed into a hut and blowing apart a grandmother and child. "Don't mean nothing." How many times had he cried himself to sleep, repeating the phrase over and over and over.

He forced himself back to the present. The flashbacks, the dissociation, the numbness, got worse when he was under stress. He could make the symptoms go away but it took effort. Exhausting effort. He had to keep busy, distracted. He had to go back to the condos. But if he went door to door without a plausible excuse, someone would call the police. In poorer neighborhoods, his county ID would be enough. Residents were used to complying with authorities, albeit in a passive-aggressive way. Sometimes outright hostile. But calling the police would just bring more unwanted governmental attention to them.

He went downtown to the Multnomah County Courthouse. He had been there several dozen times over the years, usually testifying whether someone should be committed for an extended psychiatric hospitalization. When it was built in 1914, the block-square six-story building was the largest courthouse in the West. It was dominated by limestone Ionic columns on the outside and high-ceilinged hallways with impressive woodwork on the inside, but what struck him was the different smells. Of sweat and too much perfume in the corridors and courtrooms, and that musty, dusty paper odor in the bowels of the court where the records were kept. Which was where he headed.

The building housed reams and reams of documents from civil and criminal proceedings, as well as county tax records. The files had outgrown the space and were being converted to CD-ROMs. Hanson used the microfiche to look up Tammy's case numbers. He jotted them down on a call slip and passed it across the worn counter.

The clerk, an almost albino pale young man, made his boredom evident as he said, "I need ID before you can have files."

Hanson showed his county ID. "You with the DA's office?" the clerk assumed, not really looking at the laminated card and pleased at a chance to talk. Hanson realized how all the IDs issued by the county looked the same, and felt a happy surge, as if he had gained the superpower of assuming different identities.

"I'm with mental health," he said, feeling no reason to lie.

"I wish I had some mental health," the clerk said with a dry laugh, followed by a smoker's cough. "You can use the photocopier for free, just write down your department."

The clerk hadn't read his name, and since he was not on official business, Hanson scrawled an unintelligible squiggle. The clerk shuffled into the back, eventually returning with four inches of files. Hanson said his thanks and took them to a view carousel in the back of the room. After about an hour reading, he photocopied several dozen pages from civil and criminal records that looked promising, knowing it would take more focused study to determine what was worthwhile. But none of the papers gave an address in the Eagleton condos.

Jeanie Hanson believed it was one of nicest lunches she had ever had. Instead of the sharpie come-on she had expected, they chatted amiably. Tony Dorsey talked about his wife and kids, the frustrations of being a father and a husband. She found herself naturally talking about Jeff, whom she was so proud of, and Brian, and the mixed feelings that went with that. Despite being a powerful political figure, Tony Dorsey was a good listener who smoothly refilled her glass and made her feel special. She told him about Brian's Vietnam combat experience and where he worked.

"Being a counselor must be an interesting job," Dorsey said.

"Ugh. The people he works with, they're so extreme. He used to talk about it with me, but only in vague terms to protect their identities. Like I would really care. Still, I don't know how he does it. Or why he'd want to." She sipped the seventy-five-dollar-a-bottle Prenevost Vineyards merlot. "Now what you do, that's interesting. I hear the mayor won't make decisions without consulting you."

He gave an endearing aw-shucks shrug.

"I must admit, I did an Internet search on you. Not much from before you came here. Very mysterious." She cocked her head and gazed at him curiously.

"Let's talk business, shall we?" he said, though it wasn't a question.

For several minutes they spoke about zoning variances, traffic flows, and which anchor stores would be most advantageous to the development. She could tell he was impressed with the easy way she brought up facts and figures in response to his questions, and when she didn't know, she admitted it and promised to get back to him. She could imagine the scene in a movie, the camera circling, capturing him, her, their posture, their closeness, their heat.

He sipped more merlot, stroked his chin with his free hand. "I'm going to tell you a secret. The answer to your question before, something most people don't know." He leaned in closer, lowering his voice. "You asked about my background. I was CIA."

"Really?"

He nodded. "Nothing glamorous. Analysis work. A few overseas postings. I gave the government fifteen years of service, but it leaves a hole in your résumé. I've got a lame cover story about working for the Defense Department, but I never liked it."

They locked eyes. "I've never met a spy before."

"Former spy. There are things I saw that I don't like to think about. I bet your husband says the same thing."

She nodded, not really wanting to talk about Brian, wanting to learn more about the fascinating Tony Dorsey.

"Does he have times when his emotions flare up, when he's different, scary to be around?"

"He's going through one now," she said.

"Hmm. Do you know what triggered it?"

"A client of his died. He feels responsible and won't believe it was suicide."

"An accidental death?"

"No. That she was murdered. He's read too many mysteries, thinks he's Sherlock Holmes."

They both chuckled.

"The thrill of the hunt," Dorsey said.

He patted her hand, lingering for a moment. "I've really enjoyed this lunch. I feel like I've known you forever."

"Me too," she said.

"I'm hoping we must have lots of meetings on the Springfield mall. And the inner southeast project."

"I'm sure there are numerous details to discuss."

"Definitely. I'm curious about your husband's investigation. You know if he does uncover anything, I can make sure it gets to the right people."

Tony was so sweet, even humoring her husband. "That would be great."

"But if I know husbands, I suspect he wouldn't want to know that you're coming to me for help. We'll keep it between us."

She was excited at having a secret connection with Dorsey. "I feel like I'm being recruited as a spy."

"My little Mata Hari," Dorsey said, and she felt a warm internal quiver at his use of the possessive.

Driving back to work, she found herself humming Carly Simon's "The Spy Who Loved Me." She caught herself, was momentarily embarrassed, and then began loudly singing, "Nobody does it better." When Jeanie Hanson returned late that evening, Brian had files spread across the dining room table. He greeted her with an inattentive grunt, standing hunched over the table and barely looking up.

"What've you got there?" she asked.

"Court papers and other records on the client who died," Brian said, continuing to scan the papers.

"Anything interesting?" she asked casually.

He looked up and she saw the fatigue and anguish in his eyes.

She suddenly realized how painful the death was for him. "Honey, put it aside. I'll give you a back rub."

He shook his head. "Thanks, but I know the answer is buried here."

She strode into the house and settled in.

As Hanson pieced together the life and death of Tammy LaFleur/Grundig, there was no shortage of suspects. Mainly abusive boyfriends, a few jealous girlfriends of men she dated, and a couple of drug dealers whom she had ripped off. Plus indications she had been an informant on a meth lab case. Tammy had been immersed in a world of violence and criminality. Yet she had been making progress. Her last criminal charge—possession of a few grams of marijuana—had been six months earlier. No prostitution arrests in more than a year, no charges of possession of a controlled substance with intent to distribute in eighteen months.

How had she been able to afford the Eagleton condo? A sugar daddy? Brian was frustrated over the mystery and with Jeanie, who had been so quick to breeze by him. Wasn't she willing to do more than feign a millisecond of concern?

He felt the cravings and the desire for someone to

talk to. Someone who could comprehend the beast within him. It wouldn't be Betty Pearlman or anyone from the mental health clinic. If he mentioned his concerns to anyone there, it would be categorized as an unhealthy, and unprofessional, obsession. They couldn't understand the strange energy it tapped into. He'd go from clinician to client quickly in their minds.

It was close to midnight but he called Bill McFarlane.

"Too late to get popcorn," McFarlane answered, recognizing the number from his caller ID. "How're you doing?"

"I've been better."

"Accepting life on life's terms?"

"Do I have a choice?"

"You have the right to fuck up your life. If you choose to exercise that right, anything you do can make things worse. If you can't screw it up yourself, we can provide someone who will make it immeasurably worse."

"The dark side of Miranda," Hanson said.

McFarlane snorted. "The real Miranda had his own dark side. A dirtbag rapist who supported his low-life habits by autographing warning cards. Got killed in a bar fight a couple years after the Supreme Court decision."

"I've got suspicions on the Tammy LaFleur murder."

"You're the only one calling it a murder. You're not with the ME, the DA, the police, or the sheriff. How stupid are you willing to look?"

"I'm willing to have the courage of my convictions. Then I can turn it over to you pros."

"I'm thinking you need a checkup from the neck up."

It annoyed Hanson when McFarlane lapsed into

12-step cliché speak. "And get off the pity pot," Hanson said, with an exaggeratedly tired voice. "I forgot to ask about the gun. Where did it come from?"

"That was one of the first things they looked at. It was reported stolen from a house about three months ago. John Q. Citizen type. The trail there is cold."

"How would she wind up with it?"

"Brian, she had lots of enemies and knew the streets. Even when she was doing her 'Guns are bad' rap with you, how long would it take her to get a stolen piece if she wanted?"

"Well, if she felt she needed protection, maybe she knew something. She is dead."

"And it looks like it was by her own hand. What will it take for you to get over this denial trip? What will it take for you to accept what you are powerless over?"

"I'd like to know for sure."

"That's stinkin' thinkin'," McFarlane said. "Absolutism. Wanting the world to be the way you want it. Black and white."

"Maybe I shouldn't be talking to you, maybe you're too entrenched."

"You don't feel I'm telling you the truth?"

Hanson recognized a therapeutic confrontation. He was frequently surprised when McFarlane said what a good counselor would have said in a similar situation.

"You admit the police may be involved," Hanson said. "Maybe I should try talking to Internal Affairs."

"That would be interesting. I can give you the number if you'd like."

"You think they'd listen?"

"Oh, they'd listen. Not sure how they'd take it."

McFarlane paused, like a comic waiting to deliver a punch line. "I could refer you right to the top. Captain Grundig."

"Maybe I should."

"He was her uncle. You think he doesn't know she was killed? You think he's waiting for some guilt-ridden addict counselor to bring it to his attention?"

"Okay, you made your point," Hanson said.

"Brian, I know you're doing this from a place of concern," McFarlane said, softening his voice. "Take a step back, look at things objectively. Pretend you were counseling someone in a similar place."

Hanson sighed. "Okay, thanks."

"Listen, don't hesitate to call. I know you're going through a tough time. You've built a good life, but don't forget, once an addict, always an addict."

Jeanie Hanson lay in bed, listening attentively to her husband's side of the telephone conversation. Telling Tony Dorsey would be harmless. The erotic attraction was suppressed; she was thinking how good he could be for her business connections.

She thought about the VP who currently served as liaison with the city on some of the biggest projects. He was nearing retirement. It was a high-profile position, in line for the real inner circle. But it was more than that. There was her own money, which, if invested wisely, could be quadrupled. Get her back to the lifestyle she had grown up with. There was no such thing as insider trading to worry about. As long as her investments didn't inflate what the bank had to pay, there would be no punishable conflict of interest.

While Brian shuffled papers downstairs, she drifted off to sleep, with sweet visions of herself jetting off to Europe on bank business, with time for an extended shopping spree in Rome.

CHAPTER SIX

"You've been looking into Tammy's death?" Louis Parker asked with a smug I-already-know-the-answer expression.

"What makes you say that?" Hanson said, trying to hide his surprise.

"In a lotta ways every place is like high school."

Hanson cocked his head slightly to the side and gave him a tell-me-more look.

"Every place is made up of cliques and smaller communities. Say I was dropped down in New York and needed to do a skip trace. How would I do it?"

"I don't know," Hanson said. "I don't even know what a skip trace is."

"Tracking a deadbeat or bail jumper. Anyone who doesn't want to be found. The paper trail is a good place to start. Like you did at the courthouse."

"How did—"

"I've got my sources. Particularly when someone is stumbling around like an elephant in a china shop.

No, wait, that's a bull. It's the elephant in the living room. Anyway, paper is always good. Hard to argue with what's written down. You can gather info without the suspect even knowing." Parker grinned at Hanson's befuddlement.

"Please go on," Hanson said.

"You're trying to sound therapeutic, Doc, but I know it's more than that. Remind you of your time in Vietnam?"

Hanson leaned back in his chair, keeping a poker face. "What do you know about Vietnam?"

"When I was first coming, I wondered how much of the real world you had seen. I didn't want a pansy-ass with a degree and no idea about anything outside a textbook. Sure, I checked you out."

"I passed?"

"Obviously. So let's go back to checking out my hypothetical guy in New York. I find out what he likes, whether it's a hobby, or a food, or a type of crime. Then I start narrowing it down. People know people who know people. Six degrees of Kevin Bacon." He sat back, enjoying himself. "So what's your theory?"

"About what?"

"Tammy. When you do an investigation, you usually start with a hypothesis. The butler did it. Actually, usually it's someone's husband, wife, business partner. Then, who was around, anyone seen in the area. Then look at the cause of death. Motive. Opportunity. Method. Think of MOM."

"I've heard of that. But we're getting far afield of a counseling session."

"C'mon, Doc, we usually do. You like listening to

my war stories. I can help you out on this deal. Good for my juices too."

"Louis, I appreciate the offer, but it would be a gross ethical violation of the therapist-counselor relationship. You could investigate much better than I can, but I'm not even sure if I should."

Parker leaned forward and patted Hanson's knee. "You feel it in your gut, don't you?"

Hanson nodded.

"I know you pretty well, probably better than you think. I know how you respond to what I say, what gets your interest, what you're listening to politely. You think a therapist is the only one who likes to read people? C'mon, it'll be fun."

Hanson shook his head.

Parker sat back and folded his arms. After a longer silence, he said, "Okay, you got a code, I've got to respect that. If I give you a name, would you follow up?"

"I'd have to think about it."

"What's to think? If you've got something, it'll be sweet for you and her."

"Her?"

"My niece. You tell her what you got. She's looking to make ASAC by the time she's forty."

"ASAC?"

"Assistant special agent in charge. Run a field office. It'll be easy to talk with her. She was a profiler, worked for behavioral sciences."

"Serial killers?"

"Yeah. She's had a lot of hot assignments. Organized crime in Miami. Counterterrorism in Chicago. That kid's on the fast track."

Access to someone who actually knew about serial killers. Contacting Parker's niece seemed like an ethical breach, but was it really so bad? In smaller communities, there were constant overlaps, dual relationships, blurred boundaries, he rationalized.

"I'll think about it," Hanson said.

"I'll tell her to expect your call," Parker responded.

"He's an idiot," Mayor Robinson said.

"Yes, but he's an elected idiot," Tony Dorsey responded. "A strong presence on the city council. He's popular with the west side crowd and has a respectable war chest. He could even make a run against you next time. We need to figure out a way to both intimidate and appease him."

The mayor ran his hand through his thick, prematurely gray hair. The hair, coupled with a youthful face, made guessing his age a challenge. Somewhere between thirty and sixty. Actually right in the middle. Forty-five years old, trim, with blue eyes that could shift from twinkly warmth to Great Plains chill in milliseconds. And then back again.

Robinson, Dorsey, the press secretary, and the comptroller were in the mayor's office, a floor above Dorsey's and twice as large. One long wall was dominated by floor-to-ceiling teak bookcases. Looking at the wall, a perceptive observer could have written Robinson's life story. His schooling (framed diplomas from a local high school, the state university, and Stanford Law School), career (law, with a focus on interstate commerce), family (pictures of his wife, his two daughters), hobbies (old baseball mitt, framed

old postcards of the city, books on crosscountry skiing, the U.S. Constitution).

"He's already making noises about having a hearing
on the sewage plant," the press secretary said. "The
paper's going to be having a story on it this weekend.
They called for a comment."

"What did I say, C.J.?" the mayor asked, grinning.
Her name was not C.J., but one of the mayor's
behind-closed-doors affectations was to call his closest
staff by the names of characters in *The West Wing*.
Dorsey was "Leo." The comptroller was "Josh,"
based more on his looks than his role.

The press secretary was a former TV newswoman
who had made it as far as weekend anchoring for the
NBC affiliate in Seattle before an exec with an ink-
still-wet MBA decided she "was too old and had a
low Q-rating." She'd come back to Portland, initially
bitter, but had found she loved her new job. Being an
insider was more fun than having to read from a
TelePrompter while shots of burning buildings flashed
on the screen. "You were surprised at the councilman's reaction, since he was instrumental in getting
the plant built in his district," she said smoothly.
"You noted that he was at the initial hearings, and in
fact cut the ribbon at the opening, talking about the
jobs it would provide, the environmental benefit, the
state-of-the-art technology. You suggested the reporter check their old clippings versus what he was
saying now."

"It's sounds like I was wonderfully articulate and
persuasive. Thank you, C.J."

Dorsey shook his head in disagreement.

"I know what Leo thinks," the mayor said. "What about you, Josh?"

"You're going to need his vote on the bond issue for the new transit mall next month. He's thin-skinned and will hold a grudge."

"Exactly," Dorsey said. "Getting off the snappy response is fun in the short run."

"We let him get away with his cheap shots?' the press secretary asked, scowling.

"We need to teach him a lesson, but privately, so he can save face. And he'll know that if he screws around, the next time we will ream him publicly."

"The councilman is Mr. Environmental Goody Two-Shoes, right?" Dorsey asked.

"Granola Boy in Birkenstocks," the comptroller said, and they chuckled.

Dorsey took out an eight-by-ten black-and-white photo of the councilman and showed it to the group.

"Let's say this was to get to *Willy Week?*" Dorsey proposed.

Robinson laughed out loud. "That's what I love about you, Leo. You're more Machiavellian than Machiavelli."

"What do we do about the *Portland Tribune?*" Robinson asked.

Dorsey turned to the press secretary. "How tame is the reporter?"

"She's ambitious, but she'll yank the story under pressure," the press secretary said.

"Especially if the councilman calls and says that he didn't have all the facts, is going to be working closely with the mayor, et cetera, et cetera."

"Maybe give her an exclusive on the bond issue,

how we're going to be filing the proposal next week," the comptroller suggested.

"Only you would get aroused over a story like that," Dorsey quipped, and the mayor and the press secretary laughed. The comptroller forced a weak smile. "We've had a few requests for a day-in-the-life-type story on the mayor. I bet she'd go for that."

"Front page for her, if we promise to throw in some newsy sweetening," the press secretary said. "What about the councilman?"

"I'll take care of him," Dorsey said.

"I really don't think we—," the comptroller began.

Dorsey cut him off. "I don't tell you how to count beans, you don't tell me how to handle political situations."

The press secretary and the comptroller both looked to the mayor, expecting him to rein Dorsey in. The mayor was about to say something when Dorsey glowered at him. Robinson asked, "Is there anything else we need to discuss?"

Lunchtime, and the line had formed outside the mission for those who would listen to a Bible talk in exchange for a meal. When Hanson walked by the line, a young guy with a ponytail and matted beard shoved his hand in front of Hanson and demanded, "Got spare change?"

A couple of others in line shouted out greetings to Brian, telling the aggressive panhandler, "That's our shrink. Leave him alone."

Hanson felt the warmth of recognition, acceptance. He nodded to those he knew and kept moving. Briskly. He was heading in-country.

Ostensibly, he was going out for a burger. But he knew why he had chosen the Dew Drop Inn. He found the entrance under a faded, painted sign, with a blinking neon image of a frighteningly buxom woman in the blacked-over window. The standard bar smells of spilled beer and cigarette smoke hit as he let the heavy wooden door shut behind him. Dark, with an empty, brightly lit stage and a gleaming stainless-steel pole. Ludacris's "What's Your Fantasy" blasted from cheap speakers. The brass foot rail and long, scarred mahogany bar were signs of the dive's prouder past.

He had the impression of people at the tables, their outlines confirmed as his eyes adjusted to the dim light. The place was half empty, or half full. Brian chose a table far from the stage, against a back wall, and away from the spotlights.

Two waitresses, one with fifties towering, teased blond hair and the other close-cropped androgynous, worked the tables, while a big guy with a shaved head and beetle brows tended bar. Hanson knew that his name was Vic, he owned the place, and LaFleur had dated him briefly. She had described him as "not as bad as most of the assholes I've fucked" and told Hanson that Vic often pined for his two daughters, who were with his ex-girlfriend in Las Vegas. He knew that Vic had gotten a dishonorable discharge from the Navy, liked going to monster-truck rallies, and rode a Harley. Sex with him was a condition of employment at the bar, and most of the staff also turned tricks to supplement their income. He knew from Tammy that Vic was skimming, cheating his partner, using the money to support a considerable coke habit. That could be a conversation starter.

The information gave Hanson a feeling of a slight edge, counterbalanced by being in unfamiliar and probably unfriendly surroundings. He scanned for exits, for other possible bar staff, and for anyone who might know him. Several strippers were agency clients, and he thought he saw a male client at a far table. But the man's attention was focused on the vacant stage, and Hanson leaned back farther into the darkness.

Reassured, he ordered a medium-well burger with everything on it from the androgynous waitress. She jotted it down while maintaining her bored indifference.

A woman in a robe strode to the stage like a prize-fighter entering the ring. She was a petite brunette with almost elfin features. Her siliconed breasts were unveiled as the music switched to Pink's "Get the Party Started" and she dropped her robe. The tawdry sexuality, with the underlying danger, reminded him of Saigon. The boom boom bar girls and their VC boyfriends waiting to slit your throat. There was danger in the mundane—the shoeshine boy who'd cut your tendons with a straight razor, the innocuous box wired to a clump of purloined C-4.

He mentally rebuked himself. This was not the time to get trapped in memories. That was like being on patrol and ruminating on family, friends, or girlfriends left behind. An excellent way to wind up dead.

Aside from being recognized, there were temptations everywhere: the smell of spilled beer, the clink of glasses, the neon brand names above the bar, the posters on the wall, the slightly glazed look of so many patrons. Relapse was a wave to the waitress away.

Hanson was questioning the wisdom of being there

when the hamburger was placed in front of him. He tore into it ferociously. Under fire, some guys would lose their appetites, even throw up. For him, the more adrenaline, the hungrier. Even government C rations could taste good.

The brunette, glistening with sweat, was slowing as she began her third dance. He couldn't remember what the previous number had been. Hanson's head ached from the smoke, the noise, and the sharp contrast between the brightly lit stage and the dark surroundings.

Vic was talking to the androgynous waitress, increasing Hanson's paranoia. They were looking in his direction. The waitress took over bartending duties and Vic headed toward the back with the fervor of a lottery winner about to grab his prize. A coke run.

Hanson followed, dodging between the tables, which were so close together a fire marshal could've written a book of citations. A new dancer took the stage, a statuesque African American woman with big bangle earrings. She dropped her clothing and stood defiantly, in a bikini that would have been tight on a woman half her size.

The Eagles' "Life in the Fast Lane" kicked over as the counselor followed Vic down a short, narrow hallway lined with posters touting Coors, Budweiser, and Hamm's.

Hanson paused at the door, on the edge of a precipice. He could go back, pay for his burger, and walk out. Or he could open the door and plunge off the cliff. He hesitated with his hand on the doorknob.

Dorsey had asked Edith to secretly find out where the councilman would be during his lunch hour. Using her city hall network, she had the answer within five minutes.

Whole Foods was nicknamed "Whole Paycheck," with an incredible assortment of the best foods, and prices to match. Cheerful workers lurked everywhere, smiling, offering free samples, eager to please. As the councilman picked out a couple of organic vegan food bars, Dorsey walked a few paces behind him. Just as Dorsey was about to approach, a gray-maned woman wearing a T-shirt stating "Meat Is Murder" over a picture of a sad-eyed cow stopped the councilman.

Dorsey sidled away as she harangued the councilman about the villainy of fast-food restaurants. The woman gestured savagely, with the councilman moving back several times as she pressed forward. The councilman offered well-rehearsed sincere and attentive expressions and escaped as quickly as possible.

Dorsey followed the councilman, who paid for his bars and ate them as he walked briskly down the street. He entered Powell's City of Books, which billed itself as "the Legendary Independent Bookstore," with the largest new and used inventory in the country. The main store, which required a map to navigate, had 4,700 different sections in a block-square site.

Dorsey tracked him easily as he went into the business section on the first floor and took a book on public relations from the wooden shelf.

The deputy mayor waited until he seemed absorbed. "Need help with your PR?" Dorsey asked, and the councilman looked up suddenly. He snapped the book shut and put it on the shelf.

"Not really."

"You never know," Dorsey said, leaning against the shelf and speaking in a confidential tone.

"What do you mean?"

"That big Ford Explorer."

"I, you know I've got the Toyota Prius, the electric-gas hybrid."

"That's what I thought, until I saw the picture."

"What picture?"

Dorsey took a *Management for Dummies* book off the shelf and glanced at it, keeping the councilman waiting. "Nicely done. Maybe we ought to get copies for some of our officials." Then he took the photo out of his pocket, showing the councilman getting out of a mammoth red SUV.

"This, this was when my car was getting a tune-up. I ran a quick errand, I—"

"Hey, you don't have to explain yourself to me. When that photographer talked about sending it to *Willamette Week* for their Rogue of the Week column, I said, 'This guy's a friend. Don't embarrass him.' "

"Thanks, but you didn't need to. It's no big deal. Just using my wife's car. She wants it because she likes to have lots of metal around her when she's driving the kids."

Dorsey shook his head. "So I can tell him to send it over? You wouldn't mind? I mean, I don't know how your friends at the Sierra Club would feel."

"I can explain it."

"You sure?" Dorsey's raised eyebrows made his skepticism obvious. "It probably wouldn't cost you too many votes. I mean, those environmentalists can be such single-issue fanatics. Not a reliable constituency."

"It probably would be best if he didn't send the photo."

"Hmm."

"What does that mean?"

"Well, it's a favor, but I'd be happy to do it," Dorsey said, speaking slowly, with long pauses. "If I felt we were on the same team."

"Which means?"

Dorsey's tone changed, his voice lowered. "Cut the crap on the sewage plant. We both know the city needs it. You stop grandstanding, the mayor will say he's consulting with you on it. Maybe form a blue ribbon panel, study it, bless it. Then this picture gets shitcanned."

The councilman glanced up and down the aisles like a trapped animal. "Okay," he said.

"Good. Do you want your book?"

"No. I better go." The councilman hurried off.

Dorsey glanced at his watch and decided he had time to kill. He wandered over to the spy novels and found an old Charles McCarry thriller. That was what he loved about the store, finding what he was looking for and often even more.

Hanson tested the flimsy door to Vic's rear office and was pleased to find it unlocked. He turned the doorknob slowly, then eased the door open. Not that it mattered, since "Life in the Fast Lane" was echoing down the hall.

Vic was bent over a mirror, snorting up a thick line of coke. Hanson watched him shift the thin brass tube to his other nostril and vacuum up a second line. He had three more to go.

"We need to talk," Hanson said.

Startled, Vic exhaled, blowing cocaine over his desk.

"Shit!" the bar owner bellowed.

Vic yanked open a drawer, and Hanson knew he wasn't reaching for his business card. It happened in the peculiar mix of slow-motion perception and high-speed movement. "Who the fuck are you?" Vic demanded.

"We need to talk," Hanson said calmly. He envisioned his right hand moving quickly to slap the weapon away while the left did a palm heel strike to Vic's forehead. Might not knock him out, but would definitely stun him. Was he close enough? Did he still have the ability?

"I'm a friend of Tammy's," Hanson lied.

"Bullshit! She woulda taught you better than to barge in on me like that." Vic's hand holding the gun was trembling from a mix of coke and adrenaline aftershock. His finger was tight on the trigger, and the Browning Hi Power 9 mm was centered on Hanson's chest. "You're not a fucking cop or you woulda been here with a SWAT team. You're not a rip-off artist or you woulda made your move."

Hanson silently raised his hands in an "I surrender" gesture. The gun wavered but stayed on the counselor's torso.

"I'm a friend of Tammy's," Hanson repeated.

"Like I'm supposed to give a fuck? You made me waste a couple hundred worth of coke." He raised the gun, aiming at Hanson's face. "How much you got on you?"

Hanson slowly took out his wallet and lifted two twenties. He handed them over.

As Vic grabbed the money, Hanson noted another

opportunity to disarm him. A slight lunge, grab the outstretched hand, pull him across the desk with a spin so his own arm would be blocking the gun.

Hanson had been most skilled at unarmed combat. Not very practical in a world of AK-47s, M16s, claymores, and Hueys. Where the enemies' presence was seldom seen. Where booby traps, snipers, and mortar attacks occurred far more than mano a mano confrontations. Hand-to-hand combat was more dependable. Only Spike had understood. He was the one they called whenever a sentry had to be silenced.

One time behind sandbags, in between mortar barrages, Spike had growled, "Any faggot can kill someone at a hundred yards with a gun. Takes a real man to do it up close and personal." Hanson had seen the feral gleam of his teeth. "Up close, you can feel their desperation."

Hanson had nodded and decided that Spike was a psycho. Hanson didn't like how much he understood what Spike said. Twice he had killed an enemy with his hands—one time by strangulation, another by snapping the neck. He could still hear the death gurgle and the loud pop. Spike had been killed outside of Pleiku, which was tough for him but probably best for the civilian American population.

"Old man, are you stoned or what?" It was Vic. His hand was a little less trembly, the angle of the gun lower.

How long had Hanson been dissociating? "Just thinking."

"Think about your fucking last will and testament."

Hanson was in the zone, every moment potentially his last, and not really caring. "She told me about your

Harley and how much you enjoyed the monster-truck rallies," Hanson said, trying to sound like they shared common interests.

"Big fucking deal." But his finger was not quite as taut on the trigger. Would bringing up more emotional areas, like his kids, establish Hanson's bona fides or agitate the bartender?

"She told me how much she cared about you, how much she trusted you," Hanson said.

"That shows what a dumb bitch she was." But he said it wistfully.

"She told me to check in with you, that you knew what was going on. That you could help out."

"Maybe I do. Maybe I don't. Who the fuck are you anyway?"

"A friend of hers trying to find out what happened."

Vic squinted at him. "Cops said she killed herself."

"Do you believe that?"

"Cops are either too corrupt or too stupid to know the truth if it bit them on the ass." Hanson sensed that despite his bravado, Vic had cared about LaFleur.

"That's what I think. But who would've killed her?"

Vic held the gun loosely. "Start with Aaron Aardvark and go to Zippy Zyzmanko. She pissed a lot of people off."

"You know anything about her family?"

"She told me about them. Cops."

"You think they were involved?"

Vic shrugged. "If they were, I wouldn't know. Or say anything. The last thing I need is to step on their dicks. This place would be closed in a New York minute."

"You have a theory?"

"What the fuck am I doing talking to you? Get outta here." He waved the gun from Hanson to the door.

Hanson didn't move.

"You crazy fucker, get out of here."

"I really would like to know what you think," Hanson said calmly.

Vic came closer to him, almost nose to nose. Hanson saw broken blood vessels and bloodshot hazel eyes. There were tiny flakes of dandruff in his eyebrows and beard. The Browning was up again and he shoved it against Hanson's cheek. "I could kill you and claim self-defense."

"I don't have a weapon or a record. It's easier to let me live."

Vic waved the gun again. "You are one crazy motherfucker." He pointed to the door. "Get out."

"Not before you tell me what you think."

"I got the gun and you're interrogating me?"

"I want to find out what happened to Tammy."

"You got more balls than brains," Vic said, shoving the gun into his belt. "I don't know about Tammy, but I know about some screwy things. She's not the first woman like that who turned up dead in a way that stinks. There's rumors among the girls about a serial killer. I don't know whether to believe it or not. The cops don't believe it, it ain't been on TV, but it makes sense."

"Do you have names of other women he might have killed?"

"Tiffany, Amber, Tasha."

"Last names?"

Vic shrugged again. "And those were trick names. You got to understand, these women are expendable." He said it like he was proud to know the word. "What're you going to do if you find out?"

It was Hanson's turn to shrug. "Damned if I know."

As Hanson walked out, he glanced back. Vic was trying to gather the cocaine dust that had scattered on his desk.

CHAPTER SEVEN

"They're undercapitalized," Jeanie Hanson said into the hands-free microphone connected to her Sidekick cell phone. "You call for an audit now, they'll be begging for a deal before you can say 'foreclosure.'" She listened, smoothly sped up, and then eased into the two-car-length space between two trucks on the freeway. One of the truckers blasted his horn as he had to hit his brakes. She flipped him the finger and continued her conversation. "I know, I know. Their venture to date has been expense neutral. But their budget is unrealistic. You think about it. I've got six more voice mails to return."

The clock on her dashboard read 7 p.m. She was cruising on the four low-fat double lattes she had consumed during the day. "Hey, how's it going on the project?" She switched the radio to the all-news station while going "uh-huh, uh-huh" to the contractor at the other end of the line.

"They're shortsighted," she said. "This city is on a

roll. Look at how our property values have gone up twenty-eight percent in the past two years. You tell me one other city that's done as well? I know, I know I don't have to sell you on it. Fools don't recognize an incredible value when they see it. A year from now, they'll be begging for you to call back." She listened a while more, bolstered his ego, reassured him about financing, then hung up.

Development of the mall project consumed much of Jeanie's time. But her hopes, and the city's, were in the development of inner southeast. The previous two administrations had tried to get the plan approved: to move the freeway into a man-made ravine as Seattle had, then create a thriving commercial district around it. And she had a personal reason for needing the project to go through.

A previous administration had promoted the building of the 1.5-mile east side promenade along the Willamette River from the Oregon Museum of Science and Industry to the Steel Bridge. Initially criticized as a $40 million boondoggle, it had become a popular attraction for tourists and residents alike. Bicyclists, Rollerbladers, and joggers made it appealing for sports businesses, while boat-rental businesses and eateries wanting a waterfront view added interest. But the 1-5 freeway paralleling the walkway cut it off from the rest of the city and provided an ongoing source of noise and fumes.

With the freeway moved, the factory area near the river would quadruple in value. Jeanie's firm was providing financing to the large landlords who were quickly buying land as discreetly as possible. If word got out that the major players were speculating in the area, existing property owners would bargain harder.

But Jeanie knew that the small fry who often held property that had been in their families since the Lewis and Clark Exposition land boom in the early twentieth century lacked the vision. It took big firms to produce big results. She was a true believer as she called, cajoled, and charmed the unwary. With the mayor's support, and Dorsey's willingness to apply pressure, it was as sure a thing as any real estate deal could be.

After a couple more calls, she pulled into her own driveway. Entering the house, she heard an unusual thumping noise in the rec room.

"Brian?"

"I'm here."

Curious, she went down the short flight of stairs. He had set up equipment that had long lay dormant in the closet. There was a heavy sandbag that looked like a duffel bag hung from a steel frame. At the other end of the frame was an Everlast leather speed bag the size of a small basketball, suspended from a two-foot-round wooden disk. It was the speed bag rhythmically bouncing off the disk she had heard. She watched as her husband's fists pounded the bag, a blur of motion. He wore lightweight black leather gloves that hadn't been used in more than a decade.

One of her guilty pleasures was that she was turned on by boxing, hard-muscled, sweaty men brutalizing each other in a twenty-by-twenty canvas ring. Whenever she was out of town, if she could pick it up on the hotel's cable TV, she would watch, fascinated. If there was fight news in the paper, she would go to that even before checking the business section. She maintained her facade by scoffing at all sports; the truth was that no other sport was as primal, without excuses.

Brian Hanson, stripped down to boxer shorts, hair matted with sweat, bobbed lightly on his feet, switching from the speed bag to heavy sandbag, pounding so hard that the thump echoed through the house. He grunted with each powerful blow.

After several minutes, he looked at her, smiled, and peeled off the gloves.

"Looks like you had a tough day," she said.

"Kinda."

He went to the Wing Chun wooden dummy, a thick ironwood vertical pole with a half-dozen thinner rods sticking out at various angles, like a surrealist model of a coat rack. He began slapping the rods, mimicking blocks and strikes. Not a classic Western boxing exercise, it lacked the emotional jolt for her.

She went to the bedroom and stripped off her work clothes, sliding into one of his shirts. As she returned, she could hear the bouncing boom as he worked the sandbag.

"Want me to hold that for you?" she asked.

"Sure."

She struggled to hold the bag as he pounded, rocked back with the force of each blow. After about five minutes, she wasn't quite braced right and his punch jolted her backward. She fell to the floor.

"Sorry," he said, extending his hand and pulling her to her feet. She naturally came into his arms.

Within moments they were on the couch making love with a ferocity they hadn't experienced in years.

"Wow," they said simultaneously.

"I haven't seen you with so much passion in quite a while," she said, instantly regretting it.

He untangled from her. "I could say the same thing."

"Touché. And sorry."

They kissed, put their limited clothing back on, and cuddled on the couch for a few minutes.

"Hungry?" she asked.

"Starving."

In the kitchen, he chopped vegetables while she rolled the low-fat ground beef into meatballs and started the water boiling for spaghetti. A basic meal, but one of their favorites. Starting with a jar of Newman's Own marinara sauce, they added Parmesan cheese, garlic, onion, cilantro, tomatoes, and red peppers. As the big pot simmered on the stove, she asked, "What did you do today?"

"Not much."

"You looking into that dead client?"

"A little."

"Find anything?"

"Not much." The dismissive tone reminded her of Jeff's early teenage years, when any inquiry into what he was doing garnered monosyllabic responses.

She squeezed his butt. "Whatever it was you did today, maybe you should do more of it. I liked watching you work out on the bags."

"I noticed."

They hugged, and he told her, "We finished the investigation around my client's supposed suicide today. The state decided she killed herself. The papers can be shuffled into their little folders and the bureaucracy moves on."

"I take it you're still not satisfied?"

"She did not kill herself. There may be a serial killer operating."

"Really? Did you find proof?" she asked.

"Nothing I could go to the DA with."

"Hmm."

"What's that mean?"

"Well, it's a serious allegation. Could be bad for the whole city to have a story like that get out."

"And that's what's most important, the city's image?"

"If it's true, then it is important to get out. If it's a rumor or wild speculation . . ."

"I'm going to shower. Can you handle finishing up the meal?"

"Sure."

She turned her attention to the stove, since once again her attempts at connecting had failed. But she also knew her queries were more than curiosity; she was hoping for something to tell Tony Dorsey.

And that evening when they were making love, it had been Dorsey who was in her mind.

As the warm shower washed him clean, Hanson thought about why he had been reluctant to tell Jeanie. She would think he was crazy. Maybe he was.

He adjusted the water until it was colder and thought back to Vietnam, and the precious times when he could rinse off the sweaty, fungal feelings of fear. Hanson realized he had dissociated at least twice after being threatened by Vic, but was surprised at how calm being in the zone was. A familiar, friendly place where he was in control, ironically, while facing a gun.

Could he have disarmed Vic? Yes. Could he have killed him? Possibly. Did he want to? Not now.

Under the spray of the cold shower, he knew that if he continued on this path, violence was inevitable. He decided he would call Parker's niece, just to talk. If he could get a federal law enforcement person interested, he could back away.

KBAD disc jockey Paul Potter had the largest listening audience during prime morning drive time, and Mayor Robinson agreed to go on his show to announce the latest crime statistics. At the same time, a press release was delivered to the Associated Press, the *Oregonian*, the *Portland Tribune*, the TV stations, and other radio stations.

Potter had dark circles under his eyes, a perpetual scowl, and a smug tone. He was a onetime liberal Democrat who had become an archconservative when he learned what it could do for his ratings. Mayor Robinson faced him with a neutral smile.

"Once again, the numbers for major crime are down," Potter said suspiciously.

"That's right, Paul. The trend continues. Compared with any American city the same size as ours, we're at least fifty percent safer."

"Well, that's safer when it comes to major crimes. Petty crimes run about the same as elsewhere."

"A good point, but I think most citizens if given a choice between reducing murder, robbery, rape, kidnapping, and arson, versus cutting back on graffiti, car theft, and other nuisances, would choose the former."

"What about the so-called victimless crimes, like

113

prostitution and gambling? We're higher than other comparable cities," Potter said.

"Again, it is a matter of priorities. I've worked closely with Chief Forester to be sure that resources are allocated most effectively. This may mean that a bookie gets off, while an armed robber receives the full force of our legal system. Frankly, I wouldn't want it any other way."

"How do we know these numbers are accurate?" Potter asked accusingly.

"You can send anyone you want over to study the records. But the truth is evident in our city. In how many places can a woman walk the streets after dark and feel safe? I want this trend to continue. When I was growing up, and I suspect you as well, I could play in the street unsupervised. I want our city to be that kind of place, where a kid can play hide-and-seek outside without parents being nervous about perverts and murderers."

The mayor spoke with well-modulated volume and cadence, monitoring his distance from the padded Sennheiser mike. He preferred radio to TV, enjoying the calm of the studio, the deadened acoustics, the engineer signaling through the glass window as he performed in a fishbowl. He had done enough talk shows that he could visualize the tens of thousands of people listening in on his conversation with Potter and wouldn't get lulled into a false sense of intimacy.

"Assuming you're telling the truth and have significantly reduced crime, do you credit it to mandatory sentencing, a larger police force, or capital punishment?"

"It's our community-oriented policing," the mayor

said, knowing to not get trapped in Potter's forced choice frame. "Our officers don't just ride around in cars, they're out interacting every day, getting to know the neighborhood residents as people."

"But lots of communities have community-oriented policing."

"Well, Paul, maybe we do it better than the others."

"You're saying other police departments and cities are run badly?"

Potter loved nothing more than twisting words and getting guests to overreact.

"Every police department and every city does the best it can. We've put together a phenomenal team, and of course the citizens are part of that team. Do you remember that incident last month where the burglar was caught thanks to several concerned citizens calling 911? I was never more proud of our city."

Brian Hanson switched the radio to the oldies station. He listened to Potter on talk radio most mornings, but hearing the mayor pontificate about the low crime rate was annoying. What about Tammy LaFleur? Did you count her death in your homicides? Were there other murders conveniently classified as suicides or natural causes?

Hanson had voted against Robinson. His platform was too pro-corporation, paraphrasing Calvin Coolidge with "the business of our city is business." Robinson had outspent his opponent by three to one, and won by a 75–25 percent majority. Once in power, he implemented aggressive marketing to large corporations, tax incentives for expansion, sweetheart zoning deals. Hanson had to admit there had been great successes—an expanded airport, increased tax base, booming property values, big plans for the inner east side renovation. All things that Jeanie was happy to gloat about. She had been a Robinson fan from his first speech.

Robinson's message had the hidden undercurrent that if you weren't doing well, it was your fault. Hanson had heard him speak about the work ethic, America as a land of opportunity, his own immigrant parents' story. His family had come out during the 1849 gold rush and made their fortune by buying goods cheap in town, taking them out to the camps by buggy, and charging ten times what they paid. There was no concern for the underprivileged whom the government should be helping.

Hanson parked and headed into the office, though the clinic wouldn't open for another half hour. He liked the morning time, the quiet halls, the chance to get things done without interruption. It was never that way at the end of the day, even after hours. There were leftover crises, emergency phone calls, something to be cleaned up. The morning was fresh. If something had waited overnight, there was an excellent chance it could wait another day. And most clients didn't awake before 10 a.m., so there was little going on.

Betty Pearlman was at the front desk, studying the schedule for the day. "Brian, how are you?"

He shrugged. "Okay."

"You look less frazzled," she said. "I saw you've taken time off. I hope you've been having fun."

"I don't know if I'd call it fun, but it was distracting."

She waited for more information, but he said, "I better get to my desk. I've got paperwork to catch up on." Betty, like Jeanie, would never understand what he was doing. She'd probably tell him that if he violated his discipline's ethical code or brought embarrassment to the agency by getting swept up in a vice raid, he could lose his job. Most likely she would respond like a big sister, try to convince him his actions were a death wish and talking to a therapist would help. Therapy had been his religion for so many years. Now he had a feeling that talk slowed events down, and he needed action. He wasn't sure what the action should be, but the idea of masticating it in therapy was revolting.

At his desk, he grabbed the phone book and looked up the FBI office. It took him close to ten minutes to progress through the telephone screening process. He expected to get her voice mail and was surprised when there was a final click and he heard, "This is Special Agent Parker. Can I help you?"

"Uh, I'm Brian Hanson. Your name was given to me by your uncle Louis."

"He told me you would call," she said without warmth. "I can meet you at four thirty today. But I can't make any promises."

"I'll be there."

Louise Parker hung up the phone, instantly regretting that she had agreed to the meeting. Uncle Louis, her namesake and a primary influence on her young life, had called the day before saying he wanted her to talk with his counselor about a possible serial killer.

She thought back on Uncle Louis, how he'd had the best presents for her, the funniest stories, the loving twinkle in his eye as he joked with her. She had been a sickly child, academically gifted and socially awkward. Uncle Louis was the only one she remembered loving her as a gawky girl, as an insecure teen, and then as a confident young woman. Taking her to Oaks Bottom Amusement Park, to the zoo, to Blazer games and fun places her parents never seemed to have time to visit.

She also remembered his hushed conversations, sometimes shouting matches, with her father. And visiting Louis in prison. It was ironic that he had encouraged her to go into law enforcement. He had bought her the Junior G-Men kit back when it was only *G-men*. Now, close to one-fifth of the twelve thousand agents were women.

She had been drawn to the Bureau because of expected professionalism. Something she had largely found, but not without lots of good-old-boy sexism. She had come in in 1993, when the FBI had been hit by lawsuits alleging sexist practices. She had been working in a tedious office job for a large paper mill. The Bureau recruiter had liked that she had a prelaw bachelor's degree, excellent computer skills, and two X chromosomes.

She had survived the six-month background check and the seventeen weeks at Quantico. Some of the instructors, particularly in physical training, seemed to delight in demeaning female cadets. Half of the women had dropped out. With each extra push-up or lap around the track, Louise had become more determined. She graduated the top woman in her class, with only two men ahead of her.

She contended with mind-numbing federal paperwork, fifty-hour-minimum workweeks, colleagues who thought it the height of humor to leave FEMALE BODY INSPECTOR T-shirts anonymously on her desk, and occasional bosses who were so clueless they made Dilbert's boss seem like a paragon of leadership. She maintained an above average arrest record, had earned three commendations, and could quote from the *Manual of Investigative and Operational Guidelines* by heart. Every time she passed by the locked, glass-fronted case with confiscated weapons, or the display honoring the nearly three dozen FBI agents who had died in the line of duty since 1925, she felt honored. Louise loved her job.

Though not as exciting as her previous assignments, working in Portland had been wonderful. The place where she was raised. Closer to her uncle, whom she had seen age more rapidly in recent years. She had been one of the special agents—all FBI agents were special, they joked—who had broken up a multistate fencing ring. She liked the street crimes, the gritty interviews, knocking on doors, serving warrants. She knew some colleagues whispered she had Jane Wayne syndrome, but they were the same ones who started rumors that any woman who rebuffed their advances was a lesbian.

She still had an interest in serial killings and sexual assaults, and kept her eyes on data and trends, in addition to her regular assignments. She wished she was back in behavioral sciences, even though the intense work had nearly burned her out. Pursuing white-collar criminals just wasn't as exciting.

She usually was the first one in and among the last to leave, and still never completed all she wanted.

Which was why she was eager to have her meeting with Brian Hanson be as brief as possible. She had agreed to see him purely as a courtesy to her uncle, and because there was something peculiar happening in the city. Uncle Louis kept trying to get her interested, but she really didn't have time to investigate an amorphous feeling. She focused on the details of establishing probable cause as she prepared a search warrant for a secondhand dealer on Southeast Eighty-second Avenue.

Hanson had trouble concentrating, but having been a counselor for so long, he was able to coast with a certain amount of "Tell me more" and "That sounds like it was difficult for you?" Pearlman, however, was able to detect a difference and caught him in the hallway between sessions.

"What's up?" she asked.

"What do you mean?" he responded, feeling like he'd been caught in a lie.

"I don't know, but you seem different. I can't describe it. Am I hallucinating?"

"I need to leave a bit early today. I've got an FBI agent who is interested in talking to me about Tammy LaFleur."

Pearlman sighed. "If that's what you need to do, go ahead, take some time."

"Thanks."

She sighed again and moved off.

He met with the girl who had cut herself. She showed him a report card that included two As, a B, and a couple of Cs. "But those teachers hate me," she explained. The possibility for rapid change was one of the things he liked about working with younger clients. By the time they were in their twenties, destructive patterns were so entrenched, and the environment they were in was so reinforcing of bad choices, that it could take years to see a real difference.

He finished with his last client at a little before 4 p.m. The man was a late-stage alcoholic who looked seventy but was only fifty. He appeared to have early Alzheimer's though Hanson suspected it was Korsakoff's syndrome. He had scheduled the man three times for evaluations by the psychiatrist. Each time, the client had forgotten the appointment, despite reminder calls that morning or the evening before. He missed about half of his appointments with Hanson.

But today he had come in with a rambling update on his life. His conversation reeked of confabulation, filled-in details that weren't quite right. But Hanson had continued to build rapport, trying to get him in for the med evaluation and not confronting any of the questionable facts. The session had gone well, and another medical appointment had been set.

Hanson decided to walk to Louise Parker's office. His route traversed most of downtown, from the Old Town district where his agency was housed, past the half-dozen "skyscrapers," none taller than thirty-five stories, to the civic center that was home to city hall, the administrative building, the courthouse, police headquarters, the jail, and the federal building.

It was typical autumn in Portland, where the joke was if you didn't like the weather, just wait fifteen minutes and it would be different. Frozen coating on cars overnight, then a morning fog. The streets glossy from an earlier rain. A chill wind blew leaves around the street. The bright sun had begun to fade and the chill of the night was gaining strength.

Portland FBI headquarters was located close to the edge of downtown, in a bland white eleven-story building that also held medical, financial, and state government offices. Hanson rode up to the fourth-floor area, where a receptionist eyeballed him through the thick glass window. He noticed that someone had chipped a couple of letters off the raised sign, making it the Feral Bureau of Investigation. A paper sheet Scotch-taped to the window warned that it was a federal crime to take notes or pictures in the area.

He was buzzed in through the eight-foot-high doors into the windowless waiting area, still separated from the receptionist by bulletproof glass. Sitting in the barely comfortable chair, he noted the ten most wanted poster, pictures of the FBI director and the president, a large FBI seal. Nothing to warrant a *House & Garden* spread.

Parker came through the interior buzz-in door with a stiff smile on her face. She wore a navy blue tailored blazer, and Hanson couldn't tell if she had a weapon. He searched her features, looking for similarities with her uncle. She had dark blond hair pulled back, strong cheekbones, a pale complexion, and a firm hand-shake. Parker was a few pounds over fashionable weight but carried it well. The FBI agent led him into a small, also windowless room with a table, two chairs, and no other furnishings. The finest in interrogation decor.

Louise studied him with cool blue eyes. "How is Uncle Louie?"

"Good."

"Let me guess—that's all you're going to say due to confidentiality?"

He smiled. "I'm glad you understand."

"I've dealt with counselors before."

"I've been here before," Hanson responded.

"Really?" An eyebrow went up at his confession.

"Yes. Responded to a call of an individual insisting that the federal government was using interdimensional probes to disrupt his sleep."

She almost smiled. "We get a lot of mental patients."

"Many clients struggle with paranoid delusions," Hanson said. "The supervisor handled it well. We were able to convince the individual to leave without an arrest."

"Nice to hear," she said, taking out a pen and small pad. "Let's discuss your concerns."

"Tammy Grundig, aka Tammy LaFleur, was found dead a week ago. Police call it a suicide. Based on my experience and consistent with the research, I believe she was murdered."

Parker's demeanor changed. He had cleared a hurdle with his professional speech, and she was less dismissive. "Specifically?"

"She was shot in the face. Suicides rarely do that, especially women. Her roommate and a past boyfriend both made allegations of a serial killer."

"What do the local police say?"

"Suicide. And they were quick to close the case. The Grundig family is police royalty in this region."

"I thought the name was familiar," she said, writing quickly on the paper. "I believe one of our crime scene techs is a Grundig. I worked once on a case with a Lieutenant Grundig. And of course the former deputy chief."

He nodded.

"Was there evidence that Tammy had been sexually abused?"

"No."

"Signs of forced entry to her premises?"

"No."

"And the gun?"

"A .357 Magnum revolver. It had been stolen in town about six months earlier and might have been hers." He told her everything he knew about the death without divulging any history gathered during therapy sessions.

Louise sighed. "Mr. Hanson, do you realize how speculative what you're telling me is?"

"Maybe if you would make a few calls . . ."

"There's not enough. As a courtesy to Uncle Louie, I'll run the info through HITS and ViCAP." She saw his confused expression. "Homicide Investigation Tracking System and Violent Criminal Apprehension Program. They're a regional and a national database respectively that track murders and sexual assaults."

"Thanks," he said, waiting, then realizing she expected him to leave. He was about to get up when she glanced at her gold Lady Rolex and said, "I'll do it now."

For a few minutes, she typed at her computer, scrolling through different fields. Her squint as she reviewed the words on the screen reminded him of Louis's expressions when he concentrated.

She looked up suddenly, and he turned away, embarrassed. "No hits are consistent with a serial-killer pattern. Frankly, the way her death runs counter to your experience with suicides, the evidence pattern runs counter to my experience with serial killers."

"You don't think it's murder?"

"I didn't say that, just that I doubt it is a serial killer."

"Why?"

"There's usually a ritualistic component to serial killings. Or they fit into a pattern. Or evidence of souvenir taking."

"What do you think it is?"

She steepled her fingers in front of her face, then rubbed the bridge of her nose. Clearly, she was deliberating how much to say. He knew when to be quiet.

"Did Louie talk much about me?"

"I can't go into it. Sorry."

Her face flushed and she leaned forward. "You want me to spill confidential material to you, but you won't even tell me a thing about what he said?"

Hanson hesitated, then rose. "Thanks for your time."

"Please sit down. You passed."

"What?"

"If you had broken your confidentiality at a little bluster, I'd know you couldn't be trusted. You come with high praise from Louie, and that counts a lot with me. Plus you seem to know how to keep your mouth shut."

Hanson settled down into the seat, not sure whether he felt pleased that he had passed or annoyed that he had been tested.

"I remember when I was about eight, and he would tell me stories about being a private investigator. He made it sound exciting." A slow blush rouged her cheeks. "Of course that was before he wound up in prison." She was all business again. "I'm not exactly sure what is going on in this town. Murder is a local-jurisdiction matter unless it is an act that is part of a RICO conspiracy. You know what RICO is?"

"Organized crime?"

"Right. Racketeer Influenced and Corrupt Organizations. Originally used to target the Mafia, but over the years used for everything from corrupt cops and politicians to Colombian drug cartels."

"What's the conspiracy?"

"I don't know. There are puzzling patterns of deaths and disappearances in Portland in the past few years. Things I hear about only coincidentally. Like Ms. LaFleur/Grundig. Or tips from Uncle Louie. Not enough to build a case."

"Do you have a suspect?"

She shook her head, a little too quickly. He didn't believe her.

"If anything else occurs to you, please feel free to call," she said while rising and escorting him to the door.

A light drizzle created a cool mist in the air outside. Had he been given a polite brush-off or was Louise Parker going to follow up? He walked back across downtown, listening to the hiss of traffic on rainy streets, and thinking about Louise Parker.

Louise Parker made a few more notes to herself on a yellow legal pad. She had been relatively honest with Hanson. She had theories and ideas, but sharing them with a civilian would be foolish.

She wished she had more time to spend on his speculation, but her boss, a Blue Flamer who was notorious for overzealous performance evaluations, would be interrogating her like a suspect if her progress reports on the computer-smuggling case were too slow.

Hanson was easy to talk to. He had a polite sincerity and intense way of listening that made her feel more willing to talk and to trust. She could understand why her uncle liked him.

She checked her voice mail and her e-mail, then resumed work on developing probable cause for a warehouse search warrant.

CHAPTER EIGHT

Hanson had taken the morning off and sat in the car facing Tammy's old apartment, in the stucco apartment complex where he had met Trixie. He hoped to catch her, maybe just awakening, vulnerable to questioning but not doped up.

Bright daylight treated the place unkindly. There were rusted patches on railings, peeling paint, a drooping rain gutter on the mossy roof. Trixie and Tammy's apartment was on the ground floor, sharing the corridor with one other apartment. A stairway led to what Hanson presumed were two similarly configured rental units upstairs.

Hanson strode to Trixie's door and knocked. No answer. He checked her mailbox—the masking tape with residents' names had been peeled up and there were only the sticky glue scabs on the surface. He peered into the narrow box and saw no mail. He pressed his ear to the door. Silence. He sniffed the air and noted the distinct scent of curry overpowering the stuffy scent of the hallway. He tracked the smell to an apartment at the opposite end of the hall and knocked at the door. A tiny, dark-skinned elderly woman of uncertain ethnic origin opened the door.

"I'm looking for Trixie," he said, pointing to the other apartment.

Her scowl made him momentarily embarrassed, but explaining he wasn't a customer would have been ignored.

"She's gone," the woman said, starting to close the door.

"Any idea where?"

"She's gone." The door was shut in his face.

At the apartment directly above Trixie's, a man with a Neanderthal jaw and brow and bristly facial hair said he'd heard her leave with someone in the middle of the night, a week earlier.

"Did she go voluntarily?"

The man grunted and looked perplexed. "Voluntarily?" The word was slurred, each syllable sounded out with effort. He was either drunk, developmentally disabled, or more likely both. "What d'you mean?"

"Were voices raised? Did you hear threats?"

He squinted while thinking, then shook his head slowly. "I mighta had a few beers. It's kinda blurry. Haven't seen her in a while," the man said, his hand rubbing his crotch.

Down the stairs, Hanson stared at Trixie's front door, noting the gap between the frame and the door. With a little leverage from a tire iron, it would pop.

He glanced sideways and realized that he could peer into her apartment by going a dozen paces down the driveway. Hanson eased over and on tiptoes peered in.

The kinky pictures had been taken off the wall, obvious from unadorned nails and the shadow dirt line where frames had hung. The red couch and love seat were gone, as were the piles of adult magazines. The apartment looked more like a typical young working woman's home.

"Hey, freak, what are you doing?"

A trio in their midteens, husky, with Eminem swagger and baseball caps pulled low on their heads, surrounded him.

"I'm a friend of Trixie, wondering where she is," Hanson said.

"You one of her weirdo friends," the apparent leader said. "Like a cash customer."

"No."

Hanson turned his back to the building wall and faced them. His coiled posture made them hesitate. He had let his shoulders drop, his lips curled in an unfriendly smile. He guessed the speaker would not be the first to lunge, probably the one to his right, who was the first lieutenant. The young man's left shoulder had dropped, almost imperceptibly, and Hanson anticipated a southpaw jab. The leader was stepping to the side, the third bullyboy looking for an opening.

"Bet you're a cash customer. Got a big wad you're set to blow, freak. You like her to slap you around? We'll take care of that. And your money too."

Hanson's hands were up in a conciliatory gesture, about a foot apart, chest high. His arms were loose, ready to block or plunge fingers into the bullyboys' throats or eyes. "I'm not looking for trouble. But I'm not running either," he said, his voice low and husky with a Clint Eastwood rasp. "If you've made money rolling Trixie's customers, that's your business. But if you fuck with me, you make it my business."

Fractions of seconds passed slowly; Hanson watched, waited.

The bullyboys were like raccoons that had fished a piranha out of the koi pond.

Hanson was blissfully alert as the blade clicked open. It was the first lieutenant, eager to prove himself. Hanson shifted his feet, fluid energy flowing into his arms.

"Hey, what's going on over there?" The shrill voice came from a white woman in her sixties who would be called scrawny before she'd be called slender. Sharp-featured, with gray hair pulled back into a bun, she had a solid grip on a black-bristled broom that was bigger than she was. If it had been a classic straw broom, Hanson could imagine her labeled a witch.

Before the bullyboys could answer, she waved her broom. "Johnny, is that you? You fixing to get into trouble again? Who's that with you? Todd? Aaron?"

"We weren't doing nothing," said Johnny, the leader.

The knife had disappeared and they were trying to look like they just happened to be lounging in a semi-circle around a stranger in the driveway.

"You be getting on now," the broom lady said with a hint of the Ozarks in her tone. "You don't want me to be talking to your mothers now, do you?" She gestured with the broom, as if she were sweeping them up.

"No, Mrs. Jeter," they echoed dutifully before slinking off.

Hanson leaned against the wall, feeling the adrenaline surge. He noticed a strange emotion, disappointment. Violence interruptus. He had been eager to test himself against the trio.

"Dr. Hanson, you ought to be ashamed of yourself."

He was surprised she knew his name and momentarily wondered if she was a witch. Then he realized she had called him Doctor, which so many of the older clients, like Louis, preferred to do. He searched his memory, trying to identify her.

She seemed to know. "You never shrunk my head, if that's why you're scrunching up your brow thinking." She leaned on her broom and grinned, showing ill-fitting dentures. "Was my grandson you helped, Rupert."

He nodded as if he remembered.

"I don't expect you recall him. He's the same age as Johnny and his dunderheads. Used to hang out with them, had a few arrests. You worked with him. He's in the Army now, getting an education. Made sergeant. I reckon he'd be glad you knew."

The name Rupert was unusual enough that Hanson did remember. The boy fit the classic profile—no good male role models, poverty, chaotic home, lack of job skills, lack of structure, too much testosterone. The military had been an ideal solution. Even through the trauma of his own war experiences, Hanson recognized that the military, 12-step programs, and a healthy partner had probably changed more lives positively than all the psychotherapists in all the offices throughout the country.

"I do remember Rupert. A decent kid. Liked the Mariners, always wore their cap."

Her grin grew wider. "Son of a bitch. He'd be tickled to know you didn't forget him. I'm gonna e-mail him tonight." She saw his surprised expression. "You think an old coot like me can't log on to the Internet? Heck, I get half my medications off the Web. Now, what're you doing snooping around those girls' apartment?" She gave him a lecherous look. "Maybe that's a dumb question. You *are* a man. My Ezra, he was damn close to ninety when he passed on. I was a child bride, you see. Anyway, no sooner do I get the computer, than I catch him looking at those girlie sites. I didn't mind. Put a little fire back in the old locomotive." She smiled at a memory.

"I'm not here about their business."

"Which means you're here about yours?"

"I can't say," Hanson said, lapsing back into his professional mode. Even his innocuous remarks about Rupert were a confidentiality violation, but he was still off-kilter from the adrenaline.

"I reckon either one of those girls could have created enough business for several headshrinkers. 'Cause if it weren't for men coming around like hound dogs after a bitch in heat, they wouldn't have been like that."

"Any idea where Trixie might have gone?"

She shook her head.

"Did you ever see anyone suspicious hanging around?"

"They had as many gentleman callers as a McDonald's drive-through window. Most of them looked out of place."

"How's that?"

She waved the broom in a big circle. "Too fancy for this neighborhood. They were like those white boys

133

you see going into the ghetto to get drugs. Only most of these were older, dressed snazzy, fancy cars. I guess in their minds they felt like they were going on a date."

"You have any hunches about what happened to Tammy?"

"Woman's intuition?"

He smiled. "It's more often right than not."

She smiled back. "I always said you were a smart one. The men I know ignored it. That's why they're all dead, and I'm still going out dancin' on Saturday nights." She pointed to a small, well-kept house across the alley. "That's where I live. I let the two of them sunbathe in my backyard." She pointed to an area with a six-foot cedar fence. "Made them mint juleps, shared a few laughs." She was about to cry, sniffled, then recomposed herself. "Tammy didn't tell me much, but I do know who her father is. Do you?"

"The former deputy chief."

"Right. And she's got those brothers and cousins and uncles who are poh-lice." The old woman snorted back a laugh. "Of course from what she told me, sometimes she did play a police officer. Maybe the mean nurse. Or the nasty teacher."

"You think her father knows something?"

The woman nodded. "She told me she had the feeling he was watching her. Not quite watching over her, but keeping an eye out. A couple of near arrests she got off with a warning. And the cops would call her Ms. Grundig. Another time she was beaten up by one of her customers. She told me later it had become a police priority. When they found the john, shortly thereafter he was in an emergency room looking like he had been hit by a tractor trailer."

"Anything else you can tell me?"

She took her broom abruptly and began sweeping the driveway. "No, nothing." She began moving away without a good-bye, intent on her sweeping, as if the idea of being any sort of a witness had suddenly become unappealing.

Wolf double-checked the mug shot and verified he had the right target. Police suspected Lou Ray of a couple dozen robberies of convenience stores. In an independent store, the Asian owner had reached for a pistol under the counter and learned why the big franchises had a no-resistance policy. The owner left behind a wife and their six children, ranging in age from twelve to twenty, all of whom worked in the store. The immigrant dream wiped out by Lou Ray and his sawed-off shotgun.

Wolf knew his history and had instructions that he was to disappear.

"There's no warning to be sent on this one," he had been told. "We've been having too many deaths. Just have him leave."

"How persuasive should I be?" Wolf had asked coyly.

"As persuasive as you need to be."

Wolf followed Ray to a loud North Portland bar. There were a couple of big Harleys outside, their chrome reflecting the streetlight. The windows of the bar were blacked over, in violation of state liquor authority regulations. Wolf suspected that was the least of the violations at the place. The faded sign, "The Happy Hour," was crudely painted black on white.

An occasional shout or loud laugh escaped the bar. Wolf waited in his car close to an hour before Ray walked out stiffly, with the effort of someone resisting the influence of alcohol.

He drove over the St. John's Bridge, and Wolf guessed he was heading home, to his small wooden frame house in the hills above the industrial area by U.S. 30. There was the slightest weave to his driving. Wolf hoped no cop pulled him over—it would mean an unfortunate delay in Ray's departure.

A quarter mile from the house, Wolf sped ahead of Ray. He reached the isolated street before the armed robber and parked his car by a vacant house. Wolf crouched in the overgrown brush near Ray's front steps.

Ray parked and stumbled up the steps, his intoxication more evident. He had left his front door unlocked, either confident that no one would dare bother him or not caring about his crappy belongings in his shabby house.

As he opened the door, Wolf pushed in behind, slamming him down to the floor. The sudden jolt activated Ray's bar-fighter reflexes. He rolled and came up swinging. Wolf parried easily, then punched him hard in the stomach. As Ray doubled over, Wolf brought an elbow down on the top of his neck, and Ray collapsed. Wolf lifted the barely conscious man up, at the same time taking out his K-bar. The brass-knuckle-handled knife was a daunting sight, but Ray stayed tough.

"Fuck you, I ain't got money," he said.

Wolf made a small flick of the blade. Ray yelped as blood poured from his lip. Wolf pressed the foot-long knife against his throat. "I don't like cursing. Especially from a low-life sack of shit."

"What do you want?" Ray demanded.

"Do you have a girlfriend?"

"Sure."

"What's her name?"

"Peggy. Peggy Lee."

Wolf flicked the knife again, and Ray screamed. He was bleeding from an earlobe with a half-inch cut. "I admire Ms. Lee's taste in men. I need you to come into the kitchen and write her a note."

"What kind of note?"

Wolf put the razor-sharp edge of the knife against Ray's throat. The bleeding armed robber had sobered. "I'll dictate," Wolf said. "Don't worry, I won't use big words."

Wolf kept one hand locked on Ray's shoulder and the knife by his throat as they walked to the kitchen. Flies hovered over plates of rotting food piled up in the sink.

"Who are you?" Ray asked.

"I'm from the Health Department. Get paper and a pen."

Ray noticed that Wolf had a small Army surplus backpack on and was wearing latex gloves, with hospital booties on his shoes. He abruptly realized how close to death he was.

"Here," he said, eagerly producing a legal pad and a greasy Bic from a kitchen drawer. "Whatever you want."

"Good. You write what I say, then we go to your car, you drive off, and don't come back. Understood?"

"Understood." Ray eyed a steak knife that was lying on the worn gray Formica kitchen counter.

Wolf followed his gaze and shook his head no, so slowly and confidently that Ray didn't even seriously consider the move. His only hope was in complete obedience.

"What do you call Ms. Lee as a term of endearment?"

"Huh?"

"You got a pet nickname for her?"

Ray looked embarrassed, then muttered, "Honeyjugs."

"Sweet. Write something like 'Honeyjugs, I got to get out of town. It's been nice knowing you.'"

Ray's hand shook as he tried to write.

"Take it easy, tough guy," Wolf said. "You're almost done, and on your way out of here."

Ray calmed enough to write the note, slowly printing, each letter an effort. "Hunnyjugs, I got to get owt of town." When the armed robber was done, Wolf glanced at the note, made sure it was adequate, then stepped behind Ray.

"Okay, now let's walk toward the door."

As Ray relaxed, Wolf grabbed his jaw and shoved the K-bar into the back of his head, pithing him like a frog. Ray jerked for a moment, and barely bled. Wolf lowered the body. The killer used a paper towel to wipe up the few droplets of blood from the kitchen floor. He used another paper towel to wipe the blade of his knife clean, then put both paper towels in a Baggie and tucked it in his pocket.

"A lot less painful than it was for the grocer," Wolf

said to the corpse, setting the note on the counter.

He took a six-by-eight tarp, a small carbide-bladed saw, a blowtorch, and three large trash bags from his backpack. With the indifference of a slaughterhouse worker, he severed Ray's head and both legs from the torso. He burned away much of Ray's face and fingertips. Each part went into a trash bag, which was then sealed. He carried the two legs and the head out to the car in one trip, and the torso with arms attached in another. He drove two hours east of Portland, then buried the torso about a quarter mile off a backcountry logging road. He drove another five miles and repeated the routine with the head. Then another three miles to bury the legs. All were more than two feet deep in the soft earth, with rocks casually strewn on top to keep coyotes and other scavengers from uprooting them. Jorge Gonzalez was in a similar grave about a half mile south.

"As persuasive as you need to be." With characters like Lou Ray, force was better than persuasion. One less scumbag on the streets meant that dozens, if not hundreds, of people could be safer. Wolf left a window open as he drove, blasting his face with cool night air. He was tired, but content.

"You seem more at peace," Betty Pearlman said, sipping a Diet Coke and gazing at Hanson over the top of her half-frame mock-tortoiseshell glasses. "You've taken a few days off. Good for you."

"It's been helpful," he said, feeling guilty but not telling her that the time had been spent trying to gather information about Tammy LaFleur's final weeks. Plans of tracking down a killer were not in keeping with the therapeutic ethos. If he found a serial killer, what would he do? Particularly if he thought the police wouldn't act?

"You've lost a little weight," she said enviously. "Working out?"

"Yeah. Every day." Which was true. He was sore, but pleasantly tighter.

"Good for you. I wish I could do it," Pearlman said.

He smiled and they got down to clinical supervision. They met once a week for an hour to discuss his cases—were there issues he had missed, liabilities to share, possible ethical concerns? Pearlman would often have a slightly different view on a case, which gave him a broader perspective. By being one step removed, she could be more objective, provide a counterbalance. He usually looked forward to the session as a chance for reflection and challenge.

His renewed vigor showed in his therapeutic work, and Betty commented on it. He was more confrontational, less willing to just sit and listen. He recounted some of his interventions, concerned that he was becoming too directive.

"I hear you saying that you know he's no good; what are you going to do in the next week to improve your situation?" he had asked one woman.

To another one, he had said, "You say you'll try and get to group. Every time I heard the word 'try,' I figure it's never going to happen. What obstacles are there to your saying you will do it?"

To a third, he had said, "Denial of your problems seems to work for you. That's fine, but what's the point of coming in if you're not ready to change?"

His blunt but compassionate manner had worked. He had seen more progress among clients in the past two weeks than he had in months beforehand.

"I'm trying things a little differently," he told Betty. "More active."

"Whatever you're doing, let's bottle it," Pearlman said. "Is there a framework you could pass on to staff at our next group consult?"

"I don't think so. Not really empirically grounded, more of a personal paradigm shift. I'm looking at the behavioral more than the cognitive."

"What do you think is causing this shift?"

"Not sure."

"I can speculate," she said.

He cocked his head, indicating he was listening.

"Tammy's death. The idea that life is a time-limited experience."

"It's possible."

"Make sure you're spending enough time on engagement. Not jumping into action too quickly. You know the old bromide: 'Before I care that you know, I have to know that you care.'"

"Like all the 12-step-isms. They become a cliché because of their wisdom."

"We're getting into an intellectual sidetrack. Usually that happens when there's something you don't want to talk about."

She knew him too well. Everyone's imminent mortality may have been a factor in his more directive therapy approach, but it was wanting action on Tammy's case that was pushing the shift, Hanson knew. He didn't want to tell Betty that, and shrugged.

"That reminds me, I'd like to take tomorrow morning off."

She shrugged back at him but didn't push further.

"You know mornings tend to be light. You'll be in by . . . ?"

"Before noon."

"You're going to kick back?"

"Sort of."

CHAPTER NINE

Hanson guessed that once again a surprise morning visit would be best. As he drove the Sunset Highway into Beaverton, the unique architecture of the city began to give way to the bland familiarity of the suburbs. Named for the once prolific state animal, the area was now Anytown, USA, a landscape of strip malls, franchise-infested four-lane boulevards, sprawling shopping centers, occasional swatches of artificial-looking greenery, and housing developments with pretentiously poetic names. Garden View Acres, Golden Creek Estates, Palace Vistas.

The former deputy police chief lived on a cul-de-sac in Arboreal Meadows. Based on the unmanned guard booth at the entrance, the amount of green space between the houses, and the various efforts at creating similar but not quite identical trimmings, Hanson estimated prices well into the half-million-dollar range.

He parked at the foot of the respectably long, curving driveway and walked to the ten-foot-high maple wood door. The bell chimed the "Da, da, da, dum. Da, da, da, dum" theme from *Dragnet*. Either Grundig had a sense of humor or he was obsessed with his years on the force.

No answer, though there appeared to be lights on inside when Hanson peered in through the large window near the door. He had the impression of showroom-perfect furnishings, perhaps coordinated by an interior decorator. Dark wood cabinets and subdued pattern upholsteries.

Off to the side was a gated, six-foot-high rounded-top cedar fence. There was a simple latch on the gate and Hanson opened it. He froze, staring at a stunningly beautiful garden.

"You like what you see?" Walter Grundig was a big man who had gotten smaller, a high school football player plus seventy years. He had closed-cropped gray hair and rheumy but piercing blue eyes. He held a large, silvered .45 revolver in his right hand, pointed casually at Hanson. "You've got a few seconds to explain yourself. Hands in plain view and not moving so fast that you'd startle an old man." There was a breathless quality to his words, and Hanson recognized symptoms of chronic lung disease.

"This is a beautiful garden."

"That it is." Grundig lifted the shiny gun. "Skip the chatter about my daffodils. Very, very slowly pull your shirt out of your pants, unbuckle your belt, then roll down the top of the pants all around. Good. Now turn three hundred sixty degrees, slowly."

Hanson did as directed as the ex-cop watched carefully.

"Good, now pull your pants legs up at least six

inches." Hanson was about to readjust his belt when Grundig barked, "No, no. Keep the pants loose."

Hanson felt awkward with his pants drooping, barely hanging on his hips. "Slowly take your wallet out of your pocket, using your fingertips. Keep the other hand up and out to the side. Then toss the wallet to me."

Hanson did as he was told. The ex-chief caught the wallet and glanced at the driver's license, never looking away from Hanson for more than a fraction of a second. "Ugly picture," Grundig said. "At least you didn't lie about your height and weight like most do."

Using a thumb and forefinger, and still keeping a wary eye on Hanson, he pulled out one of Hanson's business cards. "Ah, you're a counselor. You've come here to counsel me about my roses having a rust problem?"

"No, sir. I wanted to talk."

"That 'sir' shit doesn't count much with me. The politest guys I know were just out of prison or the military. Your hair's too long for both of those. Only other ones who use 'sir' nowadays are salesmen. I got respect for a military man, the others I'd just as soon shoot."

"I use 'sir' with anyone holding a gun on me."

Grundig nodded, and lowered the gun a few notches. "You have many dealings with people holding guns on you?"

"Until recently, no."

"You work at the downtown psych center," Grundig said, fingering the business card. "That was a wild place, even back when I was a desk sergeant in central. Everyone hated calls from there. Never knew if you'd get stuck with an arm-swinging mental who hadn't bathed since Roosevelt was president." He chuckled. "Of course if we found someone like that on the street and couldn't get him into an ER, we'd dump 'im at your place."

"It's probably more humane than leaving him on the street, and it cuts down your paperwork."

"Ah, the ultimate goal, less paperwork. Until I became a paper pusher at headquarters and spent my time developing new forms and procedures. Mr. Hanson, I still have many enemies in this town, and you may be one of them. You might still have a flat knife taped to your body or an accomplice watching and waiting. You look like you might be able to kill an old coot like me barehanded."

"You'd put up too much of a fight," Hanson said, knowing that the flattery both admitted a violence potential and was a compliment to the old man.

Grundig coughed. "You can fix yourself." As Hanson adjusted his pants, the retired cop said, "You'd be Vietnam era. You serve your country?"

"Pleiku and a few other places."

"I was a grunt in WWII. Did get to vacation on the beaches at Normandy. Unfortunately, the Nazis had their beach blankets set up and we had to take it from them." The hand holding the gun lowered. "Probably an old man's vanity that there's people around who'd be out to get me still."

"You can't be too careful."

Grundig coughed again. "Let's go in. This is the most talking I've done in a long time."

Inside, the smell of cigarette smoke was strong. As was the feeling it was a man's house, a giant den.

"You're wondering why I'm suddenly not ready to

shoot?" Grundig asked, as he set the gun down on a counter.

"The thought crossed my mind."

"I recognized your name. Wasn't sure if you were in law enforcement or maybe been arrested. Hard to place out of context. Ah, I used to have such a great memory for names and faces. The chief told me I could've been an old ward heeler politician." He gestured for Hanson to follow and they walked to the living room. Grundig eased into a black leather recliner and gestured for Hanson to sit in the twin. Grundig grabbed a pack of Marlboros and lit up.

"Thirty years a smoker, then I got diagnosed with emphysema. Gave it up. Two years ago got the diagnosis of the big C. So much for being good." He lit a cigarette, inhaled with passion, then coughed as he exhaled. He didn't seem to care. "That was right after my wife died. Not a good year." Another cough. "Suzie told me about you."

"Suzie?"

"Susan Tammy Grundig was the name her mother and I agreed on when she was born. I don't know where that LaFleur crap came from. But I don't know where a lot came from with her." After another deep drag on the cigarette, he said, "Ah, maybe I do have some ideas. Who was it said that it is a pity life has to be lived looking forward but can only be understood looking backward?"

"I don't know."

"The guys who knew me on the job would laugh. I'm getting philosophical. I've read Shakespeare, hadn't done that since high school. The Bible. Facing death does that. You ever find that in people?"

"Sometimes." Hanson had seen people get philosophical and others get mindlessly busy. Some people did things they had never done; others fell back on comfortable routines. Some became quiet and others couldn't stop talking.

"But you're not here to hear an old man babble. You want to know about Suzie."

Hanson nodded, attentive.

"She was second born, with three brothers. But I guess she told you that."

"I can't go into what she might have said, but I am eager to hear whatever you have to say."

"She's dead. So what's with this confidentiality doubletalk?"

"Confidentiality survives death," Hanson said.

"Nice to hear that something does. Like the man said, the good is often interred with their bones." He smiled tightly and coughed. "I probably wouldn't want to hear what she said anyway." He gazed at Hanson questioningly, hopefully. The counselor kept a sympathetic but impassive face.

"Okay, maybe before I talk to you, you'll tell me a little something that's been bothering me," Grundig said gruffly. "Like one of the headshrinkers said she was a borderline. What does that mean?"

"We try not to call people that anymore. She'd be called a person with borderline personality disorder, if that was her diagnosis. Reducing someone to just their diagnosis is dehumanizing."

"I never did well with that political correctness crap."

"Borderline personality disorder comes from way

back, when psychodynamic therapists talked of clients on the border between normal neurotic and psychotic. More modern times we look at nature and nurture, how someone can be a bad fit for their family, and it leads to emotional dysregulation. Then troubling secondary behaviors. Like drugs, prostitution, unhealthy relationships, shoplifting. Anger problems, uncertain of who she was, sometimes dissociating."

"Huh?"

"Zoning out. Black and white thinking, extreme moodiness. A lot of times it is linked to childhood traumas. Not everyone with BPD was abused, but the vast majority have been."

"Well, I doted on the boys. It was a different time. I regret it. When she got withdrawn around the time she was ten, I didn't pay attention. My wife didn't either. The boys were playing softball, basketball, attending school functions, and she just got mopier. I even yelled at her about it. A little drama queen. Trauma, yeah, trauma.

"Finally it came out that one of the coaches was molesting her. She didn't want to press charges, said she loved him. He was thirty, she was then twelve. I nearly killed him, but I didn't feel much better. He moved away after he got out of the hospital. The damage was done. You probably know the details but I want you to hear my side. I know I screwed up. Of all the things in my life, my neglecting her is what I regret most." He coughed, ground out the cigarette, then lit another. "And that includes starting smoking.

"Of course she got back at me. At the whole family. I can't count how many times I got a call from a police department somewhere in the area, that they had picked her up for prostitution, with drugs, possessing stolen property. And if I came and got her, there would be no record. Yeah, she got her revenge."

"It sounds painful," Hanson said when Grundig paused.

The former deputy chief puffed slowly, lost in his melancholy. "I got her in to drug rehab a couple of times. It seemed like she was getting better then she'd disappear and I'd get those late night calls. My wife died of a heart attack shortly after one of them. I don't think it was a coincidence." He coughed again, and angrily ground out the cigarette. "That's my wife's garden. She was cremated, had asked for her ashes to be spread there. I tend the garden. It's like my time with her."

Hanson nodded slowly, honored by Grundig's trust and disclosure.

"I was a good man. Locked up bad people. Ask anyone who served with me. Yet as I try and make peace with my Maker, this comes up. There doesn't seem to be a clear answer anywhere."

"The answer to what?"

"Why? Just that, why?"

Having been with so many people holding secrets, Hanson sensed that there was more, that the deputy chief was holding back, and ready to talk. Like a cop on a surveillance, the counselor waited.

"Suzie spoke highly of you. Felt you'd been helpful, that you cared. Was she right?"

Hanson nodded.

Grundig looked even older as he sat silently. In the quiet of the house, Hanson could hear his gentle wheeze.

"Do you think she killed herself?" the ex-cop asked.

"No."

"She didn't. That girl was a fighter. She had bad taste in men but she never gave up. Do you believe me?"

Hanson nodded.

The old man's eyes misted and he roughly wiped them with a sleeve, then glared at Hanson as if to dare him to say something.

"Your daughter was a fighter," Hanson said.

"Damn straight. When I saw that girl and her troubles and how she kept bulldozing through, I knew she was my daughter." He smiled and coughed. "I remember her as a little kid, falling down and getting up, falling down and getting up."

Hanson could feel the old man's energy winding down and was concerned that he would get stalled in reminiscence. "But if it wasn't suicide, what then? And why?"

"She was murdered, I have little doubt." Grundig paused and lit another cigarette. "You've got me smoking like a chimney. Not that it matters much." After a few slow puffs, he said, "A couple days after her death, a cop named Quimby came around. He made it clear that they didn't want me making a fuss. He was his usual smooth self, hinting that my pension could be screwed up, my family's reputation sullied, even my life in jeopardy, if I dug around. Of course I snooped. My daughter wasn't the only one with a stubborn streak. I got a couple more warnings, then gave up." He looked off. "That's why I'm telling you. I want someone else to have the memory of her the way she was, not the way they want it to seem. If you can find out anything, great. Me, I'm ready to spread my ashes in the flowers."

"Do you have a theory about who killed her?"

"She called me a few weeks before she was killed. Told me she was getting her life together. Again. I was skeptical, had heard it before. You know how it is with an addict."

Hanson nodded.

"She told me she was involved with a legit guy, not a crook. Had hopes he would straighten things out as far as getting her kid back. She said she'd been straight for a month and he was going to help her."

"Any idea who he was?"

"Someone well connected. Political or maybe a celebrity. But I never could tell how much of her stories were addict bs. She also had crazy talk about a conspiracy. Made it sound like she knew about a big deal that she wasn't supposed to know about."

"Did she give details?"

Grundig shook his head.

"I thought at one point she might have been the victim of a serial killer."

"I worked a half dozen serial-killer cases. I-5 killer, Green River killer, Molalla Forest, Ted Bundy." Grundig coughed. "It doesn't have the same feel. There's a funny feeling you get with a serial killer, like you stepped onto a stage. The scene is arranged to be seen, experienced. There's a lack of spontaneity in most cases, a planfulness that's palpable."

Hanson was tempted to tell him that Louise Parker had said something similar but decided to keep drawing Grundig out. "What would you recommend I do?"

"The smart thing to do would be to forget her.

That's what my sons have decided to do. They were always embarrassed by Suzie. But if you were doing that you wouldn't be here, right?"

Hanson nodded again.

"I'd find out what was going on in her last week. Someone must have seen her with someone unusual. Maybe she talked to a friend. But you're going to be stepping on toes."

"Won't be the first time," Hanson said.

Tony Dorsey loved the excitement of a construction site. So much of what he did involved ideas, talk, memos. Construction sites were the concrete realization of that work, abstraction made real. The wet cement and shiny metal studs, the scream of the circular saws, pounding of hammers, hard-hatted workers hurrying about, piles of material transformed into a structure. It reminded him of his past, though sites in the Pacific Northwest were nowhere near as corrupt as the ones he had visited during his previous life. The concrete wasn't watered down, nor were inspectors paid off. There were safety policies and procedures, and bosses actually seemed to follow them. Of course as the go-to guy in the mayor's office, it was often his job to provide a shortcut. To make sure a well-connected friend's application at the bottom of the pile was switched to the top or a marginally acceptable inspection had a few points shifted, to be sure it passed.

There had been community resistance to this project, a high-rise full of pricey condos in a neighborhood where nothing currently was taller than three stories. The building was part of Mayor Robinson's vision for greater urban density. At least that was the official public reason. The fact that both the major contractor and the bank financing the project had donated more than fifty thousand dollars to his past campaigns, and had committed to that much again if he ran for Senate, was not discussed.

Dorsey spotted the contractor hurrying into the white-sided trailer at the edge of the site. Walking carefully in his Ferragamos, Dorsey rapped on the trailer door and stepped inside without waiting for a response.

"Tony, good to see you," the contractor lied. A stout sixty-year-old with an oversize coffee cup in his hand, he sat at a small desk looking over papers. The cramped trailer was packed with papers on clipboards, pinned-up blueprints, racks with recharging walkie-talkies, spare hard hats, some of the more expensive pneumatic tools, and spools of copper wire.

"I know. Though it would have been nice if you returned my phone calls."

"I'm sorry, I've been busy. Got three projects going. The new Clackamas County administrative building. The mall development. And this. I been running around so much, haven't even had a chance to return calls in days. I was about to call."

"I'm sure."

"So how's the mayor?"

"Fine. Though he'd be disappointed if he heard who you chose as the artist for the city admin project." Through the public art program, 1.33 percent of the capital budget on new construction projects had to go for art.

"C'mon, you know I don't choose the artist."

"The mayor was really hoping that Candice Crossley's work would be chosen. He's a big fan of hers."

"But the commission—"

"I know what went on. I know it's not a coincidence that your cousin was chosen. His work looks like shit."

"It's not my taste either, but—"

"I suggest you talk with the commission about the inherent problems in siting his artwork, how it doesn't fit with the architect's vision, whatever you need to say. I'm hoping to hear that after careful reconsideration, Crossley's work was chosen."

"But she's a painter."

"Those long corridors demanded something to break up the monotony."

"I can't—"

"Don't tell me what you can't do. Now I believe that at least ten percent of your subcontractors need to be non-Caucasian. It looks awfully white-bread around here. I didn't recognize any minority names in the contracts. We may need to shut things down so we can review that you are in compliance."

"Tony, do you always have to go right for the balls?"

"I'm too busy to play nice. You know what I expect. Make it happen and we'll have plenty of time to be pals." Dorsey gave the contractor a small salute as he headed out.

He had to grab the errant puppy by the scruff of his neck and give him a shake or he'd pee on the carpet and grow into a disobedient mutt. Which reminded him of that counselor, Hanson, who was sniffing around. As Dorsey strode across the construction site, he hit the button for Hanson's wife's cell phone.

"Hi, how you doing?" he asked, not bothering to identify himself.

"Good. I'm in a meeting," she responded.

"You free for lunch tomorrow?"

"For you, of course."

"I'm touched. Antoinette's. Say at eleven forty-five?"

"I'll be there."

A client was late, and Hanson used the time to call Louise Parker. He was surprised, and more pleased than he'd admit, when he didn't go to voice mail and she took his call.

"Tammy LaFleur's roommate and business partner has disappeared," he said, trying to sound dispassionate. "I went to their apartment and it looked like she hadn't been there in days."

"Business partner? What business was that?"

"Um, prostitution."

"I see. Want to give me specifics?"

"On the prostitution?"

She chuckled and he felt clumsy. How could women do that, make a man feel like a gawky teen with the slightest giggle or smirky look?

"I know what you meant," she said seriously. "Come on, Brian, you work with this population. How often do they disappear in the middle of the night, no forwarding address, poof!"

"There's a creepy neighbor who—"

"Is he your serial-killer suspect?"

"I don't know if that's it. But I spoke with Tammy's father, who also thinks something is screwy. He told me he got warned off by local police."

"So the city is in on a serial-killer conspiracy?"

"Thank you for your time," Hanson said stiffly.

"Brian, I'm not as excited as you are about wild speculation. It's not even circumstantial."

"When I put together a case for you, maybe I'll call," he said before hanging up.

He sat at his desk, seething. Don't fight the anger, he told himself, channel it. He thought back to a hand-to-hand-combat drill instructor, a friend of his father's, who had first taught him basics when he was no more than ten.

"You got five S's that're gonna determine who walks away, and who doesn't. Size, strength, skill, speed, and spirit. In that order, I've seen. A big guy with no heart goes down to a little one with spirit." Then he had slapped the young Hanson around until the boy cried from frustration. "You ready to give up?" the instructor had asked.

"Fuck you," Hanson had snapped, trying to head-butt him in the groin. The instructor had laughed as he'd easily blocked him, then stood Hanson upright. "You got the spirit, just like your old man." It was a visceral memory, a defining moment in his life.

"Brian, your client is here," the receptionist buzzed in on the phone.

Hanson jolted to the present. He couldn't allow the memories to overwhelm.

"Tell them I'll be right up," he said. He focused on the texture of a baseball-sized stone he had placed strategically. Quartz, yellowish white, multiple planes and angles. Breathe in, breathe out. Time to get in character, he mused as he rose slowly from his desk and walked to the reception area.

CHAPTER TEN

Jeanie Hanson traced a finger along her husband's muscled abdomen as they lay next to each other in bed. Sheets and pillows had fallen to the floor with their thrashing. Their years of distance had enhanced the pleasure, made it more like a passionate romp than the romance of two longtime partners.

"I like your new hard body," she said.

He smiled, enjoying her touch. Was she responding to his invigorated primacy or the female attraction to the dark side? Eros or Thanatos?

She stretched and rolled away, on her back, hair splayed, looking like a posed picture of postcoital bliss. Her hand rested on his thigh. He growled appreciatively as she kneaded and squeezed higher and higher.

"You've been a changed man the past few weeks," she said. "I'd been getting worried about you being burned out."

"My supervisor said something similar."

"Things changed at work?"

"Not really. It's more about that client whose death I was investigating."

"Are you still?"

He hesitated. Her hand gently stroked him and he could feel the blood throbbing to his loins.

"Yeah. I've been taking time off, talking to people. The FBI, her father—who used to be deputy police chief—neighbors, friends."

"What've you learned?"

"You really want to know?"

"Yes. If it's important to you, it's important to me. What've you been up to?" she asked huskily.

"I've told you most of it already."

"I don't mind hearing it again."

"If your hand goes much higher, I'm going to forget what we're talking about."

"Naughty boy," she said, and squeezed his thigh. She rolled onto an arm, facing him. "I bet what you've been doing is exciting."

He nodded. Deep down, for reasons he couldn't identify, he didn't want to talk with her about it. The death and his digging felt too personal to talk about with the woman he had just made love to, whom he had fathered a child with, who had been his wife for so many years.

But he told her everything he could recall.

Jeanie Hanson felt the thrill of seducing her husband. She could see it in his eyes, feel it in his motions—he was hers. She was momentarily caught up in his intensity as he told of his quest for Tammy LaFleur's killer.

Then she realized how silly it was, a middle-aged man wanting to play Don Quixote with his idealized whore. Maybe Dorsey could help her husband and make sure Brian didn't blunder into trouble. She thought of what a hunk Dorsey was and how he could further her career.

"You've got a funny smile," Brian said, interrupting her thoughts.

She responded by kneading his thigh again. "Is this funny too?"

"Mnnnnn."

She rolled over to him and bit his chest lightly. Then his stomach.

"Still think I'm funny?" she asked.

She suspected he could snap her neck with his hands. She had seen his strength and skill as he worked out. She also knew he wouldn't hurt her. And that ultimately gave her greater power.

Early morning, and Hanson met with AA sponsor Bill McFarlane in Fuller's Coffee Shop. All that remained of the bacon and eggs with sourdough toast was a few greasy smears and crumbs on their plates. Seated on the hard stools around the U-shaped counter, they sipped the coffee.

"Why are we here?" McFarlane asked.

"You mean that in an existential way?"

"Cut the bullshit, Jean-Paul Sartre."

"I'm impressed. A cop who knows existentialist philosophers."

"Is that as unusual as a counselor who doesn't ask 'How do you feel?' in response to everything? Or you expecting me to drag my knuckles on the ground while looking for minorities to beat to death with a nightstick?"

"You sound cranky," Hanson said.

"Up all night on a case. How's your recovery?" Mc-Farlane asked abruptly.

"Pretty solid. I haven't gone to a meeting, but I did read the Big Book a bit. A lot of wisdom there."

"Damn straight. I'm glad you're doing okay, and I'm asking again, what are we doing here? Surely you can come up with a better breakfast buddy."

"I wanted to ask your opinion of former deputy chief Grundig."

"I'm here as an informant, not a sponsor?"

"You're here as someone I trust and respect, who knows the guy."

"Why do you want to know?"

"He also doesn't go for the suicide explanation. Led me to believe there's a cover-up. I need to know if I can believe him."

McFarlane's coffee cup was empty. He signaled for the waitress to refill. When she did, he slowly rotated the worn, warm white ceramic cup in his hands. "He had a reputation as a straight shooter. Everyone knew what was going on with his daughter and felt bad for him. For the whole family."

"Any chance someone would want to get back at him by killing his daughter?"

McFarlane smiled. "You're getting that kind of paranoid thinking that cops thrive on. Warms the cockles of me heart, even if it is bullshit. The old man's been out of the loop for years. Besides, whacking Tammy would be more of a favor to him than a message."

"He said Quimby came by and he was encouraged to keep his mouth shut. I'm wondering why."

"Our fair city is getting famous for low numbers on serious crimes. Any deaths are bad publicity. They're hoping to win some of the big employers back to Oregon."

"Who's they?"

"Who stands to gain? The mayor, the police chief, DA, businesses, homeowners. America's Safest City. Even you benefit if property values go up."

"That sounds like something my wife would say."

"You keeping her satisfied?"

"What's that mean?"

"It means you've told me about her and I've seen her. She's a pedigree. You're a mutt."

"I'm not here to talk about my marriage," Hanson said tersely.

"You're sounding snappy there, Fido. Want to tell me what's going on?"

After a sigh, Hanson told him about their renewed passion, how he had told her what was going on and how uncomfortable he felt with the disclosure.

"Maybe you're not used to really talking with her. Got to accept life on life's terms. Nothing wrong with being a mutt. You just need to know it. Accept that you're less inbred and she's going to get her ass sniffed at the dog show."

Hanson squinted at him. "What's the message in all of this?"

"You think there's a message? Did you just get on

this bus?" The cop swigged down the last of his coffee. "Your turn to pay," he said, standing abruptly and sauntering out.

As Hanson settled the check, he wondered about McFarlane's canine observations.

Tony Dorsey waved his ID card from the mayor's office and was buzzed through the thick glass doors to police headquarters. Most visitors had to go through a rigorous check-in, a symbolic border crossing, making it clear they were entering a sanctum sanctorum. Photo IDs logged in, even for those who visited almost daily. Reporters who fell out of favor could find themselves waiting a half hour in the sparsely furnished lobby. Not Dorsey, who got the express-lane welcome. As the mayor's liaison with the bureau, he was there to resolve citizen complaints, review budgetary issues, and sit in on review board hearings. His unstated job, at Mayor Robinson's behest, was to make it clear to Chief Forester who was really in charge.

Dorsey liked cops—the legal connivers, the adrenaline junkies, the burned-out heroes, the zealous rookies. He liked the macho atmosphere, hardly tempered by the female officers. Virtually anyone with handcuffs, a nightstick, a gun, and a badge became macho.

He kibitzed with a couple of sergeants as they rode up in the elevator, then flirted briefly with a young female clerk. Leaning on the top of her cubicle, looking down her low-cut top, he made an obvious double entendre about enjoying the view. They bantered for a few minutes and he parted with a remark about "spending a weekend climbing the beautiful peaks of the Pacific Northwest." She laughed, blushed, and gave him her home phone number when he asked. He felt particularly powerful, with the novelty of an outsider and the intimacy of an insider.

Andrea Jayson's office was a warm, windowless room about the size of three cubicles. The sign on the door said "Computer Geographic Surveying." She had a couple of seventeen-inch flat-panel computer monitors connected to a confusing array of gear. There were two ergonomic keyboards on her large, unadorned desk. Jayson was a plain woman in her late thirties, with unbecoming eyeglasses, stringy hair, and a nervous habit of rubbing her nose. She also had an IQ close to 200 and had twice turned down offers from Microsoft and Sun Microsystems to stay with the city. No one understood why.

"How is my digital darling today?" Dorsey asked after a quick knock on her open door.

"I'm doing okay."

"I was asking about the computer," he said playfully.

For a moment she took him seriously, frowned, then realized he was kidding. She smiled, as if they were joking about a favored child. "You're such a kidder."

"I try. How are you doing?"

"Keeping busy. Can't complain, wouldn't do any good."

He chuckled as if she had made a quip worthy of Oscar Wilde.

"Well, darling, any interesting stats as far as numbers in our fair city?"

Mayor Robinson had implemented a program modeled on the Compstat system developed in New York by Mayor Giuliani. It involved almost real-time tracking of data, and then meetings where all responsible parties had to account for crime increases. No excuses that information, or key personnel, were unavailable.

"Nothing bad. Things have quieted down recently." There had been a string of armed robberies starting a month or so ago. She tapped a few computer keys, and a map of the Southwest Terwilliger area appeared on the screen. A few more keystrokes, and little symbols in the shape of a gun popped up in a cluster on the boulevard. More keystrokes, and the names of businesses that had been robbed were filled in. Largely bars, a couple of restaurants, a couple of convenience stores. As she tapped on the keyboard, the computer rotated through screens showing census data, socieoeconomic profiles, arterial highways. "But it doesn't make sense."

"What do you mean?"

"Here's another example." Tap, tap tap.

"What's this?"

"Rapes, all a similar MO. Entering the premises of a lone woman in the early-morning hours, usually through an open first-floor window." The symbol on the computer screen was a cruelly grinning Satan. "You know the way they classify rapists?"

He shook his head.

"There's sexual-gratification rape. Usually impulsive, the most prevalent, a lot of date rapes fall in this category." She spoke as if she were reading from a textbook. "The anger rape is also unplanned, often with physical force in excess of what is necessary. It's an act of revenge. There's usually long periods between the assaults, as the perceived wrong increases. Power rapists are planners. They feel like losers and take it out on women. Then there's the sadistic rapists. Into torture, bondage, mutilation. Often they've got a fascination with violent pornography. The real freaks. They collect souvenirs, like serial killers. Make audio-tapes, steal items of intimate clothing to masturbate over." She blinked her eyes.

Dorsey nodded. "They all sound like freaks."

"Definitely. Here's another case where we had a cluster of incidents. Same MO." The satanic faces appeared in a few broad clumps. "Then the crimes stopped."

"Maybe they were arrested, or better still, hit by a truck."

"I've checked with Robbery-Homicide and Sex Crimes. No arrests that would fit the profile. Believe me, that's a big part of my job. We also check the morgue and for long-term hospitalizations."

"Moved away?"

"Possible. This rapist would fit the pattern of either an anger or a power rapist. The data don't add up."

"You've discussed these concerns with anyone?"

"Several people, including the chief. They all say be grateful for small favors."

"Well, I appreciate your hard work."

"Thanks. You know, they had a suspect in mind for both of these crime patterns. I checked with the detectives. The suspect disappeared."

Dorsey shrugged. "I suppose that happens."

"Does the timing strike you as strange?"

"You know what I say?"

"What?" she asked.

"Be grateful for small favors." He winked, then headed out.

During his first morning session, Hanson suffered a vivid flashback to a time when he'd listened to the sound of a buddy dying next to him. Hanson and his platoon had been pinned down by a sniper for more than an hour and had listened to the soldier screaming in pain and fear of dying unattended. Unable to stand it, Hanson had finally jumped up and charged directly into the line of fire. The sniper had apparently disappeared into the forest moments before Hanson's suicidal attack.

The client was so absorbed in her own problems, she didn't notice the sheen of sweat on Hanson's brow or the tremor in his hand. The counselor managed to reground himself in the moment, finish the session, then hurry to the bathroom to splash cold water on his face.

He blamed the flashback on Vic and the terror of being helpless in front of a gun again.

Betty knocked at his door, interrupting his brooding. "You're up on the crisis board. Got time for a call?"

When the crisis team supervisor was out, Hanson provided backup. Just like his being de facto security guard. But Betty knew that he liked the chance to get out of the office for fieldwork. He had been on the crisis team for years, initially resisting becoming "trapped in an office."

"I've got a two-hour chunk free," Hanson said after glancing at his calendar.

"Shouldn't take too long. It's a welfare check at the Mark Twain. Greg Burkett. He's in the computer as a closed client." She handed him a printout and he scanned it quickly.

Burkett was a forty-two-year-old unpartnered male white with a primary diagnosis of polysubstance dependence and a secondary diagnosis of chronic depression. Burkett, perennially unemployed, had gotten occasional jobs as a day laborer but now had a bad back. His health problems also included hepatitis C, high blood pressure, and several dental disasters. He had no family in the area and was intermittently homeless. There was a note that he was chronically suicidal, particularly when lonely, which was most of the time. He had made two serious attempts and had had six hospitalizations.

The Mark Twain was a notorious single-room-occupancy hotel about ten blocks from the agency's office. It would've rated negative stars in the AAA tour book. Small rooms with saggy, stained mattresses, broken windows, and shared bathrooms that smelled like they vented the entire city's sewer system. There were said to be tunnels in the basement, connecting with the waterfront. Many of the Old Town businesses were rumored to have been recruiting stations for the many shanghai artists who worked Portland in the early part of the century, trapping drunken sailors who awoke fifty miles out to sea.

The four-story redbrick building looked almost habitable in the subdued gray light of the drizzly day. The desk clerk, a slender Pakistani with a pencil-thin mustache, recognized Hanson.

"It has been a long time since I have seen you," he said.

When Hanson asked, "How've you been?" he got a detailed account of how the man had had another son, had started community college, and was trying to get enough money together to make a small down payment on a house.

"You called about Greg Burkett?" Hanson asked.

"He was down in the lobby before, mumbling about suicide. I think he was drunk. Very bad. Room 310."

Hanson remembered that the slow-moving elevator was almost as foul as the bathrooms. He walked up the worn stairs, mindful of the grimy green walls, the smell of body odor and cigarettes, the dim lighting. The narrow corridor, not much wider than his shoulders, was lit by exposed lightbulbs hanging every dozen feet.

Hanson rapped on the flimsy wooden door. "Mr. Burkett, Brian Hanson, I'm with Rose Community. Can you open up?"

Silence.

A little louder. "Mr. Burkett? I'm here to see how you're doing. People are concerned." A few more raps of his knuckles on the door. "Please open up."

A cheap lock clicked and the door opened a few inches. The man peering out looked better than Hanson had expected. A salt-and-pepper beard was neatly trimmed; his eyes were clear, his clothes clean. Burkett looked a lot healthier than most of the residents Hanson knew. "Who are you?"

"Brian Hanson, with Rose Community." The counselor pointed to his ID tag and passed a business card in through the six-inch gap where Burkett held the door open. "You worked with Polly from our agency," Hanson said.

"Yeah, Polly. Kinda cute, but naive."

Hanson didn't say anything though he agreed with the appraisal. "You were talking about suicide?"

Burkett harrumphed. "What about freedom of speech?"

"I've no desire to interfere with your freedom of speech, just wanted to be sure that you're safe."

"No one's safe in this world."

Hanson made a mental check in the paranoid column, while aware that for anyone living in Old Town, it could be a dangerous world.

"Can I come in?" Hanson asked.

Burkett threw wide the door and gestured grandly. "Come right this way."

The cramped room was neat, sparsely furnished. A battered laminate night table had a couple of newspapers and a dog-eared Dean Koontz book. A mismatched dresser had only cigarette burns on top. The metal-frame bed was covered with a splotchy sheet. There was no evidence of alcohol or drug paraphernalia. No signs of a weapon, rope, or pills. Two stories up, it was doubtful that jumping would be a serious option.

Burkett's sinewy bare arms gave testament to his troubled history. There were numerous scars across his wrists, as well as evidence of collapsed veins and abscesses from intravenous drug use.

As Burkett complained about the injustice of the world, Hanson had the feeling he was pretty close to sober and probably had a Cluster B personality disorder. He externalized responsibility for his problems and showed no insight into his chaotic interpersonal relations. Hanson felt the powerful desire to get away that so often went with the personality disordered.

"What's an old guy like you doing fieldwork for the Rose?" Burkett asked, though he was only a couple years younger than Hanson.

Hanson struggled to not respond defensively. "You're used to working with younger staff?"

"Yeah, usually pretty young women. Gives me something to think about when I'm alone in my room. Can you get me some female room service?"

"If you're feeling depressed or upset in any way, please call," Hanson said.

Burkett fingered Hanson's business card. "Crummy stock. And I see you're not a Ph.D."

"It was a disappointment to my mother," Hanson said, regretting the wisecrack even before he was done saying it.

"Hey, if I'm suicidal, could I get better housing?"

Hanson found himself fighting the urge to say, "A mausoleum with a view." Instead, he said, "No. If you come in, you can talk with one of our housing specialists to see about options."

"We'll see," Burkett said, as if he were considering doing Hanson a favor.

"How's my favorite up-and-coming real estate mogul doing?" Dorsey asked, as Jeanie slid into the booth at the back. They had been there four times and it was "their" table. Since the deputy mayor had been a regular for years, the VIP treatment was no surprise. But the restaurant staff was savvy enough not to act like his female guest was merely another in a long string of conquests.

"Pretty good," Jeanie said.

"I should think so. I was at the permit office yesterday, took a look at your paperwork." He had started a bottle of 1999 Moutaine Gris merlot, and poured her a glass. "I did notice one glitch."

"Really?"

"A primary subcontractor on the electrical work—his license isn't current in this state, just Washington."

"Damn."

"It'll take a few weeks to get an emergency application through. And you're at a crucial part." He smiled. "Sometimes, these things can be expedited."

She looked at him hopefully. "What do I need to do?"

He took her hand in his. "Be my friend."

She smiled coyly. "What does being your friend entail?"

"You have a dirty mind." He stroked her hand slowly, generating a tingly heat. "But I'm not that kind of guy. You really just need to be my friend."

"I consider you a friend."

"Excellent. Let's see what's good today."

The waiter, who had been waiting for his cue, came and recited the specials. They both ordered clams *de brucca* in a white sauce.

"How's life?" Dorsey asked.

After several minutes talking proudly about deals she was negotiating, she asked, "And for you?"

"Oh, meetings on top of meetings, relieved only by tedious paperwork and an occasional lunch with a pretty woman." She felt warm, woozy, and blamed it on the half bottle of merlot they had finished. His hand on her forearm, fingertips gently rubbing the soft skin, was amazingly erotic. "Family life is little relief. The kids are okay but my wife gets on my nerves. She's so, so boring."

She nodded.

"How about your husband?"

"We have our differences, but I guess we're okay."

"A woman like you could do better."

"What do you mean?"

"You're bright, beautiful, successful."

"He's an okay guy," she said defensively.

"That's true. Can you look me in the eye and say you don't want more than that?"

She avoided his gaze.

"Okay, let's change the subject. How's Sherlock Holmes doing with his investigation?"

"He's fiddling along."

Dorsey chuckled. "Sherlock Holmes, fiddling."

She looked at him perplexed.

"Holmes played the violin."

"Oh."

"What kind of fiddling? I'm curious."

"Nothing interesting. I saw the mayor quoted in the paper the other day about the possible city hall retrofitting and expansion. What's that going to mean?"

"You're trying to change the subject," he said.

Fortunately the main course came and she got him talking about the city hall renovation. When they were done with the meal, he ordered another bottle.

"I've got work this afternoon," she said.

"Ohh. You don't want me to drink alone, do you? Particularly when it's such a very good year." He raised the wineglass, swirled it, and watched fluid the color of blood flow slowly down the inside. "It's got legs, you see. Not as nice as yours, of course."

His hand returned to stroking her arm. The talk circled, but he brought it back to her husband's investigation.

"You're holding back on me," Dorsey was saying. "Friends don't do that." He stopped rubbing her arm. "You don't want to hurt my feelings, do you?"

"No, it's just . . ."

"I watch out for my friends. Do you know what I do to my enemies?"

His Mona Lisa smile disappeared, his expression instantly intimidating, his eyes as cold as a shark's. "What's he looking into?"

"I don't really know."

"Jeanie, never try to bullshit a bullshitter."

The relatively mild obscenity seemed shockingly coarse. He wiped his hand with the cloth napkin and pressed his fingertips together, making a sharp popping noise. "What's he up to?"

"Why do you care?"

"I only care to the extent that you won't tell me. It makes me feel like you don't trust me."

What harm could it really do? Her husband's actions were silly. There was no point in alienating Dorsey. She didn't need to tell him that much. "He's still obsessed with that client of his that was killed."

"Tammy LaFleur."

"I guess that's her name."

"Do you think he was sleeping with her?"

The thought had occurred to Jeanie but she'd dismissed it. Hearing the possibility voiced by Dorsey gave it some credibility. She felt angry with her husband for wasting time on the dead woman when he could have been using it to further his career.

Under gentle but insistent questioning, she told him about Hanson's visit to the FBI and to the former deputy chief. When she was done, she felt horribly guilty, and Dorsey sensed it.

Dorsey's lips were tight, his brow furrowed, as he asked, "What's with your husband anyway? Doesn't he have anything better to do with his life?"

"Can we talk about something else?"

"You feel bad. You didn't really want to share all that." It wasn't a question. "You know in spy trade-craft when you're developing sources, you do them a small favor, build trust, then get them to give up confidential information. Once they do that, you've got them. No turning back."

Jeanie suddenly felt cold, queasy, the food a heavy ball in her stomach.

Her feet were planted on the floor. She felt Dorsey's foot, under the table, wiggling in between, forcing them apart.

"If I were a spymaster recruiting you, now you'd be mine." He moved his other foot between hers and slowly moved her feet wider apart. "You'd be an asset. I'd take what I needed, whenever I needed it."

Her legs were spread wide apart under the table and she felt painfully vulnerable.

His smile hadn't changed. "No turning back," he repeated.

"What do you mean?" she asked, trying to sound stronger than she felt.

"How would your hubby feel if he knew about this conversation?"

"He wouldn't care."

"Want to bet?" He took out his cell phone. "Let's

call him. I can say I heard from you about what he's doing and would like to help. I'll bet you the cost of lunch he's not amused."

Dorsey began punching in numbers.

"No," she said, so loudly that the people at the next table turned to see what was going on. "He's a very private man."

"Of course." Dorsey put the cell phone away. "My treat for lunch. I enjoyed it immensely."

He moved his feet away and she was able to close her legs. She locked her knees together and demanded, "What's with you?"

"It's a game. I know you like them. I want you to know who owns Boardwalk and Park Place here."

"I don't want to meet for lunch again."

"But we will." Dorsey took out his wallet and paid for the meal with cash. "Portland is a surprisingly small town. Our paths are destined to cross. I'll make sure of it." He left without saying good-bye.

Jeanie played with her napkin nervously until she noticed that the waiter was watching. She hurried from the restaurant to her car, unusually unsteady in her high heels.

She drove off, noticing that her hands were shaking. It was only when she settled back into her desk at her office, checking voice mail and performing routine tasks, that she began to wonder. Had she ever told Dorsey the name of Brian's client? And had the deputy mayor really known her husband's work number well enough to dial it from memory?

CHAPTER ELEVEN

Hanson tried to schedule as his last appointment of the day a client who was either easy or enjoyable to work with. Many times during his earlier years he had been challenged by a suicidal or homicidal client at 4:55 p.m. His own emotional resources were depleted, most hospital beds were taken, and there was no overtime pay in community mental health.

Louis recounted amusing anecdotes about Portland as if he were socializing at a Kiwanis luncheon. "How come you're letting me just shoot the breeze?" he asked, interrupting his tale about an irate farmer who dumped a ton of manure in front of city hall as a protest against urban development.

"Does it seem helpful?"

"No, but it beats watching *Jerry Springer*." Parker laughed. "You hear about the support group for compulsive talkers? It's called On and On." Parker laughed again. "I hear you've been a busy boy."

"What do you mean?"

"Seeing old Chief Grundig and Louise. What did you think of her?"

"Louis, we're not here to talk about how I spend my off hours."

"Yeah, she can be a bitch," Parker said, as if Hanson had answered his question. "But get her on your side, and she's great. What's your next step?"

"Louis, I think we should revisit your treatment goals."

"To get rich and healthy, and move to a warm climate."

Hanson maintained eye contact with Parker and said nothing.

"Oh great, one of them therapeutic staring contests," Parker said. He leaned his head forward, mimicking Hanson's posture and locked eyes.

It was Hanson who broke contact a few moments later. "Louis, maybe you should be doing therapy on me."

"But I do. I can tell you got a bee in your bonnet over Tammy's death. It gives you a sense of purpose but fucks up your head. Like going to that strip bar."

"How do you know about that?"

"What's the point of being old if you ain't wise? I got lots of friends in town. That's why you should work with me. You wanna know more about Vic."

"Such as?"

"Now I've got your interest." Louis sat back in the chair. "I won't make you beg. Tammy was hoping to bring him in on her big deal. She told me she didn't trust him, didn't want to cut him in, but thought she might have to."

"What big deal?"

"That I don't know. I do know you've been bit by the investigating bug. You can't tell if snooping is the right thing to do, but it feels like something you've got to do."

"What makes you say that?" Hanson asked, trying to not show surprise at Parker's insight.

"A good investigator is like a good shrink. Thinks a lot about people and what makes them tick. Asks questions, makes observations, tests hunches. You probably call them hypotheses or something, but that's 'cause you got the fancy plaque on the wall."

"You continue to educate me, Louis."

Parker beamed. "Gotta go, Doc. You think about what I said. We'll check in at our next appointment."

"I look forward to it."

Parker nodded and headed out. Hanson sat back, amused and confused. Given budget constraints, it was hard to justify the meetings with Parker, but Hanson had been around long enough that he could write a managed-care-acceptable, evidence-based practice progress note that showed that Parker still met criteria for medical necessity. "Explored and addressed symptoms of isolation and loneliness which had the potential to aggravate his age-related dysthymia. Identified and challenged negative cognitions. Blah, blah, blah, yada, yada, yada. Continue treatment plan."

He was tucking the note in the chart when Betty Pearlman waved for him down the hall. He guessed that there was some crisis, one of the young clinicians dealing with a 4:55 suicide caller.

"You got a tux?" Pearlman asked when he stepped into her office.

"Huh?"

"Tux. Or a fancy suit?"

"I've got a gray suit I haven't worn in years that came from Nordstrom."

"Dust off the mothballs. You're going to be our agency representative at the civic awards ceremony this Saturday."

"I hate that crap. Why don't you send someone who likes monkey suits and rubber chickens? Maybe Hanrahan." Hanrahan was a young man with large ambitions, who had his eyes on being at least a director within the next few years. The kind who would shake hands while looking over your shoulder to see if there was anyone better to suck up to in the room.

"Someone put in the word with the CEO. They want you and your wife as the guests. You must've done something right."

"Or wrong."

"No, for wrong they don't give you the seven-course dinner. You know which fork to use for the salad?"

"The same one I use to clean my ears?"

"You see, you are getting refined. Ten years ago, you would've chosen another part of your anatomy."

"Over the past ten years I've learned how delicate a flower you are."

"Screw you too," she said fondly. "Go home and read Emily Post."

"I think I prefer *The Anarchist Cookbook*. Seriously, would you like to go instead of me?"

"Seriously, no," she said. "Besides, they wanted you."

"I don't understand why."

"Maybe because of that pregnant woman you talked off the bridge."

"That was four, five months ago."

"Yeah, but it got a fair amount of press. You never know when a politician is going to decide to cash in on it. All I ask, see if you can get more funding out of them."

On the ride home, Hanson mulled it over. Maybe it *was* the pregnant-jumper case. She had been in her twenties, from a well-established family, pregnant by a lower-class boyfriend her parents didn't approve of, who had dumped her after finding out he was going to be a father.

Hanson had been driving home from work, seen her at the railing, and spent more than an hour talking with her. There had been a photo in the newspaper of her leaning over the edge with him a few feet away, his face showing compassionate concern. Every time Hanson drove over the bridge, he thought of her and wondered where she was. He was still wondering about the young woman when he pulled into his driveway.

"Hey, Jeanie, I'm home."

He could tell right away from her stiff posture that something was wrong. After so many years together, reading each other's mood was as easy as guessing whether it would rain in the Northwest winter. Knowing what was driving the mood was a lot harder. "What's up?" he asked.

"Nothing. I had a tough day. What about you?" she asked with more intensity than the question called for.

"Not bad. But something a little odd. We have any plans for Saturday night?"

"I don't think so."

"Well, get out one of your nice outfits. We're going to the mayor's civic awards ceremony."

She blanched and said, "What?"

"We were invited. Maybe because of that pregnant woman I talked off the bridge. Not really sure why. But it's definitely a command performance."

He had expected her to be excited at the chance to socialize with the elite. Instead she hustled into the bedroom and shut the door.

He made himself a TV dinner. After a half hour, he knocked at the door, then opened it slowly. She was sitting on the bed staring at *Wheel of Fortune* on the TV. She never watched *Wheel of Fortune*.

"Honey, what's going on?"

She shook her head.

"This isn't the reaction I expected," he said.

"What did you expect?" she asked angrily. "Oh, goody. I'm supposed to be available to go wherever you want whenever you want. Well, I've got a life too, you know."

"You had something planned for Saturday?"

"No, but I could have."

"I told you this was sprung on me today. I—"

"Leave me alone," she said, turning up the volume. The player spun the wheel, it came up bankrupt. The audience groaned while Pat Sajak offered his sympathy.

Brian stood in the doorway, looking at his wife, who sullenly stared at the TV.

"Is there anything you'd like to talk about?" he asked.

"No."

Sajak's voice brought back memories from when

the TV personality was an Army disc jockey, with a hearty "Good morning, Vietnam" his tagline.

He went to his gym and worked out, pounding the bag to exorcise frustration. He was unsure what the dinner invitation meant and needed to discuss it with her. Once again, she wasn't there for him.

An hour later he had worked up a sweat, but his anger had only deepened. As he'd pummeled the bag, he'd kept thinking about Vic throwing him out. Louis's comments had made it clear that there was more to be discovered there. With each punch, Hanson had gotten more determined to find out what Vic knew. The counselor convinced himself that assuaging his own pride was a very secondary motivation. He pulled on a black hooded sweatshirt and left his wife a note saying, "Went out. Back by midnight." Driving to the bar, he thought of all he could lose by getting in a fight. He dismissed being physically injured, but the damage to his reputation and licensure was considerable. He turned on an oldies station and Mick Jagger urged "Sympathy for the Devil." Brian felt like a cartoon character with a devil on one shoulder and an angel on the other. The devil was much more persistent.

With his sweatshirt hood pulled around his head, he looked like someone trying to hide his identity. Which wasn't unusual at the strip bar.

The spotlighted stage area was actually brighter lit than the street outside. As he scanned the crowd, he barely registered the dancer, a voluptuous white woman with a big butterfly tattoo on her back. Vic was nowhere in sight.

A six-foot five-inch thick-necked type in a leather vest was eyeing him suspiciously. The bouncer had a broken nose and a ridge of scar tissue he wore proudly along his brow. Hanson took a seat toward the back and ordered an overpriced Seven-Up. It was the same androgynous waitress he had had before, but she didn't recognize him.

Hanson was in his "spider sense" threat-evaluation mode. He scanned the crowd, looking for cops, troublemakers, anyone who might know him. Nothing. He sipped the drink and waited. The bouncer spent most of his time ogling the dancer, occasionally talking to one of the female bartenders or a waitress. His overmuscled presence was deterrent enough for most rowdy patrons.

While the bouncer was distracted by a loudmouthed drunk at the far end of the bar, Hanson moved briskly back to Vic's office. He padded on the balls of his feet, silent, even though the thumping beat of Gloria Gaynor's "I Will Survive" muffled any sound he made.

The moment before the raid. No matter how much noise, the pounding of the pulse in his temples was always loudest. War isn't seen, it's heard and felt. Where would the first shot come from? Who was going to die? Was there a hidden trip wire, a Bouncing Betty mine? An AK-47 trained on him as he prepared?

Then there was the great wash of adrenaline, the surge that would carry him in screaming, his comrades by his side, killing anything that moved. VC, NVA, or any poor peasant who happened to be in the way.

The bar was more than a trigger for his addiction. The sweaty smells, smoke laced with spilled beer. The noise of a thumping bass through cheap speakers. A writhing, nearly naked female surrounded by darkness and shadowy figures. It was every dive in Saigon, on Patpong Road in Bangkok, Olangapo in the Philippines, or anywhere horny young men found solace.

The door to Vic's office was open and he slipped in. Vic sat behind the desk, laying out lines of coke.

"You're not very smart, are you?" Vic asked, quickly pulling a gun from the drawer.

Hanson raised his hands wordlessly. At the roughly six feet between them, he couldn't reach Vic in the time it would take the bar owner to fire. Best to stand still and let the bar owner, who thought the gun in his hand gave him complete control, close the distance.

Vic got up from behind the desk and moved toward him. His glittering eyes and jerky movements betrayed the coke already in his system. "This is what I get for being a nice guy. I'm going to make up for my mistake."

"I want to talk."

"Really, how special," Vic said. He was about four feet away. Hanson was unconsciously calculating distances, times. One foot closer. Vic paused. "I'd fucking blow you away if it wouldn't screw up my liquor license. Instead, I'll give you time to think about things. Like, say, a week in the hospital."

The bar owner threw a left jab first while keeping the gun aimed at Hanson's middle. But as Vic's attention focused on his punch, Hanson gently blocked it with a fast-moving slap from his own left. His right hand slapped the gun sideways, back toward Vic. Hanson grabbed the bar owner's throat, catching his Adam's apple in the webbing between thumb and index finger.

Vic struggled to breathe and lift the gun. Hanson

grabbed the barrel with his right hand and twisted back hard, breaking Vic's trigger finger. He yanked the gun free and smashed the butt on Vic's head. The whole fight had taken a little over a second.

Vic was bleeding from his temple, gasping for breath, and dizzy from the pain of his broken finger. Hanson twirled the gun like a cowboy and tucked it into his waistband.

Vic, moaning, was bent double.

Hanson's voice was soft, barely audible, as he growled, "You're in a lot of pain from that finger. It would be unfortunate if I had to break another one."

"You fuck, you fuck," Vic said through gritted teeth.

"That's your right index finger. What should be next? I've heard pinkies are surprisingly sensitive."

"You fucking fuck fuck," Vic said, heaving and dribbling spittle.

Hanson reached for him and Vic cringed. "Stay away from me."

"You've got something to tell me about Tammy, something you forgot to mention."

"Fuck you, you fuck, I'm gonna fucking kill you."

Hanson moved quickly, grabbing Vic's wrist and twisting it in a *kote-gaishi* lock that rotated his palm toward the pinkie edge of his hand and dropped him to the floor.

"Tell me about Tammy. What're you holding out? What's worth a few broken fingers and maybe a broken wrist?"

The bar owner winced as Hanson applied a few ounces of pressure. "She came in here about a week ago, with a guy who looked like one of them ZZ Top characters."

"What do you mean ZZ Top? Give me a better description."

Vic hesitated and Hanson applied pressure.

"White guy, long beard and dark glasses. Couldn't tell eye color."

"How old, anything I can identify?"

"Somewhere between forty and sixty. Average height and weight, brownish hair, if it wasn't a wig. The beard was fake, I'm pretty sure." Hanson held his index finger tight and moved it slightly, making a noisy pop. Vic continued, "She had been in a few days earlier, without anyone. I asked if she wanted to pick up a shift. Told her another girl was out sick. She said no, that she had some big deal cooking. Wouldn't give me details."

The door swung open suddenly, and the doorway filled with the bouncer's bulk. "You okay?" he asked Vic.

"Do I look okay, you dumb fuck? Get this guy out of here."

The bouncer tried to surprise Hanson by raising his hands as if he were going to throw a punch but attempted a snap kick as the initial attack. A foot in the belly or groin would have been a stunner for most drunks. Hanson was neither drunk nor an amateur, and the bouncer's movements were as clumsy as if he were doing his moves underwater.

Hanson sidestepped the kick, caught the foot, and yanked it up higher. The bouncer landed flat on his back, knocking the air out and bashing his head on the cement floor. Hanson stood over him, ready to deliver a kick, but the bouncer was unconscious. Hanson felt his neck—there was a strong pulse.

"I would've thought he had a harder skull," Hanson said to Vic, who was leaning on his desk for support. "Now, what else can you tell me about ZZ Top?"

"That's it."

"Anything about his voice, his movements?"

Vic seemed to really be considering the question. "Didn't hear his voice. Him and Tammy were talking in each other's ears, playing kissy face. I saw him go to the john once. He didn't move like an old man, but I'd guess he wasn't a twenty-year-old either. Maybe fifty to sixty or so. Skin wasn't pale, but not dark either."

"Now what about Trixie?"

"Trixie? Which one? I know about four."

"Friend of Tammy's. In her twenties. Brunette, kinky, swings both ways?"

"She never danced here. Not that I can remember them all, they come and go so fast."

The bouncer groaned.

Hanson thought back to Vietnam, to interrogations that had gotten out of hand. The little man, down on his knees, eyes taped shut, hand tied behind his head, might have known who killed your buddy the night before. Hanson would leave when the spooky-spooks came, the CIA and their flunkies, the ones who liked inflicting pain, offering prisoners flight lessons from Hueys.

"Pity we couldn't chat peacefully," Hanson said. "Maybe next time."

"You're a fucking head case," Vic said.

"I suppose I am," Hanson said, abruptly walking out on Vic and the reviving bouncer. As Hanson passed through the bar, the smells of alcohol, cigarette smoke, and sweat called to him like sirens to Ulysses. How many times had he lost himself in a Saigon bar? Sweet, petite barmaids, with squeaky giggles and girlish ways. Most were more hardened than a Marine Corps drill instructor. The distraction of sitting at a bar, smoking a cigarette, sometimes a joint, and having another combat vet with drying ears around his neck come up and go, "Yeah, that says it" when nothing had been said. "Don't mean nothing." And the fights, which had been a discharge as powerful as sex, after a mission gone well. "Get some."

Brian focused on the current moment. The women looked different. There wasn't the sound of mortar or cannon, or the thump of bombs in the distance. Nor the fertile, mildewy humidity that enveloped the tropics. No one was wearing camos, and there wasn't a gun in sight. Brian made it to his car without stopping or melting down. One minute at a time.

Hanson drove halfway home, then pulled into a gas station and called the only person who he thought might understand. McFarlane's machine was on. It was reassuring hearing his voice.

"This is Hanson. I had a relapse. Not using substances, more of a dry-drunk episode. I'm feeling grounded right now, but it would be good to talk sometime soon." On his way home, after a brief internal debate, he detoured to toss Vic's gun in the Willamette River.

CHAPTER TWELVE

"It felt good," Hanson said, as he and McFarlane sat on the green-slatted park bench. There were names carved into the wood of young men whose major achievements was that they could carve their name into park benches, and of lovers wanting to proclaim their passion.

The popcorn gone, they sipped Starbucks coffees and stared at the pond, where ducks quacked harshly. A low-lying fog concealed the birds and softened the scenery. The park had been designed by the same family of landscape architects that did Central Park in New York.

"So good it was scary," McFarlane said.

Hanson nodded and said, "I was closer to relapsing than I've been in years."

"You were high on your anger. Rage-aholic."

"I guess. But there was more to it."

McFarlane rotated the hot paper cup in his hands. "You sure it's not just stinkin' thinkin'?"

"Doesn't feel like it. I was in the groove."

"Why'd you call me, then?"

Hanson hesitated. "I don't know."

"That's the smartest thing you've said this morning."

A pretty redheaded woman jogger passed, being tugged forward by a large, gleaming black Labrador. McFarlane's eyes followed the woman until she disappeared into the fog. "Nice." He returned his attention to Hanson. "Even if the war was screwed up, you served your country."

Hanson remained focused on the coffee cup, head down.

"You may have done things that you can't believe now. I know I did," McFarlane continued. "But they were right at the time. And you lived to talk about it, to think about it, hell, to feel guilty about it. Most guys feel guilty about what they did, but glad to be alive, and maybe guilty about that too. Ever since you became obsessed with the death of this LaFleur woman, you've been on a downward spiral. Risking throwing away the life you've built up."

"I feel more alive than I have in years."

"There's a group in town spun off of Cocaine Anonymous. They go skydiving every couple weeks, bungee jumping, that sort of thing. They need the jolt. Maybe you ought to consider that. Or join a gym where you can do kickboxing."

Hanson looked up, face-to-face with McFarlane. "It's more than the thrill of physical confrontation," Hanson said slowly. "I'm making amends to the universe, trying to do some healing to undo the hurting. I can't bring back the dead, or ask forgiveness of people I wronged over there, but I can work to balance the karmic scale."

McFarlane sighed. "Sounds like you're determined to play it out."

Hanson nodded. "I guess."

"I suppose you've got to learn the hard way." McFarlane stood. "Call me if you want help."

"With my addiction or the investigation?"

"My advice is to drop the investigation. I'm not going to enable you on that. You need to think about how all of this plays into your addictive thinking. Like you know more than everyone else, can control things, paranoid bullshit."

"I'm not saying that Elvis and the CIA are behind it," Hanson said with a weak smile that McFarlane ignored.

"Leave investigating to the pros," McFarlane said. "Stick with what you know. You've carved out a good life. Don't ruin it." He walked off without waiting for a response and was soon invisible in the fog.

At the office, Hanson left a message for Louise Parker before meeting with his first client, the young woman who had been cutting on herself.

She was doing much better, had not cut or taken drugs for more than a week. Hanson took a solution-focused approach, asking her with a Columbo-esque naïveté, "How did you do that?"

She boasted how she had stayed busy. "I started thinking about scoring, then kept doing stuff until the urges passed."

"That's great."

"Shit, I think I did about everything on that list you gave me. I watched videos, cleaned, exercised. Did crossword puzzles, called a friend. Did I leave anything out?"

"You got busy and didn't do anything to make the situation worse. Good for you."

"My mom was giving me grief, like she wanted me to screw up. To confirm the crap she's said about me over the years."

"If you screwed up, that would make your mother happy, you think?" Knowing her family system, Hanson suspected the girl was correct.

"Hell, I'm going to stay out of trouble to piss her off."

His next client was a perennial no-show, but ever since LaFleur's death, Hanson had been much more diligent in his follow-up. He called the client's home, and the man answered the phone groggily. The client had stayed up late the night before, was annoyed that Hanson had called, and expressed no regret for missing the appointment.

"Maybe counseling is not what you're needing right now," Hanson said.

"My PO says I got to come in."

"But it's not a high priority for you. The hour I had reserved for you could have gone to someone else."

"Gimme another appointment. You got anything tomorrow?"

"My next free slot is a week from Friday."

"I'll take that. What time?"

"Two. If you don't make it in, I will assume you're not interested in treatment and close your chart."

"Will my PO be notified?"

"That is standard procedure."

"What if I revoke my release of information?" he asked cagily. "Would you have to keep my record confidential?"

"Our agreement with you was that in the event of

any revocation of releases, we would notify the referring agency. So yes, I would keep it confidential. But I would have to let your PO know you revoked it."

"He'd yank my ticket."

"That's a distinct possibility."

"I'll see you next Friday," the man said, then hung up.

Hanson noted the conversation in the chart, along with his assessment, which didn't take a degree in psychology, that the client was unmotivated. Hanson liked motivational interviewing, where the potential for change was viewed as having five stages. Precontemplative clients didn't see there being a problem. Contemplative clients thought there might be a problem, but didn't know how, or necessarily want, to attack it. Clients in the plan stage were ready to think seriously about change, and perhaps move to the next stage, actually taking action. Then came the maintenance stage, keeping up the progress that had been made.

The client who'd overslept was precontemplative. He was counter-balanced by the teenage cutter, who was in the action mode. It was a pleasure to have clients who actually were willing to attempt change. Teens could be much more extreme, whether in suicidal depression or suddenly getting an epiphany and changing before they had done irreparable harm. So many of his adult clients had the unwanted children, the physical illnesses, the criminal justice record, the overwhelming debts, the entrenched harmful patterns that came from years of mental illness.

Hanson was immersed in overdue paperwork when he got a return call from Louise Parker.

"I'd like to talk," she said.

"Go ahead."

"I'm at the courthouse. I'm not sure when they're going to call me in to testify. Can you swing by?"

His eleven o'clock appointment had canceled, and unlike many days he had no clients scheduled during lunch. "I've got a gap in my schedule for the next couple hours."

"I'm on the fourth floor. I'll be out in the hall by courtroom C."

At the Mark O. Hatfield United States Courthouse even most of the criminals were well dressed. Small-fry drug dealers were left for the local district attorney; the U.S. attorney pursued only the multimillion-dollar operations or white-collar criminals. There were larger-scale bank robbers, but even they took off their backward baseball caps and dressed up when going to federal court. Whereas state court often took on a shabby bazaar atmosphere, with attorneys loudly plea-bargaining in the hallways like bazaar traders, in the federal court a solemn dignity prevailed.

The sixteen-story structure had, because of its overhanging roof, been nicknamed the "Schick Razor Building" by irreverent Portlanders. Visitors passed through a metal detector, attended by a half-dozen blue-blazered guards, that served as a threshold from the commoners' world. The doors, moldings, and wainscot were bloodred cherrywood. The gleaming stainless-steel elevator rose almost silently and bore none of the scratches or graffiti that local court buildings suffered.

Louise Parker, wearing a navy blue pantsuit, with white blouse, small pearl earrings, and a single-strand pearl necklace, was jotting a note to herself in a Palm Pilot as he approached.

"You look more like a lawyer than an FBI agent," Hanson told her.

"What's an FBI agent supposed to look like?" she asked, tucking the Palm into a pocket.

"I meant that as a compliment," he said.

She nodded. "Lots of agents are lawyers." They walked down the hall.

"This place has a royal feel to it."

"It's the federal judges. They're appointed for life, set a dignified tone. I'll tell you a joke if you promise not to repeat it."

He nodded.

"What's the difference between God and a federal judge?"

Hanson shrugged.

"God doesn't think he's a federal judge."

Hanson chuckled and took a quiet joy at the little intimacy. Gray-haired and gray-suited lawyers moved quietly down the hall, hunched over, deep in discussion about pleas to be negotiated, motions to file, or the best place to get a good roast beef.

Hanson and Louise Parker sat on a hard wooden bench. The position at the end of the corridor let them watch the courthouse ballet from a dispassionate distance.

"Courthouse seats remind me of pews," Hanson said.

She held the thought for a moment, then nodded. "A different kind of worship here. Pictures of judges on the wall."

"And the flags. Definitely a shrinelike feel." He enjoyed Louise's cynical side and suspected that whatever case she had been called to testify on was not going well.

"Thanks for coming over," she said. "I prefer talking face-to-face. Too much time listening in on wiretapped phone conversations."

"I bet you've heard interesting conversations."

"The signal-to-noise ratio is actually pretty disappointing." She seemed about to say more when a tall Hispanic attorney with jet-black hair came out of the nearest courtroom. She tensed and lapsed into her professional mode.

"Is he opposing counsel or an ex-boyfriend?" Hanson asked. She stiffened even more and he regretted his observation.

"I heard from a confidential informant that you roughed up a bar owner and his security guard," she said.

"It was self-defense, but I'm impressed by your resources," he said placatingly.

"What have you been up to?"

He told her, ending with, "I'm thinking of going back to see Deputy Chief Grundig. I think there's more he'd be willing to tell me."

"Why's that?"

"I got the feeling he was going to open up. He had an eagerness to talk coupled with indifference to the consequences. Plus a healthy dose of guilt about his parenting of Tammy."

She hesitated momentarily, weighing what she wanted to say. "When exactly did you see him?"

"About a day and a half ago, in the morning. Why?"

"He's dead."

"How?"

"Natural causes. Heart attack."

"That can be faked a dozen ways."

She put on a mock surprised expression. "You're kidding? Like maybe the CIA sprayed him with shellfish toxin that evaporated?"

"Okay, of course you'd know that."

"I heard about it because his nephew works down the hall from me. Grundig was in bad health, his daughter who he has a highly conflictual relationship with dies, and then he dies. Do you really think that is so suspicious?" She paused, then asked, "Want to go visit Trixie?"

He was so surprised his mouth literally dropped open.

"Yeah, she's not dead. In fact, she's back in her apartment."

"How do you know?"

"She called me."

"Why you?"

"That's one of the things I'm interested in. The case I was here for is continued until next week."

He stood. "Let's go."

They took the Hawthorne Bridge out of downtown. Once called Asylum Avenue, since it dead-ended at the first insane asylum in the state, Hawthorne was now a funky boulevard, with mini brewpubs, bookstores, and offbeat restaurants. The rich street life was clogged with the perennially cool and the cool wannabes. Pierced skateboarders, shaggy panhandlers, black-clothing-clad shopkeepers, stores selling nothing but beads or esoteric cards. And of course, numerous coffee shops.

"I enjoy the street scene here," she said.

He tried to imagine her walking down the street, how she'd stand out in her straight-and-narrow way. She seemed to read his thoughts. "I've got my basic black turtleneck and jeans outfit. Even Doc Martens."

"I can't decide if you'd look like you fit in or like you were getting ready for a covert op."

"Maybe both. That lawyer, Handsome Dan, he's both." To Hanson's perplexed expression, she responded, "The attorney you saw at the federal courthouse. Dan Ortega. He's opposing counsel, and an ex."

"That must be tough."

She nodded. "It was a couple years ago but a bad ending." She paused. "Not sure why I'm telling you this. Anyway, how'd you know?"

He thought for a moment, having to reexamine his own perceptions. "You were leaning forward, saw him, and leaned back. You blinked hard, almost a miniflinch, tightened your lips, and then quickly regained your composure with me."

"Oh."

"I made half of that up."

"Impressive. It sounded real."

"You seemed to be remarkably in control, except for that fleeting moment. It's what made it more noticeable."

"If you're calling me a control freak, I take that as a compliment."

"I'm wondering, is it standard FBI practice to take civilians along on investigations?"

"You're here as a trained mental health professional."

"Why do I not believe that's your sole motivation?"

"I do owe you more information," she said, smoothly taking the turn onto Southeast Thirty-seventh. "I don't know why she called me, but I had the feeling she was lying to me on the phone. I want to shake her up. If there's any indication of trouble, I want you to either hit the floor or get your butt out of there ASAP."

"Of course."

"Now, why don't I believe that?"

They pulled to the curb before he could come up with a snappy answer.

CHAPTER THIRTEEN

Folding metal chairs covered much of the basketball court in the city's West Side Community Center, located at the edge of Forest Park. The walls echoed with angry shouts and barks.

Off-leash areas for pets in parks was one of the most volatile issues the mayor's office had to deal with. Wherever possible, attending the meetings was delegated to a junior staff member. Angry dog owners who believed their beloved pets should be allowed to roam wild and free warred with those who complained about dog attacks, unscooped poop, or pets running in front of cars. There were designated areas in a few parks, but there was a constant demand for more space, with the opposition wanting no off-leash areas at all.

Dorsey was stuck at the meeting because the head of the community association, a major contributor to Mayor Robinson's campaign, had requested that the mayor attend. Dorsey substituted to save his boss from having to listen to impassioned tirades that were long on emotion and short on logic.

The woman speaking was in her late sixties, had hair dyed an intense black, and held a yapping corgi in her arms.

"Dogs have been faithful companions to humanity for tens of thousands of years," she said. "To place unnecessary and unwanted restrictions on their freedom is to do an injustice to all the brave dogs who have served us throughout the ages." The meeting had just settled down from the previous ruckus, when an Asian man had complained about his daughter being knocked over by an overly friendly golden retriever, and a Caucasian man with a Chihuahua had loudly commented that the Asian didn't understand because people in his country ate dogs. The Asian man, a Japanese banker whose family had come to the U.S. shortly after the gold rush of 1849, had to be restrained as he lunged for the Caucasian. The Chihuahua got free and ran up an aisle, promptly getting in a fight with a skittish Doberman. The Doberman was backing up while the Chihuahua yipped and snapped.

Dorsey pretended to be taking notes on the meeting while actually jotting notes on chores and roughing out a memo. He nodded seriously, as if each speaker were making a good point.

His mind wandered as the speakers got less articulate, more redundant, and wildly passionate. He doodled a woman on the page who looked roughly like Jeanie Hanson, but naked, and Dolly Parton buxom.

As he thought about Jeanie and the dinner that night, he recalled that he had not called the usual babysitter. He was hoping that fact, plus his wife's distaste for politics, would be enough to keep her home. He had married Arlene when he first moved to the city. The expectation was that he would grow into eventually managing his father-in-law's three hardware stores. He surprised her family by volunteering on Robinson's first campaign, ultimately being hired as an advance man. His rise was quick enough to please even his father-in-law, particularly when Dorsey arranged a zoning variance so he could open a larger store. When the expanded store opened, Dorsey got the mayor to declare it "Honest Dave's Hardware Store Day," and give an interview which ran on two channels about how vital store owners like Dave were for the economy.

As the dog meeting dragged on, the deputy mayor wondered what Brian Hanson would be like in person. He had a strong impression from Jeanie, but of course that was filtered through a wife's eyes. She described her husband as John Wayne sitting on a powder keg of repressed emotions.

"Physician heal thyself," Dorsey had said.

"It's one of those clichés that is true—many who go into the counseling field are messed up in the head themselves," she had said. "One of these days, I think he's going to hurt someone."

The thought gave Dorsey a thrill. He'd have to take precautions.

"I'm going to go in and talk with her for a few minutes," Louise Parker said, glancing at the Lady Rolex on her wrist. "In ten minutes, you come and knock. Listen at the door first, and if it sounds like anything other than a friendly conversation, go back to the car."

Hanson nodded as if he would obey.

As she got out of the car, she smoothly adjusted her jacket, allowing her better access to the fourteen-shot SIG-Sauer 9 mm on her hip. "Ten minutes," she said firmly.

Hanson was used to female supervisors, but he was conflicted over the idea of a woman going into a risky situation and ordering him to stay back. At five minutes, he was out of the car and heading to the apartment. He was alert for the youths who had given him trouble. No one was around. He stood at the door and heard conversational tones, like two old girlfriends chatting. He knocked and the voices stopped.

He heard a gasp from the other side of the door and then Trixie opened it wide. "You see, you see," she said shrilly.

"What's going on?" he asked.

"He's been like this, stalking me," she said. "He's crazy, he was obsessed with her."

"Why don't you come in and we can shut the door," Parker said softly to Hanson.

Hanson stepped into the apartment, and Trixie cringed like Fay Wray avoiding King Kong.

"I don't understand," he said.

"Stay back," Trixie said. "She's an FBI agent. If you bother me any more, I'll have you arrested."

"Mr. Hanson, how do you respond to these allegations?"

"It's a lie. I've been here once before."

"I thought you said you were here twice," Parker said evenly.

"Twice, but once there was no one here."

"You see, he's a liar," Trixie said.

"What do you want me to do?" Parker asked the young woman.

"Keep him away from me."

The femme fatale was now the ingenue in jeopardy. She was dressed in sweats, with hair pulled back in a ponytail, a typical college girl. Hanson felt like a teacher accused of improprieties with a student. He stood awkwardly, looking to the FBI agent, trying to figure out what was going on.

Parker sat on the small couch, watching the two of them like a bored housewife enjoying Dr. Phil. In a small leather flip notepad, she jotted a few notes.

"I didn't realize you were setting me up," Hanson said to Louise.

"You brought him here?" Trixie asked.

"I wasn't," she said to Hanson. "And yes," to Trixie. "I thought it best that you two discuss misunderstandings you might have had."

"Keep him away from me," Trixie said.

"You were talking like you wanted to press charges. I made a few inquiries before we came here. They confirm what Mr. Hanson said. That you had disappeared. And that when Ms. LaFleur was alive, you both were active in the sex trade."

Trixie wrinkled her brow, then pouted.

"I have no interest in arresting you for that. You're as entitled to protection as Laura Bush. But I do need you to be honest with me."

"I better speak to my lawyer," Trixie said. "In the future, all contacts have to come through him."

"Thanks for taking the time."

The FBI agent and the counselor rode wordlessly in

the car for several minutes before Hanson said, "Want to tell me what that was about?"

"She called me making those allegations that you heard. I wanted to check them out. See you two face-to-face." Parker said it without malice or triumph.

"What did you decide?"

"It confirmed my initial perception."

"Which was?"

"That she's a bad liar."

Even though he was confident in his own innocence, Hanson felt a wave of relief. Which was followed by an equally strong surge of anger. "It would have been better if you had let me know what was going on."

"Brian, my impression of you was favorable but that doesn't mean much. C'mon, you're a counselor. You ever make judgments about someone, then find out you were grossly wrong?"

"But I don't deliberately deceive them." Hanson, feeling like he had sounded petulant, was eager to change the subject. "Why was she making up a story?"

"One possibility is you somehow did scare her and she's fabricating it to get you out of her life."

"That's possible."

"I'm not convinced. I couldn't get a straight answer about where she'd been. Of course she could be nervous talking to a federal officer."

"But it could also be someone put her up to it to discredit me, keep me from pursuing an investigation of Tammy's death."

"Could be. If it is, they made a lousy choice as far as a witness."

"What do you recommend I do?" Hanson asked.

"Don't screw up. And watch your back."

On the ride to the dinner, Jeanie Hanson had the tight-lipped expression that Brian knew meant conversation would lead to an argument. They parked in a nearly full lot a couple blocks from the twin glass-towered Oregon Convention Center.

The thirty-five-thousand-square-foot Portland Ballroom had been partitioned off into a four-thousand-square-foot rectangle. Large floral baskets were centered on white tablecloths on the twenty dozen-person tables. With thirty-foot-high ceilings and cinder-block walls, and despite more than two million dollars' worth of public art in the hallways, the fifteen-year-old structure had all the charm of a Wal-Mart.

Waiters and waitresses distributed breadbaskets and water pitchers as hundreds of guests settled in. Ushers moved smoothly through the throng, guiding people to their reserved seats amid a drone of voices, greetings and chitchat, chairs being moved, backs being patted.

The large room was three-quarters filled. Hanson didn't know anyone at his table. He did recognize several people at the long dais, including the mayor, the police chief, former U.S. senator Jake Charmaine, and several state, county, and city officials. They smiled, shook hands, and posed for pictures with the smaller fish that swam in and out of their presence.

Hanson felt claustrophobic. He hated the noise, the people, the tasteless catered food, the fake socializing. His clothing was too tight. He remembered the last time he'd worn it, some bank function arranged through Jeanie. She had a talent for mingling, easy smiles, polite laughter, feigned attentiveness while searching for the right table to hop to.

Sitting on her other side was a guy about her age who chatted with a woman next to him, then shifted his attention to Jeanie. Because of the ambient noise, Brian couldn't hear what was being said. Jeanie was surprisingly stiff, as if she knew and didn't like him.

Hanson turned to the elderly woman next to him and they swapped introductions. Then the woman returned to talking with the man on the other side of her, who had briefly been introduced as a well-known cardiac surgeon. All around the table were little dyads and triads chatting. Hanson bit into a breadstick, still wondering why he had been invited.

He was halfway done chewing it when the man on the other side of Jeanie reached across her, extended his hand, and said, "Hi, I'm Tony Dorsey with the mayor's office. You must be Brian Hanson."

Hanson shifted into his assessment mode, something he was comfortable at, something he knew he did well. Dorsey was trim, well groomed, with a genuine smile that was well practiced. Hanson noticed a small scar on his eyebrow. Dorsey was comfortable enough with Jeanie to reach across her for the handshake. The deputy mayor's grip was firm but not impolitely bone-crushing. Good eye contact, no signs of tics, tremors, or psychomotor agitation.

As Dorsey sat back, Hanson recognized a telltale gun bulge near the deputy mayor's hip. Why did the deputy mayor need a weapon? The mayor was seated at the dais with no bodyguard in sight, and Dorsey was more than a dozen yards away. Was there a threat expected at this dinner?

Hanson leaned back in his chair and focused on relaxation breathing. Within a few moments he was calmer. He watched his wife, tense but smiling, talking with others at the table. Dorsey chatted smoothly with people coming over to pay respects. His speech had normal rate, rhythm, and volume.

Hanson was in the zone, senses humming. He was like a sniper on a perch, saving his energy, studying the action with a cautious neutrality. His eyes swept the room, assessing threat potential, options, escape and evasion possibilities. He was as aware of the sharpness of the steak knife under his hand as he was of the nearest exit.

Then Dorsey was up and moving, artfully table-hopping as soon as the entrée was done. The deputy mayor was talking to the police chief. No love there, the counselor deduced. Dorsey seemed to dominate, standing close, gesturing, while the chief looked off into the distance with a pained expression and nodded politely.

Dorsey seemed comfortable talking with a state senator, a congressional representative, an elegantly dressed woman with tens of thousands of dollars' worth of pearls around her neck, a doddering senior whom Hanson recognized from newspaper photos as the former head of the largest lumber company in the region. Dorsey returned to the table for dessert.

Tony Dorsey finished the required schmoozing and now could focus on Jeanie and her knuckle-dragger husband. Dorsey began discussing the rainy weather they'd been having with the woman to his left as his right hand snaked down and rested on Jeanie Hanson's knee. She barely masked her startled expression and tried to brush his hand away. Dorsey continued talking to the woman on his left while sliding his hand higher up Jeanie's thigh. Jeanie struggled to remove it, but his grip was too strong. She clamped her legs together and stared straight ahead.

"Is everything okay?" Brian whispered.

"Fine."

Dorsey leaned over her and said to Brian, "Quite an event. Have you been to many of these?"

"Not really," Hanson said.

Dorsey smiled a Cheshire cat grin. "They get tiresome pretty quickly. I have to go to a couple a week. Boring speeches, the same cast of characters." Dorsey's hand crept higher on Jeanie Hanson's thigh. "My job is really not that interesting," Dorsey said with false modesty. "But your job sounds intriguing."

"Mine?" Hanson asked. "What do you know about what I do?"

"Jeanie and I have met a couple times," Dorsey said. "She speaks highly of you."

With Dorsey's hand at the top of her thigh, Jeanie held a tight-lipped smile, a slight flush in her cheeks. "She's told me of the challenging folks you work with. Very admirable."

Hanson gave his wife a surprised look. Jeanie shrugged.

"What else have you two talked about?" Hanson asked.

Jeanie looked even more uncomfortable.

"The usual boring political news," Dorsey said.

"Zoning issues, promising developments, who's sleeping with whom." Dorsey kept his bemused expression. "Of course that's figuratively, not literally. I'm surprised Jeanie never mentioned it to you. She was telling me the other day how much she enjoyed our lunches, wanted to schedule them more often."

Then the head of the city's water bureau came over, and Dorsey, seemingly annoyed at being interrupted, was forced to shift his attention. He removed his hand from Jeanie's thigh.

"Everything okay?" Brian asked her.

"Fine. I'm not feeling so hot."

"Want to leave?" Brian asked hopefully.

The attorney who was master of ceremonies cleared his throat and spoke into the microphone. "Thank you all for coming. We've got some important people to honor tonight. I promise we'll keep the speeches to a minimum." He then went on for about five minutes, thanking various sponsors of the event and dignitaries who were present.

About a half hour into the speeches, Hanson decided to use the restroom. As the counselor headed down the corridor, Dorsey wiped his mouth with the white cloth napkin, stood, and winked at Jeanie.

"Wait, where are you going?" she asked.

He leaned over and whispered, "To spend quality time in the men's room. His tongue flicked out lightly and touched her ear. She jumped like she had been given an electric shock. "Don't worry, I only like women."

Dorsey sauntered down the corridor after Hanson. The counselor was at the sink, washing his hands.

"Great bladders thinking alike," Dorsey joked as he emptied into the urinal. He glanced around, making sure the bathroom was empty. "Your wife did mention one other thing to me. Tammy LaFleur."

Hanson dried his hands and stepped closer to Dorsey. "I'm not sure I know that name."

"It's okay. I want to help you. I understand you've been asking around about her."

"Confidentiality laws don't allow me to say anything about anyone who might or might not be a past or present client."

"Sure, sure. Let me tell you some of what I know. She's a woman who shot herself in the face a few weeks ago. Daughter of the former deputy police chief. A troubled girl, getting counseling through you. Don't feel bad about it."

Hanson folded his arms across his chest and said nothing.

"Jeanie was trying to help you. She said you were upset, going on a wild-goose chase. She wanted me to look into it. I know lots of people in the police bureau."

"I didn't realize Jeanie knew you so well."

"We hit it off. She's great. You're a lucky man."

"Thanks," Hanson said flatly, taking a step toward the door.

"I did check into it," Dorsey said. "She committed suicide."

"Okay," Hanson responded.

As Hanson put his hand on the door, Dorsey said, "People are not happy about you snooping around."

"People?" Hanson said, turning back to face Dorsey.

"You know Tammy comes from a well-connected

family. They'd like her buried in peace. For things to settle down. You therapists call it closure, right?"

"If I did have a client named Tammy and she had died in a suspicious suicide, I think her family and friends would want it followed up on."

"It depends on who is defining it as suspicious. Maybe you've got a guilty conscience. Maybe you had a questionable relationship with her."

Hanson stepped in toward Dorsey. The deputy mayor pushed back his jacket and let the gun in a belly holster show.

Hanson growled, "You think you could get that out before I'd shove it up your ass?"

"I hit a hot button," Dorsey said.

Hanson took another step in. Dorsey held his ground, resting his hand on the gun butt like Clint Eastwood in an old Western. "Wouldn't look very good for a psychotherapist to be acting like a dropout from an anger-management group," Dorsey said. "Now listen, I know you were a tough guy during the Vietnam War. But your time is past. I know about you bothering her father right before he died, about you making a ruckus at a strip club. Go back to listening to your psychos tell their stories. Drop the LaFleur death. Your reputation is a fragile thing. So is your marriage. So is your life."

"Is that a threat?" Hanson asked, the blood pounding at his temples.

"Friendly advice. Drop it. Or else."

"Or else what? That's a nine-millimeter Beretta you have there. Elegant, but it won't stop me at this distance." Hanson moved quickly, his left hand pinning

Dorsey's right arm against his body. Hanson pushed in, shoving Dorsey up against the wall, immobilizing his gun hand. Hanson's right hand went to Dorsey's throat and applied pressure. "How long would it take me to kill you?"

Dorsey gasped and struggled, as helpless as a fish on the dock.

The bathroom door opened. Hanson quickly stepped back. "Here, let me finish adjusting your tie," Hanson said, straightening out Dorsey's collar. "Nice to see you again."

Dorsey sucked air in, coughing.

"Tony, good to see you," said the new guest to the restroom. "Paul Rankin, I'm with the fire bureau. Gotta put out a fire right away."

He hurried to the urinal, grunted, and began relieving himself.

"You will regret this," Dorsey muttered as Hanson walked out.

CHAPTER FOURTEEN

Brian drove with eyes straight ahead, arms stiff, head sitting atop his neck like a stone pile. Jeanie could tell that something was bothering him but was afraid to ask. Did he know what had gone on under the table with Dorsey? She reached over and kneaded his tight shoulders. "Everything okay?"

"Yes."

A hard rain fell on the city streets, and the lights of oncoming cars reflected off the roadway. Traffic was heavy, a symptom of the city's constant growth. What used to be a fifteen-minute drive from one side of the city to the other now took at least a half hour, even during off-hours.

They rode in silence for a while before Brian asked, "How well do you know Tony Dorsey?"

"The deputy mayor?"

"The guy sitting next to you," Brian said levelly.

"I've met him at several meetings."

"How did it happen that you told him about my client who was murdered?"

She was grateful that Brian didn't seem to realize what had been going on at the table. "I don't remember exactly. Probably the subject of crime came up at a meeting. We started talking. I thought he could help."

"I shouldn't have told you anything. You shouldn't have told him."

"Well, excuse me for trying to help."

Miles passed with nothing but the sound of their tires on the wet asphalt.

"He had a gun," Brian said.

"What?"

"He was carrying a gun. Showed it off in the bathroom."

"Showed it off? What kind of macho scene did you two have?"

"The testosterone was flowing but we came to an understanding."

"What does that mean?"

Brian shrugged and they rode in silence for a while.

"He used to be with the CIA," Jeanie said.

"I can see that."

"What do you mean?"

"I had dealings with people from the Agency in Vietnam. Occasionally an upper-class-twit type. Mainly these cold-ass motherfuckers. Hard to describe."

She tried to get him to say more but he switched on an oldies station and hummed "Street Fighting Man" as the Rolling Stones sang. When they began to play Led Zeppelin's "Heartbreaker," he sang along. She knew better than to try a conversation. Which was fine with her. She needed to decide how she would handle Dorsey the next time they met. How she would relate to her husband was secondary.

At home, Jeanie hurried in and went up to undress. Brian sat at their computer and read through his e-mail: a couple from friends and family around the country; jokes that had been forwarded; details about a cousin's wedding he probably would skip but send a fifty-dollar gift to; and spam inviting him to get rid of his mortgage, increase his penis size, win at casinos, meet sexy Russian women, make a fortune by helping a Nigerian banker, and get cheap drugs over the Internet.

He switched to Google and typed "Tony Dorsey Oregon Government." He noticed the shading on a link and realized that there was a cookie in his computer, indicating that Jeanie had already visited the site. With a couple of keystrokes, he reviewed her search history.

Brian stared at the professional portrait of the deputy mayor. What level of intimacy was there between Jeanie and Tony Dorsey? He had been betrayed emotionally; was there a physical part to it as well? The deputy mayor seemed like her type—powerful, well connected, more concerned with getting projects done than doing the right thing. A typical political weasel. Was he ex-CIA or using that to hustle Jeanie?

Hanson looked over Dorsey's bio, which was vague before his time in Portland. International consulting for the U.S. government, including work for the State and Defense departments. Then a bunch of bureaucratic babble about "infrastructure development in emerging nations" and "liaison with developing Balkan nations." Transparent cover, Hanson thought.

What Brian really wanted was a drink. It was nearly

1 a.m., and he debated whether he should call McFarlane. He knew the cop would be available to him with no concern for the hour, but Brian also anticipated a lecture and 12-step clichés. He decided he could get solace from reading the Big Book instead. By handling the dog-eared copy, he felt a connection with the troubled souls who over the years had found solace by working the program. He read a dozen or so pages, and then the Serenity Prayer came into his head.

"God grant me the serenity to accept what I can't change, the courage to change what I can, and the wisdom to know the difference." Probably invoked more than any other message, at least in the Judeo-Christrian world. Though the Twenty-third Psalm, particularly the "Yeah though I walk through the valley of the shadow of death I shall fear no evil, for I am the meanest motherfucker around" version, had been popular in Vietnam.

He forced himself to stop thinking about Vietnam and refocused on the Serenity Prayer. Repeating it, breathing in, breathing out. Was Tammy LaFleur's death something he needed to accept or something he could change? He couldn't bring her back, but if she had been murdered, was he responsible for finding her killer? And what would he do then? Don't mean nothing. Don't mean nothing. Don't mean nothing.

After a long while, he was ready to try sleeping.

Hanson was at his desk by eight the next morning, struggling to stay awake with just four hours' sleep.

"You're here bright and early," Betty Pearlman said cheerily, sticking her head through the doorway. "You look like you had quite a time last night."

He fixed her with his bleary gaze, trying to decide if she knew what had happened.

"Tell me about it," Pearlman asked, dropping herself into one of Hanson's patched office chairs. Like most of the mental health center's furniture, it had been donated to the nonprofit by a wealthier corporation after a few years of use. In the nonprofit world, it would be part of the decor until the stains got too gross or the patches constituted more than the original fabric.

"About four hundred people, the mayor, a senator, some faces that were vaguely familiar so they've probably been in the paper. No Brad Pitt or Angelina Jolie."

"Not even Carrot Top," Pearlman joked. "So why were you invited?"

"Damned if I know."

"No special recognition of the fine work you've done? No one offering to build a wing in your honor? No secret handshakes and invitations to join the Freemasons?"

He instinctively knew the deputy mayor had been behind the invitation. Was it to see the man he was cuckolding or to try and intimidate him? Brian asked, "You know anything about Tony Dorsey?"

"He used to sit on the board of this agency," Pearlman said without guile. "Deputy mayor, sharp dresser and political operator, good-looking and he knows it, has a rep as a womanizer. He was a go-to guy—if you want something done sooner rather than later, get him on board. Why?"

"Nothing. I spent a few minutes chatting with him."

She waited for more information but Hanson said nothing.

"You look like hell, Brian. You can't do the late-night carousing you used to do when you were twenty."

"Nowadays, if I did the kind of carousing I did when I was twenty, I'd be dead," he said. At twenty, just back from the war, he had been teetering between numbing intoxication and destruction.

She stared at his serious face and knew where his mind was going. "You take care of yourself."

When Pearlman was gone, he shut the door, leaned forward into his hands, and covered his face. How quickly was he reverting to his Mr. Hyde self with the actions that had kept him alive in Vietnam? Violence without thought. The reactions he had grown up with. His father was an alcoholic carpenter who would beat his wife and kids when things were going badly. When sober he was a great dad. Always willing to toss a football or baseball, or teach Brian how to cut wood safely, make a bookcase or a step stool. Gave solid advice like "Measure twice, cut once" or "Dull blades cut flesh easier than wood."

But when the construction business was slow or he had exceeded his tab at the bar he would stagger home and slam the door with a fury that let Brian, his mother, and his brother know they should hide if they could. He had the feeling his mother willingly let herself be battered, rather than have the kids take the force of his father's fury.

No one noticed the pattern until Brian discussed it with a therapist a decade and a war later, that the day after his father's violent drunken binges, Brian would inevitably get in a fight at school. Brian didn't fight for adolescent braggadocio, he fought to hurt. An A student in middle school, he was already a known troublemaker by high school. After Brian was caught high on pot and joyriding with a couple of friends, a judge suggested the discipline of the Army or jail. The choice was easy, even with the war beginning to heat up in Vietnam. His father died, driving drunk, while he was overseas. Hanson missed the funeral. Hanson's mother remarried after a couple of years and was absorbed with her new family. He exchanged Christmas and birthday cards with her.

He loathed the violence within himself, so close to the surface, so easily provoked by the smug deputy mayor. Would he have maimed or killed him? And then what, left him on the floor of the bathroom to be discovered by the police chief or some other big shot? Was Dorsey really ex-CIA or a dweeb with a gun showing off?

Brian rubbed his face, pressing against his eyes until he saw stars. He glanced at his wall clock. He had forty-five minutes until his first client. Maybe there was something in Tammy's file that could answer his questions, convince him one way or the other.

Although he had no clinical reason to be looking through the chart, Hanson strolled to the chart room.

"Hi, Mary, how's my favorite guardian of endless paperwork?" he asked.

"The state's doing an audit and I've got to pull fifteen charts in the next few hours. Don't ask."

"I need one I closed not that long ago, Tammy LaFleur."

"I remember, you pulled that one before."

"Yeah, the joys of paperwork."

"Hold on." She went back to the closed chart room. Even before she returned, he knew something was wrong.

"Her chart's not where it's supposed to be."

"Misfiled?"

"Doubtful. We usually keep the closed charts in good order. It's better back here when we don't have you clinicians coming in and messing things up."

"Could I take a look?"

"Suit yourself."

They went into the back room, where floor-to-ceiling metal shelves housed several thousand manila file folders. All the clients that had been seen for the past seven years. A secured warehouse held another twenty thousand charts detailing the lives and suffering of closed clients. The agency was hunting for a grant to fund scanning them and storing data electronically. He watched as she ran her finger down the tabs, lips moving slightly as she quickly read the letters. "It's gone," she said with a frown. "I'll put in a lost-file form."

Numerous active charts were misplaced, usually because one member of the staff had a file out that another one was looking for. For a closed chart to be AWOL was unusual, and both he and Mary knew it.

"Let me look at the tracking record," Mary suggested. With federal HIPAA requirements, all health care entities had to diligently record any time a file was reviewed by someone outside the agency.

"It was last checked out to an Adam Dawson, deputy district attorney."

"A copy?"

"No. He had the original. Viewed it on site, then

it's signed in. See, here's Ginger's signature." Ginger was the young receptionist and file clerk who Hanson suspected had a meth habit. He had argued vehemently for more serious screening of the low-paid file clerks who had access to the most confidential material. One file clerk had been caught arranging drug deals on a company phone in the chart room.

Hanson asked Mary a few questions but she grew increasingly defensive, like a Pentagon general not wanting to believe anyone could breach a fail-safe missile system. He left her muttering and looking over the papers.

The counselor had ten minutes before his first client, and called the district attorney's office. "Adam Dawson, please?"

"I don't have anyone in my directory with that name," the operator said.

"Uh, could you double-check? It's important," Hanson said.

"One minute." The operator got back on the line after close to two minutes. "I checked both new and former employees. No one by that name."

"Thanks." Hanson hung up, feeling a heady mixture of relief and concern. It was evidence that something was going on, but what did it mean that someone had made the file disappear? What was in the file that was so valuable?

He hurried to Ginger, who was, as he had expected, useless.

She had no recollection of checking the file out, and launched into a monologue about how busy she was. He was pondering his next step when the receptionist buzzed and told him his client had arrived.

* * *

Dorsey had enjoyed humiliating Jeanie Hanson right in front of her husband with the jerk not even knowing it. But then there had been the bathroom scene, where Hanson had been in control, even though Dorsey had the weapon. The deputy mayor had gone home filled with anger and arousal and pretty much raped his wife. Arlene's docile acceptance had added to his fury. He had fallen asleep to her pathetic stifled weeping. Not the first time either.

At work he ruminated on the horrid panicky feeling as the counselor had held him by the neck. His voice was still scratchy—Edith had even asked if he was coming down with a sore throat. Clearly Hanson was a sadistic psycho, a danger to the community.

Dorsey could barely concentrate as he reviewed his morning e-mail. Nearly fifty messages had piled up. He fumed as he waded through a dozen or so between the water bureau and the city comptroller, arguing deferred billing practices for the city's larger commercial properties. The water bureau chief and the comptroller were like little kids calling each other names, wanting as large an audience as possible. His index finger savagely jabbed the Delete key.

He was snappish with Edith and terse with the press secretary, who was trying to arrange for him to fill in for the mayor at a library-opening photo opportunity. "Listen, C.J., no one gives a fuck about this ribbon-cutting bullshit. Let some lightweight from the county get his picture in the paper." He'd hung up before she could respond.

Dorsey dialed a phone number. After three rings, the machine picked up. "Let's talk, Doc."

CHAPTER FIFTEEN

Jeanie Hanson shuffled through the stack of papers on her desk a couple of times, in no mood to interpret or analyze spreadsheets. She gazed at the papers, but all she could see was Dorsey's smirky face. And her husband's placid face afterward. There had been flashes of anger, which she had been grateful for. She could understand anger. But then Brian had gotten that calm, distant expression. She recognized the irony in the situation, that her always alert husband hadn't known what was going on under the table right next to him. Or maybe he had. How much did Brian know? What would he do to Dorsey? What could Dorsey do to him? She had to salvage what she could.

Hanson met with a couple of clients who fortunately were in a maintenance mode. One needed validation that staying clean and sober and not returning to live with an abusive girlfriend was the right thing to do. The other had housing and food basket problems.

Hanson did a little basic case management, hooking the client up with an advocate. His mind, however, remained stuck on the night before.

Greg Burkett was a surprise to Hanson. He had come in for a second appointment after their initial crisis session in the hotel. Though guarded in his comments, Burkett was less antagonistic, and had an almost playful air as he bantered with Hanson. He admitted that his parole officer was pressuring him to get treatment.

"So what should we focus on today?' Hanson asked, after Burkett talked about a Trail Blazer game he had seen on TV, the weather, and a woman he had dated several years earlier.

"You ever think about drugs?" Burkett asked.

A clinical dilemma, since as an addictions counselor he'd be open about being in recovery, while mental health counselors were guarded in disclosure.

"We can talk about it, but I'm curious as to why you ask."

"You can't understand it unless you've been there."

"Whatever my experience, it's not exactly the same as yours. Are you feeling like I can't understand you?"

"You ever get the hunger down so deep and so strong that you can't think of anything else? Feel like you can't go another second without a hit? Like the world just isn't complete?"

"It sounds like it's very important to you. When did you last use?"

"It takes a doper to know a doper," Burkett said with a smile. "You still got the cravings, don't you? Want it so bad you can taste the taste, smell the smell."

"We may think about things but never do them," Hanson said. He could feel he was on the defensive. The session progressed, not really therapeutically, but at least not harmfully, Brian hoped. Afterward, Hanson reflected back on the session. A good counselor used his feelings the way a musician used an instrument, monitoring the vibrations and trying to compose something artful. The session had struck a discordant note. Did it mean Burkett was suicidal? Homicidal? Did I miss something? Hanson wondered. But he had to field a crisis call from a school counselor, and then his next client was waiting.

Anna was a trauma survivor with trait-level borderline personality disorder. She instantly knew he was distracted. She was the kind of client that, while completely overwhelmed by emotional dramas of her own creation, had highly developed antennae for picking up the emotional state of those around her. Growing up in a home where physical and emotional violence was the norm, knowing whether it was an ill wind blowing in could save her from abuse.

An old phrase stuck in Hanson's head even as he welcomed Anna. He was in Indian country. Not politically correct, but the way they thought of it in Vietnam. In the wilds, and not really sure who was going to be shooting at him from behind which tree. What should his next step be to avoid a trap?

"You don't care about me, do you?" Anna asked. Petite, usually wearing fashionable clothing that she boasted she had purchased at the Goodwill, she had a pretty heart-shaped face, marred only by the crooked teeth that gave away her impoverished background.

She had initially made it clear she was coming to see Hanson only because her Department of Human Services caseworker mandated therapy as a condition of getting her children back. But gradually she had opened up, talking about her abuse by her stepfather, her feelings of failure about parenting, her desire to be a better mother than her mother had been to her, and anxiety over what would happen if she got her kids back.

Hanson had worked, successfully, to build her trust. He knew that lying to her would take them a couple steps backward. "You're right, I'm distracted," he admitted.

"What happened? Did DHS tell you they wouldn't give my kids back?"

"No, Anna, it's more about me than you. I'm sorry, I'm caught up in an outside problem. Not really here with you the way I should be."

"You're telling me the truth?"

"Yes. I always do."

She stared at him. "Want to tell me about it?"

"They don't pay you enough to listen to my problems."

She giggled, a sound he had never heard from her. "You're an okay guy, Brian."

"Thanks."

"If you ever need anything, you let me know."

"Thanks. Now, let's get back to how you are doing."

It was a simple prearranged meeting code. They had a half-dozen different sites. Dorsey would get there first. Wolf would arrive a couple minutes later and watch, making sure no one was tailing either one of them. Wolf would follow Dorsey as he walked at a leisurely pace to an out-of-the-way location where they could talk. If there was anything out of the ordinary, Wolf would avoid contact. It had happened a couple of times, when people who knew Dorsey had come up and begun conversations. Dorsey had politely chatted, and then been forced to reschedule.

By using the name "Doc," Dorsey had signaled that they should meet on Pill Hill, home to Oregon Health Sciences University, the Veterans Administration, Doernbacher Children's Hospital, and a half-dozen major medical institutions. By using three words, Dorsey had signaled to meet at 3 p.m. Dorsey had learned early on that hospital complexes were a good place to meet. Lots of people moving in a hurry, lots of strangers. Most people were either worrying about life and death or expensive medical procedures, or they were overworked medical staff. The hospitals and clinics offered a warren of confusing multilevel connecting passageways, with numerous entrances and exits. Even if he was recognized, he would say he was visiting a friend.

Dorsey had chosen the pedestrian cable-suspension sky bridge, the longest in North America, connecting the ninth floor of OHSU with the second floor of the Veterans Administration Hospital. Meeting midway on the 650-foot-long bridge, Dorsey and Wolf could see several hundred feet in either direction.

They stood a few feet apart, gazing out the window at the great view of Mount Hood and the east side of the city, leaning slightly toward each other, but not directly facing. A casual passerby wouldn't even know they were talking.

"I've got another one for you," Dorsey whispered.

"The pace is picking up," Wolf said.

"We're making inroads," Dorsey responded. "We're at a tipping point. I already heard from a law enforcement source that we're getting a reputation in the criminal world. You know Los Angeles, back in the early to mid part of the twentieth century, used to have the goon squad that would beat up lowlifes trying to get established in town. And look at how Los Angeles grew."

"I always thought it was the stars on Hollywood Boulevard that pulled people there," Wolf said cynically, his lips barely moving. "So your goal is to have Portland be like L.A.?"

Dorsey shot him an annoyed glance. "The target's name is Brian Hanson. All the information is inside the paper." Dorsey had an *Oregonian* folded under his arm. He laid it atop the railing between them, and pretended to check his pockets.

"How do you want this Hanson handled?" Wolf asked. "Does he disappear? An accident, or should he be made an example?"

The latter was the least-used option, since the death showed up as a crime and defeated the purpose of Dorsey's project. Every now and then, it seemed most effective to have a target found horribly victimized. The police and press had speculated that it was some sort of retribution on a drug deal gone sour.

"The target passes as being legit but he's really up to his eyeballs in criminality. It would be best if there were signs that he was having a mental breakdown. Then we can decide whether he'll kill himself or be murdered because he pissed off a bad guy."

"Like what?"

"I have an in at his clinic—maybe we can plant drugs in his desk. We can connect him tighter with the Tammy LaFleur killing or her wacko roommate. Pour booze down his throat and set him up for a drunk-driving wreck. If we want it to look like an organized-crime revenge hit, use your imagination. Pull his nuts off or take out his tongue, I don't care. Be creative. I want people to know this guy is dirty."

Wolf nodded. "What's going on with him?"

"Need to know, need to know," Dorsey said.

"I do need to know," Wolf insisted.

"He uses his position as a counselor to recruit young women for the sex trade and deal drugs. He's in a major position of trust and has abused it. When he thought one of his young victims was going to squeal, he killed her."

"I haven't heard anything about it on the street."

"He's been cautious. I was lucky to get good intelligence."

"Are you sure about him? Maybe it's a head case spreading rumors."

"Positive. I can get you more evidence if you'd like. Begin scouting him out."

Wolf nodded. "When would you like this to happen?"

"Be ready."

Wolf nodded as Dorsey walked away, leaving the newspaper on the railing.

Wolf picked up the paper without looking at it and

slowly walked in the opposite direction. He rode the elevator up a couple floors in the hospital, then walked down a corridor. Confident no one had followed him, he returned to the parking garage. Seated behind the wheel of his nondescript gray Taurus, he looked at Brian Hanson's home and work addresses. Wolf began to plot his options.

Louise Parker put her arm through her uncle's as they walked into the dark polar bear exhibit building.

"You remember?" he began.

"I do," she said, but knew he would reminisce anyway.

"We used to come to the zoo every week back then. The MAX didn't exist, the children's museum was still across the parking lot, they hadn't had the big expansion."

"I remember." She put on a bad impression of his voice. "This zoo goes back to the 1880s, when a sailor who owned a pharmacy downtown began collecting animals during his travels."

"Go ahead, make fun of your uncle," he said without any malice.

She squeezed him affectionately. Two bears played in the inside cave. The Parkers watched while one bear held a hard plastic globe that looked almost like a bowling ball and gnawed at it while bobbing in the water.

"They look so cute," she said.

"Could snap a bone the way I'd break a pencil. Probably even easier," Louis said.

"Aren't you the cheery one. How're you feeling?"

"Can't complain," Louis said. "I vowed I'd never be

one of those old folks who talked about their bodily functions and doctors' appointments. But if you want to know when I last went to the bathroom . . ."

She slapped him playfully and he gave an exaggerated wince.

"Assaulted by a federal officer. I'm gonna talk to my attorney."

"Uncle!" she said, like a little girl rebuking a silly adult, and pulled his arm into hers while they continued their walk.

"The zoo. Oaks Amusement Park. Alpenrose Dairy."

"Snow tubing on Mount Hood. Going to a Trail Blazer game," she said, continuing their list of past favorite activities.

"We do have some good memories, don't we?" Louis asked rhetorically.

They moved to the outside exhibit. The other bears lounged luxuriously, licking their giant paws, stretching, simultaneously looking cuddly and deadly.

"I've never asked—why'd you do it?" she asked him.

"Do what?"

"The stuff that got you indicted."

"Let's find a bench, I'm getting tired."

She thought he would use that as an excuse, but after they sat on a bench near the monkey house, with the shrill sounds of annoyed capuchins and spider monkeys behind them, he turned to face her. "I don't know. It's the kind of thing that with twenty-twenty hindsight, I can't believe I did. You know the boiling-frog story?"

When she shook her head, he continued. "You drop a frog in a hot pot, it jumps right out. But put it in a pot at room temperature and slowly increase the heat and eventually the critter boils to death without even knowing it. I'm not making excuses. I was surrounded by people taking shortcuts. Some legal, some not so legal, some flat-out illegal. I liked the power, didn't want to give it up." There were a few seconds of silence. They watched a young couple towing two kids in a wagon. "I've got a question for you. You ever think about settling down, starting a family?"

"Now you're sounding like your sister."

"Them's fighting words," he said. "How's she doing?" Louis hadn't spoke to his sister, Louise's mother, in close to a decade. She had never forgiven his fall from grace.

"She's okay. Might be showing a bit of Alzheimer's. Hard to tell if it is just normal forgetfulness."

"Maybe she'll stop holding grudges."

"You wish," Louise said, and he clucked agreement.

"Since we're being so open, what's the story with that counselor you sent to me? What do you want to happen?"

"I don't know."

"Uncle Louis, ever since you taught me chess, I know you've been three moves ahead of everyone. I don't believe it was a casual thing."

He wiped his brow, feeling fatigued after the slow walk. "You always knew me best," he said fondly. "And I know you too. You think this is a good way to avoid answering my question?"

"Okay, I'll answer yours. Yes, I've thought about kids. There've been times when I was dating someone and I thought, This could be Mister Right. What would our kids look like? But then something important would happen at work and my energy would go there."

"It's still possible," Louis said.

"Possible, not probable." They people-watched for a few minutes. Young couples, gaggles of giggly girls, noisy families, and an occasional older couple. "So why did you refer Brian to me?"

A few long moments passed. "You may find it hard to believe, but it was an impulse."

She fixed him with her best interrogating-a-suspect look. They locked eyes, then both burst into laughter.

"Okay, I still cheat on my income taxes," he said.

"That's IRS and I don't care. I do too."

"There's something screwy in this town," Louis finally said. "The crime rate being so low doesn't add up. I know plenty of the cops, the prosecutors, the judges. None of them are such whizbangs that the city should have the lowest serious crime rate per capita in the country."

"Maybe it's something other than the criminal justice system?"

"No. I know the social service system, the mental health and drug treatment systems. I understand what you're saying, like maybe they do a great job of treating drug addicts, so there's less drug-related crime." He paused and wiped his brow again. "From people I got to know in prison and at the mental health center, I hear about folks disappearing. Not nice people necessarily, but disappearing in ways that don't make sense."

"Uncle Louis, with all due respect, these people are

bottom-feeders, probably not the kind who keep a daily planner and never miss an appointment."

"We're talking about screwy stuff, stuff that even lowlifes wouldn't miss. Like picking up drugs that had been paid for. Or setting up a hot date and not show-ing up."

She frowned. "Suspicious, but hardly enough to convict. Have you spoken with the locals?"

"They may be part of the problem."

"A police conspiracy?"

"It's happened before."

"In Third World countries."

"I can rattle off a half-dozen cases of police vigilante justice in the U.S. in the past twenty years. Who else knows who the creeps are and is more frustrated?"

"Then you should have come to me. We could've gotten a task force going."

"I don't have enough to convince you," Louis said. "If I had a solid case, I would have given it to my fa-vorite niece on a silver platter. Of course, there is a flip side."

"Which is?"

"Maybe this vigilantism is the right thing to do. Look at what it has done for Portland. The great press, the booming economy. An old geezer like me can walk the streets late at night and not worry."

"At what price?"

"Some dirtbags being executed."

"I can't believe you're saying this," Louise said. "What if they kill the wrong person? Or the power of being judge, jury, and executioner goes to their head?"

"Sweetie, can you tell me in all your years with the FBI you haven't seen the guilty go free?"

"Isn't it worse to have the innocent punished?" she asked.

"You're talking to someone who did a longer sentence than lots of murderers because my case was high profile and I had a judge who was a hard-liner. Was that fair?"

"This is a country built on laws."

"And the finest justice money can buy. I couldn't afford as skilled an attorney as my coconspirators. Guess who got the longest time as a guest of the government?"

"It's not completely fair, but no system can ever be. By short-circuiting the process, you increase the chance of dangerous inequities."

He patted her arm. "Oh, this takes me back. Our heated debates. They started when you were in middle school. Does the end justify the means? Is a majority always right? What is the morality of being outside the law if the law is immoral?"

She squeezed his arm back. "It was much better than the late-night conversations I had in coffee shops during law school. You taught me to think and respect the law."

"The system is not good . . . ," he began.

"But it's the best there is," she said, completing his oft-repeated phrase. "I was wondering whether you were trying to set me up with your counselor."

"Matchmaking?" He laughed. "I hadn't thought of Brian that way."

She blushed.

"He's married," Louis said. "But I hear rumors that it's not real solid."

"I, I'm not really interested," she said.

"Of course."

"Listen, the roommate of that dead woman made allegations against him. Stalking, harassment, maybe even murder. He's more than a witness or an informant at this point. He's got to be ruled out as a suspect."

Louis snorted.

"You know him as a counselor, Uncle Louis. I've seen him. There are definitely rough spots."

"Sure, sure," Louis said. "I don't doubt that he could commit a crime, maybe even a crime of violence with the right provocation. But not harassing a young woman. He's too much of a damn Boy Scout. Do you honestly have any worries over whether he is guilty?"

"There's evidence that—"

"Not evidence, your gut feeling. Can you honestly look me in the eye and say you think he's not legit?"

After a moment, she shook her head. "I should be heading back to my office," she said, glancing at her watch.

"You never would've said that when you were a kid. You know Packy the elephant, the first born in a U.S. zoo in decades, was born the year you were. The elephants were your favorites. I sometimes thought you were part pachyderm," Louis said. "Well, I appreciate your taking the time to humor an old man."

"Ahh, things will keep. Let's go look at the elephants."

Brian had left the final hour of the day for paperwork. Besides chart notes and assessments, inevitably there were reports for the Department of Human Services over possibly unfit parents, assessments for voc rehab, notification and coordination with probation or parole officers. He checked his voice mail and began slogging through the fourteen calls.

Four of the calls were hang-ups. He had had clients who fixated on listening to his voice mail recording, and wondered if it was happening again. Then the phone rang and he picked it up.

"Hi, this is Trixie." A hesitant girl's voice, and his mind ran through his teenage clients before he realized who it was. "You know, Tammy's roommate."

"I know who you are, Trixie," he said.

"I, I wanted to say I'm sorry about what I told that FBI agent. He said that if I didn't make trouble for you, he was going to make trouble for me."

"Who's he?"

"I can't say. I shouldn't have called." She burst into tears. "I'm sorry. I haven't been thinking right since Tammy died. I'm scared."

"Are you in danger?"

After a long silence, she said, "I think so."

"What can you do to get yourself safe?" She was not a client, but assessing for specific threat, lethality, obstacles to getting to safety, coping skills, resources, and likelihood of action was automatic.

Trixie's response was heavy breathing and soft tears.

"Do you need to call 911?"

"I can't trust the police. They wouldn't believe me anyway."

"What's going on?" he asked slowly, trying to convey calm.

"I can't talk. I can't talk over the phone. Can you come over?"

"It's not really a good idea. The police can—"

"Pleeease. You gotta help me. For Tammy's sake."

"Okay. I'll swing by as soon as I can."

"Thank you, thank you. Please hurry!"

As he hung up, Hanson debated calling her back to ask more questions, refer her to the authorities. Instead, he picked up the phone and dialed a familiar number.

CHAPTER SIXTEEN

"I've got a moral dilemma," Hanson said into the phone.

"My favorite kind," McFarlane responded.

"This is one where I need your opinion as a cop as much as my sponsor."

"Do we need to meet somewhere and talk?" McFarlane asked.

"There isn't time."

"Act in haste, repent at your leisure," McFarlane said.

"This isn't a made-up time pressure. A young woman is probably in trouble. I can't ignore it." He gave McFarlane a quick run-through of his conversation with Trixie.

"Because you think your ignoring Tammy is what got her killed? Assuming she was murdered. Assuming that you could have prevented it. Assuming that you're not jumping in on this Trixie will have a bad outcome? You know what they say about 'assume'?"

"Yes. You make an ass out of u and me. Forget about whatever my issues are. As a cop, what do you think?"

"You get a call with unspecified threats from a woman who has already accused you of harassment and you're thinking about going there? You think the same thing is going to happen to Trixie that happened to Tammy if you don't play the white knight? If I were you, I'd call it in. Ask dispatch to send a patrol car for a welfare check."

"But they may take too long. And she doesn't trust the police."

"If she's paranoid, what's to say you get there and she thinks you're trying to kidnap her for a satanic cult? Your going there is about as smart as you dropping a few hundred mikes of acid and watching *Apocalypse Now* and *Full Metal Jacket*."

"But what if she—"

"Take care of yourself. Call it in and let the professionals worry about it. Let's meet and talk about this self-destructive shit."

"Thanks, I'm okay."

Hanson made a quick phone call to Louise Parker and hurried to his car. The rush-hour traffic seemed interminably slow.

Jeanie Hanson finished making notes in the margin on a leveraged-buyout report. The deal had possibilities, though several provisions needed to be renegotiated. It was the end of a long, busy day. She had a dozen e-mails left to respond to, and nearly as many voice mails. Her phone beeped once, an internal call. Her secretary was gone, but it was not a call that would be screened. The LED display told her it was Hank Love-joy, from the twentieth floor. Executive vice president and company hatchet man. A call from Lovejoy's office, particularly at the end of the day, was as welcome as an Enron IOU. The joke around the office, never said to his face, was that Lovejoy was neither loving nor joyful.

"Hi, this is Jeanie."

"Please come to my office," the silky voice said.

"Sure. I'll be right up."

She paused only to adjust her makeup and her composure. The trip was as scary as the visit to the principal's office when she'd gotten caught cheating in the sixth grade. Her father had bailed her out, posturing as if he were angry with her while in the elite Caitlin Gable School, chuckling as soon as they were alone. She wished he were around now to muzzle Lovejoy.

She mentally reviewed her recent projects, though she deduced that her summons was due to Tony Dorsey. He was going to sabotage either the inner southeast freeway project or the mall on the city's edge. Probably because of the blowup between Dorsey and her husband. The deputy mayor would find a way to screw up a major project, and Jeanie would get blamed.

She thought about others in her position who had been linked in one way or another to failing projects. The senior partners were swift in their retribution. At best, she would wind up in a closet office, doing internlike scut work at a reduced salary. Maybe that was worse than being fired.

The elevator chimed at the twentieth floor and she

walked slowly across the thick maroon carpet, through oversize heavy glass swinging doors, into executive row. Each office had a drop-dead gorgeous view and a drop-dead gorgeous assistant. Plus a second assistant, more mundane in appearance but gifted at secretarial and administrative skills. The anteroom was empty, his assistants gone for the day.

Lovejoy had a corner office with views of Mount Hood, Mount Adams, and Mount St. Helens. With clouds rolling in, the floor-to-ceiling windows seemed barely to hold back the oppressive engulfing gray. Through his open door, she saw him at his mahogany desk. "Come in, Jeanie," he said, continuing to study a sheaf of papers.

She didn't have much time to wonder how he knew she was there.

He glanced up and gave her a smile as warm as an Alaskan winter. She wasn't sure whether he wanted her to sit, or whether that would imply or encourage a longer visit. No one wanted to spend more than the minimum amount of time in his office. Lovejoy had the nickname "Mr. Burns," since he reminded people of the frail, evil billionaire on *The Simpsons*. Since the cartoon creator came from Portland, there was speculation that Lovejoy or a relative had been the inspiration for the character.

"Have a seat," he said, gesturing with a slender, age-spotted hand toward one of two matching cordovan leather chairs that faced his desk. The chairs coordinated with his high-backed chair, as well as the matching couch, which could seat five people comfortably. Off to one side was a marble pedestal with a bust of Simon Benson, in front of an oil painting of the lumber baron and another of his son, on wood-paneled walls. Benson's name was on one of the city's premier hotels, and his land in the Columbia Gorge had been donated to become highly utilized parkland.

She sat primly, waiting. Lovejoy returned his attention to the papers on his desk. After several minutes, he looked up and gave her another chilly smile. She could see his eyes this time, a cold, bright blue. He reviewed papers slowly for a few more minutes. When he looked up again, he seemed almost surprised she was still there.

"I knew your father," he said. "Good man." He ran his hand through his thinning hair and rubbed the back of his head. "I can see his lines in your face. Good Christian blood."

She nodded.

"Too many Jews in this town nowadays. They've even been mayors, buying up the place." He ran a bony hand over his face, then pointed to the Simon Benson bust. "Things were better back then. You know about the Benson Bubblers?" Lovejoy was notorious for his Portland history quizzes.

"The fountains?"

"Yes, the bronze drinking fountains all over downtown. He gave them to the city. You know why?"

Lovejoy was related to one of the founders of Portland, Asa Lovejoy. Originally a Bostonian, Asa had tossed a coin and lost naming rights to Francis Pettygrove, who hailed from Portland, Maine. "A charitable act?"

He laughed. "I don't really believe you're naive

enough to think someone as successful as Simon Benson would do anything out of the kindness of his heart. His workers got drunk during summer months, claiming they had to drink beer to quench their thirst. He put up the bubblers for free water and garnered the support of the women's temperance groups. Pretty clever, eh?"

"Indeed," she said, trying to sound fascinated. "I've heard what an intriguing man Benson was. And he was your grandfather?"

"Great-grandfather. Quite interesting. Sometime when we don't have important concerns to discuss, I'll be happy to provide details."

"I look forward to it," Jeanie said, cocking her head and trying to look demure.

Lovejoy smiled with teeth almost as white as his hair. "Jeanie, twenty years ago that coy look might have distracted me."

"I didn't mean—"

"I don't care what you meant. You're off track. This mall project you've been working on is falling apart."

"Not really falling apart, it's—"

He slapped the papers he'd been reading down on his desk, the sharp report as harsh as a gunshot in the quiet office. "Permits canceled. A detailed EIR ordered. A contractor arrested on an outstanding warrant. Do you want to tell me what's going on?"

"It's the deputy mayor. Tony Dorsey."

"I know who the deputy mayor is. I also know about his reputation. If you were romantically involved with him, breaking up in the middle of a project is exceptionally poor timing."

"Mr. Lovejoy, I'm married."

"Yes, and I'm sure that's an insurmountable obstacle to sleeping with him. Listen, I've seen how you are in meetings, making googly eyes at the men. Getting them to lose a dozen IQ points. I'm not criticizing you, obviously your tactics worked. The partners have been watching you for a while and recognized your potential."

Hanson felt as if she'd been pimped off by the rich and powerful partners, even though it had been her own decision.

"I haven't slept with Tony Dorsey. Or any other clients," she said.

"Well maybe you should have."

"I can't believe you're suggesting that."

"I never did," he said smugly. "All we've discussed is problems with this development. A $350 million deal going awry is a serious matter for our firm. And your career."

"What do you want me to do?" she asked, her tone a mix of challenge and desperation.

"That's up to you. I would suggest making peace with Tony Dorsey. Whatever that takes."

"I think this actually stems from my husband and him having heated words."

Lovejoy looked amused, as if everything she said was digging her in a bit deeper. "I don't care what goes on with you and your husband. I do care if it is spilling over into the workplace. If your husband is annoying people who can affect our business, he needs to be reminded of his proper place. Your husband is the one who does that low-paid counseling work, isn't he?"

"It's important to him to serve the community."

"Admirable, but he needs to know his place," Love-joy said. "His salary couldn't afford your monthly bill at Nordstrom. Figure out what you need to do." He returned his attention to his papers without saying good-bye. Jeanie wasn't sure the appointment was over. After a couple of minutes of being ignored, she backed out of the room.

She rode the elevator down, absorbed in her thoughts, ignoring a late-working colleague who greeted her. She had known as soon as she had gotten the summons what she would have to do. She called Tony Dorsey.

"This is Tony," he said.

She had expected voice mail and sputtered for a moment before saying, "Hi, this is Jeanie."

"You're working late," he said.

"So are you," she responded, after a moment's hesitation.

"Want to work late together?"

"Tony, I'm calling because a whole bunch of things seem to be going wrong with the mall project."

"Really. That's too bad."

"They're all connected with the city."

"Really," he repeated, and she knew for sure he was behind the problems.

"I need your help in clearing things up."

"Well then, maybe you should come by. We can talk about it."

"I should be getting home."

"Suit yourself. I'm booked out a few weeks. Call my assistant tomorrow and see if she can help. But I'm not optimistic. City bureaus are getting much tougher.

Cracking down on a few high-visibility projects is a great way for them to get the message out about tough enforcement."

"You think you could help if I came by tonight?"

"Definitely."

"I'll be by within a half hour."

Brian Hanson drove quickly, weaving in and out of the sluggish traffic, getting a few beeps and more than a couple of obscene gestures. Heavier traffic meant longer, more unpleasant trips and more belligerent drivers. He remembered when Portland was a city that prided itself on its politeness. Gone now, due to the urban growth his wife adored.

What would he say to Trixie to convince her to trust authorities? Even his most eloquent talk didn't guarantee someone making the right decision.

He parked, looked around, saw no one in the street, and hurried to Trixie's door. "Trixie! It's Brian Hanson. Trixie?" he shouted, pounding on the door. He tried the knob and it opened. He looked back at the street, momentarily wondering if he should call 911. He was in combat mode, senses alert, moving forward quickly, silently.

"Trixie! Trixie?" No response. She was not in the kitchenette near the front door, or the living room. He heard the sound of the TV from the bedroom and felt a momentary sense of relief.

"Trixie? It's Brian. You here?"

She was sprawled on the bed in front of the TV cabinet, a needle still hanging from her arm. He felt for her pulse. Nothing. He took a step toward the telephone and saw it had been ripped out of the wall.

Brian lifted her off the bed and laid her on the floor, needing the hard surface to begin CPR. He wanted the cell phone from his car, but for right now getting her breathing was more important. She was a blue-gray color, cyanotic, a few minutes away from death. He bent over her, scanning the room while continuing to give her CPR.

The closet door was partially opened. He positioned himself so that if someone came out, he could evade and counterattack. The roaring whine of a NASCAR race blasted from a Toshiba TV, loud enough to mask the sound of an attack. The thirty-two-inch set balanced precariously on a cheap pressed-wood shelf set.

Fifteen compressions, two quick breaths. After four, check for a pulse.

Even before he saw the movement, he realized there was someone under the blanket that was tossed too casually on the sofa. The figure rose up, throwing the blanket and swinging a blackjack toward his head. The millisecond awareness had given Hanson a chance to lift his shoulder. The sap bounced off his deltoid. Hanson's right arm went numb.

At the same time there was a knock at the front door and it quickly opened. Louise Parker had her gun drawn as she stepped into the room.

Hanson's attacker wore a ski mask. He swung again at Hanson and then rolled to the side as Parker's weapon wavered and she tried to get a clear shot. The attacker kept Hanson between himself and the FBI agent.

"FBI! Freeze!" Parker yelled repeatedly.

Hanson launched a back fist with his left arm. The attacker dodged the blow and rapped his wrist with the blackjack, sending shooting pains up Hanson's arm. Brian was forced to abandon Trixie as he surged toward the attacker, who swung a roundhouse right at Hanson's head. Hanson evaded, pivoted, and landed a solid kick to the attacker's ribs. He heard the satisfying *ooof* of air being knocked from the attacker's lungs and felt a crunch. The attacker yelped in pain and Brian was confident he had broken at least one of the man's ribs.

The attacker kicked the TV shelf, and the thirty-two-inch screen fell, taking the shelving with it. After the loud crash, the images stopped, but the noise of racing cars continued. The attacker drew his silenced Colt 9 mm, firing it with a sharp *spliiiiit*. A hole appeared in the wall behind Parker. She dove to the ground as he fired a second shot. Parker smashed into the side of the sofa and was momentarily stunned. The attacker aimed at her.

Hanson lunged, knocking the gun up. The bullet grazed the FBI agent's head. Brian grabbed for the gun and the attacker swung the blackjack, catching Hanson flat on the temple.

Then there was darkness.

The potbellied guard in the white shirt and dark blue pants smirked as he had Jeanie sign in the log book at the front desk and told her, "Mr. Dorsey said to expect you."

"Where's his office?" she asked, trying to sound professionally distant.

"Second floor, end of the hall, next to the mayor's. He's waiting for you."

"Thank you," she said crisply.

She sensed his eyes on her backside as she walked swiftly down the hall. She turned around suddenly and caught him looking. He leisurely began to read his *Oregonian*.

She had expected there to be more after-hours hustle and bustle but only a couple of offices were lit. The Hispanic cleaning crews didn't seem to pay attention to her.

Each click of her heels on the marble floor felt like the tread of a prisoner on death row. She had already destroyed her marriage for her career, and now her career was in jeopardy. She would do whatever she needed to preserve her job. And she knew that Dorsey knew that as well. She found his office and knocked at the partially open door.

"Come in, come in," he said cheerfully. "Would you like a drink? Anything from Perrier to Chivas Regal?"

"I'll have the Perrier," she said, noticing how dry her mouth was.

"My pleasure," he said, and spun his chair around. He took a few steps to a wooden cabinet and retrieved a bottle of water and a Sam Adams beer. "Your husband staying clean and sober?" he asked, handing her the water.

"I'm not here to talk about my husband."

He put on an exaggerated pout. "Are you feeling like a protective little wifey?"

"I came here to talk about what's been going on with the project, how all of a sudden there are so many problems."

"Do you know what this is?" he asked, holding up a report that appeared to be a dozen pages long.

"How could I?"

"You're being feisty. I like that in a woman."

"Tony, I want to clean up any questions that have come up and then go home."

"How touching. The point is, you've already betrayed your husband. It doesn't need to be in the bedroom. You've been co-opted. An easy recruitment."

He gestured toward his bookcase, which had several dozen espionage novels and nonfiction tomes. "They make it sound glamorous, but a recruitment is simple. Greed, glory, patriotic fervor, lust, fear. There are a few classic motives to be worked. It's human nature. Don't feel bad. Everyone is vulnerable to something."

"You got me to tell you things I shouldn't have. What's to stop me from walking away right now?"

"Your marriage is a train wreck or you probably wouldn't have been so easy to recruit. Your love has gone into work, where you were properly rewarded." Dorsey held up the report and waved it. "But now the partners are overextended. They need this project, for which they've gotten all kinds of publicity and more than a few million dollars. A birdy told me that you've got quite a personal interest in it as well. You've got everything short of your husband's IRA bet on this succeeding. If the city has problems, changes principal contractors, word gets out, banks get nervous, the reputation spreads of failing on a major project."

"We have a contract with the city."

"A two-hundred-ninety-seven-page contract, to be exact. Our counsel has found about fifty pages' worth of conditions that are problematic. Unfulfilled promises, deadlines not met."

"But that's typical. We'll have it made up by—"

"Have you ever foreclosed on a mortgage where the lender promised to have it resolved by the end?" He finished his beer, leaned back in his chair, and stretched.

"What do you want?"

Dorsey rolled his chair back from his desk. "I want you to get on your knees in front of me and beg for my help."

"We've got lawyers. We can fight this."

"Yes, and six months down the road plus a few million in billable hours, you might win. Of course your firm would have been so dragged through the mud you'd be lucky to get a contract for a McDonald's in Estacada. And who's going to take the fall? One of those proper old gents who run the show? Mr. Lovejoy? Or maybe an overly ambitious female who showed once again that women don't have the rocks to make it happen."

She breathed in and let out a heavy sigh, seething and struggling not to say anything that would make it worse.

Dorsey grinned, his pleasure at her discomfort evident. "Yeah, I can picture old man Lovejoy rubbing that bust of Simon Benson, waxing poetic about the good old days when women knew their place."

"Tony, I thought we were friends. I thought we had this deal going forward."

"It can still happen." Dorsey swiveled in his chair so he was facing her. "I need a sign of your dedication, your willingness, your respect." He gestured with his finger for her to go down.

Very slowly she knelt.

"Good. Now tell me how important this is."

"Tony, I really need you to straighten this out.

There appear to be significant misunderstandings and overzealous enforcement that could wreck the deal. Hundreds of jobs could be lost, reputations damaged, the project set back months, if not years."

He rolled his chair forward, reached over, and began stroking her hair. Initially she cringed, but then allowed it. He petted her as if she were a well-behaved dog. "What would you like your buddy Tony to do for you?"

"Make calls. Get it straightened out."

"Straightened out. I can do that. But there's something I want you to do for me."

"What?"

He began to unzip his fly.

"No!"

"Suit yourself." He rolled his chair back a few inches. "Call back tomorrow and we'll see if my assistant's intern can get some of this cleared up. She's a sweet kid, barely twenty, just learning the ropes, but enthusiastic."

"You know she can't get these changes made."

"But I'm very busy." He sat, with his open fly less than two feet from her face. "Except for my friends. You show me how friendly you can be and I make a couple of phone calls right now."

They stared at each other. He tugged at her hair, pulling her forward. She didn't resist.

CHAPTER SEVENTEEN

Tony Dorsey rested in his office, savoring the moment. Jeanie Hanson had been gone for a half hour. Great sex was about power and control, enhanced by the joy of deception. The bound papers he had waved in front of Jeanie, allegedly about her firm, were actually an auditor's report on the fire department's progress at hiring women and minorities.

While Jeanie serviced him, he called Arlene to tell her he had to work late. She docilely accepted the news, probably suspecting what was going on. Then he called a few bureau chiefs involved with Jeanie's construction contracts and left voice mail messages that he'd like to talk about the project. He'd turn down the heat to a low simmer to keep her coming in for a while. She was neither an enthusiastic nor an imaginative participant, but that wasn't what he was looking for.

Brian Hanson would be neutralized soon enough. After a few weeks of troubles, the discredited and obviously disturbed counselor would take his own life. With a little help. Before he did it, Dorsey would have to give him a call, while Jeanie Hanson was under the deputy mayor's desk. The thought gave Dorsey a ripple of pleasure.

Dorsey had grown up an Army brat, the son of a captain who had served in Germany, England, Spain, and a half-dozen different postings in the U.S. He'd excelled at political science and geography. Attending Johns Hopkins on a full academic scholarship, he'd been approached by a CIA recruiter.

His first few years he'd been an analyst, but always intrigued by the ops side. He applied for, and successfully completed, a transfer. He'd had a posting at School of the Americas, working with police departments from several Latin American countries. He'd never forget his first time sitting in on a Peruvian interrogation of a suspected Shining Path supporter. The two cops had violated the woman in ways he hadn't imagined. By his third interrogation, he was invited to join. He said no. By his sixth, he was an active participant. His fluency in Spanish coupled with an acceptance of "extraordinary measures" during questioning made him popular with local officials. He participated in several grisly interrogations that resulted in valuable information. By the tenth time, he was leading the interrogations.

He was about to be made station chief in Paraguay when his career plummeted. A young woman whom he had been involved in torturing turned out to be related to a Mexican senator. The senator raised a fuss over his relative's abuse, and only Dorsey's quick return to the United States kept him from being exposed and arrested.

But Dorsey couldn't kick his acquired tastes. Several prostitutes in the District of Columbia metro area were abused before word got back to the CIA. He was ordered to therapy with an Agency-approved counselor. Once the administrators felt he was not an obvious danger to civilians or a potential leak of confidential information, he was discharged.

Sitting in his office, he brooded over what to do about Brian Hanson. In the hospital, perhaps Wolf could slip in and overdose him with medication. If not, the whole incident with Trixie would just be the first step in the campaign.

Hanson awoke to bright lights and harsh sounds, which worsened his explosive headache. He was about to ask where he was, when the tired-looking young man with the white coat leaning over him asked, "Do you know where you are?"

"Hospital." It hurt to talk. The paging system called for Dr. Druker, and Hanson winced from the sound.

"Your name?" the intern asked. He looked like he was trying to make up for his youth by being extremely serious.

"Brian Hanson." Hanson tried to sit up but fell back on the bed from a dizzying wave of pain. "I know the year and the president."

"Good," the intern said. "Headache?"

"Mother of all headaches," Hanson said.

"There's swelling, probably tenderness, on the outside." He produced a flashlight, shined it in Hanson's eyes. "Yup. You got a concussion. Your left pupil is about twice the size of the right. The nurse got your vitals already and nothing extraordinary. We'll keep you for observation, give you limited painkillers. Not too much. We won't want you dozing off."

"I know about traumatic brain injury," Hanson said, gently rubbing his head. "Tenderness" was an understatement. It felt like a mule had kicked him.

"I'll write up my orders. Be back to check on you soon," the intern said, already halfway out the door.

Louise Parker had been standing quietly a few feet behind the intern. She stepped forward and patted Hanson's hand. "How you feel?"

"Crappy. Did she make it?"

"Trixie? No."

"Cause of death?"

"Not yet."

"Did you get him?"

"No. He fired several shots at me. By the time I could get up and return fire, he was gone. Then I was hustling to get you here."

"Thanks."

"No sweat. You saved my life."

"No sweat. You saved my life too."

"No sweat," she repeated with a smile, and he smiled back. "Ballistics will be able to get information out of the holes in the walls."

There was more noise from the waiting room, a mentally ill man screaming about the FBI stealing his brain waves. "Think I should offer to give them back?" she asked.

"If you could close the door, I'd be forever in your debt," he said, flinching from the ER noise.

She slid the glass door shut and they were alone in the eight-by-ten-foot room. An infrared monitor hooked up to his finger monitored his pulse and oxygen level. The readout oscillated normally on the small screen above his head. The rest of the wall looked like a kitchen, with sink, long counter, and cabinets. But the cabinets had labels like "Gloves," "Gauze Pads," and "Antiseptics." She leaned against the counter.

"I'd like to call my wife."

She handed him her cell phone; he dialed home, and got their machine. "Hey, it's me. I'm going to be home very late. I'm in the ER. Nothing serious but they want to keep an eye on me. I'll explain when I get home." He clicked off.

"You could have given her my cell number."

"Didn't know how long you'd be staying."

"For the duration."

"You don't need to."

She shrugged.

It was harder for Wolf to get around the ER than most parts of the hospital. On most wards, an unknown formally dressed middle-aged man with a confident air was assumed to be a visiting doctor, and no one dared question ID.

Now he moved slowly, police badge pinned to his chest. There were enough cops coming in and out of the ER that no one paid extra attention. It was a good place to silence someone—people did die there on a regular basis. The general hubbub could be an asset or a liability. Lots of people around, but most were distracted.

Wolf moved toward Hanson's room.

* * *

The door to Hanson's room opened and sound flooded in. "You can't shut this door," snapped an officious nurse with gray hair pulled back in a severe bun.

Parker took out her badge. "FBI. This man is a witness to an attempted murder on a federal officer. Shut the door unless you want to be charged with obstructing justice."

The nurse hesitated, then said, "I'm going to check with the doctor." She closed the door behind her.

"I'm impressed. I've never met anyone tougher than an ER nurse." Hanson settled back into the bed, adjusting it electrically so he could be half reclining. "What do you think happened back there?" he asked.

"That's one of my reasons for being here. I'd like to discuss it."

"Should I be getting a Miranda warning?"

"I don't think you're a suspect. If you killed her, calling me was either part of some brilliant scheme or very self-destructive. If you were working with the guy with the silenced gun, it doesn't seem to be a viable partnership. Though one thing does make me suspicious."

"I can guess. It's clear he didn't want to kill me. He was masked and only using the blackjack on me until you arrived."

"For a guy with a swollen brain, you're thinking pretty clearly."

Even with his pain, he noticed that she had a very nice smile. "I'm motivated. I'd like to find the SOB who did this." He tapped his head. "My arm where he rapped it doesn't feel so great either."

A nurse came in, set up a stainless-steel IV pole, and

hung a bag with morphine solution. He realized for the first time that his clothes were gone and he was in a hospital gown. She attached a tube to the port they'd put in while he'd been unconscious in the ER. The morphine bag began to drip.

"Busy night?" Parker asked her.

"Always busy. Tonight's busier than most," she said quickly. "Two car wrecks, three psychos, an overdose, a cardiac, a probable stroke, two kids with ear infections, one with an unknown fever, and someone we're waiting for a translator for because we don't know what the heck is going on." She hurried out.

"Is this thing going to get publicity?" Hanson asked Louise.

"The Bureau's not doing a press release. Any attack on an agent is taken seriously, and if we don't get results after a while, they might decide it is in the best interest of the investigation to go public. For now, every agent is offering 'get out of jail free' cards to snitches if they have information." Parker pulled over the small, round rolling stool and sat down near the bed. "You want to tell me your theory?"

"Trixie called me, either really scared or on orders to get me there. A staked goat. Maybe she was supposed to lure me over, then the guy with the gun kills her with a hot shot, knocks me out, calls 911. I'm found at the sordid scene with the overdosed corpse of a sex-trade roommate of a former sex-trade client, who is also dead. I'd be lucky if I just lost my job and license."

"Who would have the motive and access to a professional like the guy with the gun?"

"I don't know." The morphine was kicking over, and his thoughts about Dorsey were difficult to put into words. Though his headache and arm throbbed, they no longer caused him to wince with every move. There was something about her touch, her attentive expression, the way she held herself and watched over him, that made Hanson feel better than he had in a long time. Even before the attack. He reached over and squeezed her hand. "You don't need to stay."

"You're a witness. Someone needs to watch you."

He began to doze.

"I don't think you're supposed to do that after a concussion," she said. "Could be signs of a coma. Better stay awake."

"Mmm. I know," he said with a sluggish slur. "Got to stay awake."

There was a woman in the room with Hanson. Wolf pretended to be talking into the wall phone but had Hanson in clear sight. Could be his wife, but she had a no-nonsense air that smelled like cop to Wolf. Then she moved and he saw the hint of a gun butt under her jacket.

Not a good time to visit, Wolf thought, and moved briskly toward the exit.

"Any other thoughts about the attack?" Louise asked.

"Feel bad. I was in dozens of firefights, shoulda done better." Brian struggled to keep his eyes open.

"We're both alive. You did great."

"Shoulda been aware of the blackjack. Coulda had him."

"You did good."

He was quiet for a long while.

"Brian. Brian, are you awake?"

"Hmmm, yeah. Dozens of firefights. Never this out of it. Parrot's Beak. Pleiku." He breathed in and out slowly. "By the time I was in-country, there was already the hint that U.S. policy was fucked. This wasn't World War II, a noble intervention. It was geopolitical power plays by Nixon, Kissinger, and McNamara."

He fought the urge to cry, desperate not to let her see. "Hard to admit, but it may have been the best time of my life. No one who has never been in combat can understand. It was like a drug."

She waited. "No, I can't understand it. I've had to draw my weapon twice, never used it. One of the times someone else killed the bank robber. Every time I break leather, even if it's at the shooting range, I think about it. I can't imagine what it was like for you, week after week, month after month."

"I wish someone had said that when I first came back. It sucked. The war winding down. No heroes, no welcome. Remember when psycho-Vietnam-vet was one word?"

"Vaguely."

He realized that she was probably about ten years younger than he. A different generation. He felt older and wearier. The drug in his system was roiling bad memories, familiar feelings. "Shouldn'ta taken that morphine. Shouldn't give drugs to a druggie."

"You needed the painkiller."

"Painkiller. Babykiller. They called us that. I never killed a baby. I saw them dead though. VC made examples. We'd help a village, they'd punish them. Poor peasant bastards stuck between both sides. Bad things, very bad things. The body is a weak thing. Metal so much harder. Does horrible stuff, horrible. Pieces of arms, legs, a head. Faces peeled off. We knew the rice field was mined. North Vietnamese army coming in, battalion strength. The villagers knew where the mines were, walked around them while working. We forced this family forward. Mama-san made a mistake, stepped on a mine. Her daughter, maybe eight, ran to her, hit another mine. One minute people, the next minute, pieces." Hanson struggled to focus on the present, clenching and unclenching his fist, breaths coming in deep gasps.

"Shouldn'ta done it, shouldn'ta taken the drug. Not enough to sedate me. Just enough to remind me. Make 'em disconnect it." Hanson was panicky, wanting it, fearing it, and that fear making him want more.

Parker buzzed the nurse, and got the gray-haired one.

"Take it off," Hanson said, trying to sound well composed. "No more morphine."

"Doctor's orders," she said, and turned to leave.

"He's a witness," Parker said, standing up and speaking authoritatively. "I need him to be completely conscious."

The nurse was not impressed. "Doctor's orders. I'll check with him when he's available." The nurse marched out.

"So much for federal clout," Parker said.

Hanson bent the IV tube over and clamped it. The morphine drip stopped. An alarm started beeping. Louise found a switch, flipped it, and the noise stopped.

Hanson sat up with a slow, painful effort. "Do me a favor. Call my sponsor." He gave her McFarlane's cell number; she dialed, then handed him the phone.

The cop answered on the third ring.

"Hey, Bob, it's me."

"Are you high?"

"Only took you four words," Hanson responded.

"I guess. But under a doctor's stuperdvision." Hanson stumbled over the word "supervision."

"What happened?" McFarlane barked.

Hanson gave a quick recital of what had occurred at Trixie's apartment.

"You did what I told you not to do, and it got fucked up," McFarlane said.

"I appreciate your sympathy."

"Are you on the pity pot?"

Hanson nearly said he had a bedpan, but even during good times, McFarlane had little tolerance for humor. "The girl's dead. Maybe I should've done more."

"Is that your way of saying maybe if I had jumped when you said 'Let's go over there,' she'd be alive?"

"Well, maybe," Hanson said.

"This is where you should be more attuned than most to boundary issues. What do you think a police officer would have done in this situation normally? Should I let our relationship alter my professional judgment?"

"Well, you know me. That should count for something."

"It does. I know you as a human who has holes in his character. As do we all. Could a young damsel in distress drive a bulldozer through them?"

Hanson looked over at Parker, who was watching and listening to his side of the conversation. "I guess. I'll think about it."

"Want me to come over?"

"Nah, I think I'll be okay," Hanson said.

"I do too," McFarlane responded before quick good-byes.

"Did you get the support you needed?" Parker asked when Hanson ended the call.

"I don't know if I'd call it support. Not necessarily what I wanted, but hopefully what I needed."

Jeanie Hanson had heard the phone ring, and hadn't picked up. The volume on the answering machine was turned down low and she couldn't hear who it was. Not that she cared. Brian wasn't home, and that was unusual, but she preferred not to face him anyway. Images of her own degradation dominated her thoughts. She felt trapped, hopeless, victimized.

She had gargled and then swallowed two shots of Chivas Regal, then brushed her teeth for several minutes. She thought about how easy it would be to sic Brian on Dorsey. If her husband had any idea of what had happened, she suspected, he would kill Dorsey. The violence under the surface of her do-gooder husband. It helped her feel better, as if she had a Rottweiler on a leash that she could turn loose on the deputy mayor at any time.

The scotch kicked over and she felt numbed enough to stop pacing. After another large scotch, she threw the tumbler against the fireplace. She sat in the chair, staring at the broken shards of glass.

CHAPTER EIGHTEEN

The doctor offered Hanson the chance to stay overnight, but made it clear it was for observation and he would probably be better off at home. It was a little after 2 a.m. when Louise Parker, following hospital procedure, rolled Hanson out the door in a wheelchair.

As soon as they reached fresh air, Hanson promptly stood up. He failed at trying to conceal how wobbly he was.

"We can go right back in. You haven't even cut your beautiful bracelet off yet," Parker said, pointing to his identifying wristband.

"I don't want to be admitted," Hanson said. "I'm grateful to the gods and goddesses of managed care to keep the docs motivated to discharge me."

She dropped him by his house and he walked as quickly as he could to the door, hoping that he looked better than he felt. The morphine drip had worn off and he was fighting the pain with a few ibuprofens.

He didn't want to show Parker how sore he was, or discuss it with his wife.

From the threshold to his house Brian waved at Parker, and she drove away. After easing open the door, he stifled a groan as he slipped off his shoes in the foyer. He stripped down to underwear and shirt with a minimum of wincing and walked stiffly to the bedroom.

Jeanie groggily sat up in bed. "Where've you been?" she asked.

"Minor accident," he said.

"Are you okay?"

He finished undressing slowly. "Sore. Best thing is for me to get to sleep."

"Okay."

He didn't ask why she hadn't answered the phone; she didn't pursue details about the accident. He could tell she had taken a sleeping pill and was glad when she quickly drifted back to sleep.

He lay in bed, mindful of the pain, not avoiding it, letting it come and go without attachment. Sleep was often difficult, a problem he traced back to trying to stay awake in Vietnam. There were days back then when he didn't sleep, not trusting those on guard duty, painfully attuned to the sounds of the jungle, waiting for the subtle changes that would mean an attack.

His mind reviewed the shoot-out at Tammy's, and he decided he had done a good job for an unarmed middle-aged guy. He went to sleep smiling. The real attack had validated the hypervigilance from his PTSD.

Back in her spacious but cozy one bedroom condo in Johns Landing, Louise found herself surprisingly alert.

She poured herself a glass of Smoking Loon Riesling and wrote notes for the FD204 investigative report forms she'd have to do.

Sitting in a Herman Miller Eames chair, bare feet tucked under a small wrought iron and clear glass table, she gazed through the large window at the Willamette River, moving sluggishly a hundred or so yards away. Gusts of wind kicked up tiny whitecaps. It reminded her of Hanson. Quiet, with hints of turbulence.

She's been married briefly to an FBI rookie/account-ant she'd met at Quantico. Somehow he'd expected she would drop out of the Academy and become a contented hausfrau. They clutched each other for support in a stressful time and lasted less than a year.

With her job that had a fifty-hour-a-week minimum, irregular hours, and lots of secrets, dating opportuni-ties were limited. The tough exterior she developed to survive her job intimidated many men.

Hanson was not a good choice. He was older by a decade, married, and a possible person of interest in the investigation. But seeing his heroics in the apartment, and watching him struggle with his issues in the ER, she'd had strange thoughts. Like how good he looked despite what he had been through, and with no effort at grooming. Or how his body conveyed a restless power, and attractive energy. Like what kind of father he'd be to the child she'd just about given up on having.

She pushed the thoughts from her mind until she fi-nally lay down to sleep. Then she drifted off, savoring a fantasy that her minister would not have approved of.

Abundant fish in the Columbia River and soil rich with river nutrients had made Sauvie Island the Mall of America thousands of years before white men first arrived. Now it was covered with farmland and a huge nature preserve. Blue herons, bald eagles, and hundreds of other birds roosted there. The wildlife competed with herds of cows, leading to periodic flare-ups of farmers versus environmentalists versus weekend bicyclists and beachgoers.

Former senator Jake Charmaine's three-million-dollar estate was on a low hill that was the highest spot on the relatively flat island. The retired senator worked as a lobbyist with a client list that included several lumber companies, two electronics giants, and one large sneaker and sportswear firm.

Mayor Robinson mentally reviewed Charmaine's background as he drove Highway 30, parallel to the railroad tracks, past the industrial complexes and the shipyards until the man-made development—which some saw as ugly but the mayor saw as triumphs—thinned out and the trees took over.

He was driving his wife's Lexus. Usually a police officer–bodyguard chauffeured him in the dark blue Crown Victoria that served as the mayor's official car. But he knew the cop would have dual loyalties and every move would be dutifully reported to Forester. Usually Robinson was amused by the pressures of being under political surveillance. But this was a meeting he didn't want noted. He had no idea what the purpose was, a rebuke or a reward.

Robinson stopped at the intercom mounted next to the metal gate with the big "JC" on it. He was quickly buzzed in. The driveway curved between drooping willow trees; past a tennis court, a stable, and an Olympic-sized swimming pool; and up to the sprawling old farmhouse that looked well kept but unassuming from the outside. As Charmaine's butler–secretary–man Friday led him in, however, it was evident that millions had been spent to upgrade the home. Rich oak paneling, recessed museum-quality lighting, bronze busts on marble pedestals, brooding oil paintings, high ceilings with detailed woodwork on the beams. A large brass telescope on a wooden tripod sat in front of the picture window, facing the beach. One wall was dominated by a sixty-five-inch-long, two-inch-deep flat-panel plasma Emerson TV. It was tuned to CNN, with the sound muted.

"This place is beautiful," Robinson said sincerely.

Charmaine smiled ruefully. "It's going to be like Hearst Castle before my wife's done."

Moving with an old man's fragility, he fetched a thick Cuban cigar from a rosewood humidor. "I'd offer you one but I know you're not a smoker," Charmaine said, lighting the cigar. The politician puffed on the Cohiba for a full minute, savoring the taste. Robinson watched the tip on the cigar grow red, the ash beginning to expand with a seeming life of its own. The mayor studied the lined face, with piercing blue eyes and thick white hair that showed no signs of receding from his high forehead.

"Why did you invite me here, sir?" Robinson asked after a few minutes of polite pleasantries.

"You're being talked about as a candidate on a statewide or national level," Charmaine said.

"Really?" Robinson tried not to sound too eager.

"I know you well enough to know you've been thinking about the next step. Cleve Cavness has made it clear he's going to be leaving the Senate by the next election. The timing could work out perfectly. He'd be willing to endorse you."

"That's great."

"It could be. But you've got to put your house in order."

The senator leaned close enough that Robinson could see the capillaries under his pale skin. "The committee is not going to take chances on premature flameout. We have checked into you and your immediate associates, your *West Wing* cast."

Robinson stiffened, since only his inner circle knew about his *West Wing* nicknames for the staff. Clearly Charmaine and the committee had exquisite resources.

"There is a whole different level of scrutiny you must be attuned to," Charmaine said. "You run up a tab at a casino, hire an undocumented alien as your nanny, take home a tart from a bar, and it will turn up on the news. Or on one of those Internet Web sites. Of course we checked you out before this conversation."

"I gather I passed?"

"You did. We also checked that you weren't finessing the numbers on the crime stats. That's going to be the hot issue in the campaign. Crime is much easier for John Q. Public to understand than fiscal reform or the national debt. Crime is such a core issue, affecting economic development, civic pride, allocation of resources. That mugger in the alley will get them to the polling booth. Imagine if the crime-fighting strategies you implemented are translatable to New York, Los Angeles, Washington, D.C. What would those places be like with a crime rate cut in half?"

"The tactics should be applicable to a larger city."

"We didn't honestly see what you're doing differently. Some is the 'broken window' approach, addressing problems when they're small nuisances. Then there's community-oriented policing, an adequate staffing ratio." Charmaine paused and puffed. "Chief Forester deserves credit. He's job hunting, you know."

Robinson didn't, but didn't want to admit it. He nodded.

"The chief has put in for a couple of big-city jobs. Boston, Chicago. Plus sniffing around for the directorship at ATF."

Robinson nodded as if it weren't news to him. "What're his chances?"

"So-so. He's not perceived as a great leader or visionary, more someone who lucked out. Some think the DA deserves more credit. And there are rumors."

"Of what?"

"A vigilante-type thing going on."

"I can't imagine that."

"This is the West," Charmaine said with a contented puff. "It wasn't that long ago that there were about as many unsanctioned hangings as legally approved ones."

"Going back to what you were saying, what is the perception of me? Am I seen as someone who just lucked out?"

"You wouldn't be here if you were. You've got the media presence. Even if your success is attributable to luck, you've capitalized on it nicely. The economy of the city is better than most of comparable size. You've put together a competent administration. There are concerns, though."

Robinson leaned forward, attentive.

"The police chief's relationship with his son. Either he has got to cut the ties altogether or make peace with him. He loses the gay vote by being homophobic and the fundamentalist vote by not being condemning enough. That'll pull you down if you are tied to him."

"Okay."

"Your press person, she's got a drinking problem."

"Had one. She's in recovery."

"Not for the past six months."

Robinson shook his head. "I'm impressed with your sources, even if I'm skeptical."

"The comptroller has a gambling problem. Not enough to be an issue, but he'd better be careful. You don't want your man holding the purse strings to be revealed as financially irresponsible."

"I'll talk with him."

"I'm glad you're so receptive. But they're not the biggest potential problem."

Robinson waited.

Charmaine took a puff, as if carefully choosing his words, though Robinson was sure he had thought out exactly what he'd say much earlier. "Tony Dorsey. He's a dangerous womanizer."

"Many pols have had an eye for the ladies," Robinson said defensively.

"He likes to abuse and exploit."

Robinson was shocked, like a parent hearing an unwanted truth about his child. He had had suspicions, even heard the rumors, but Charmaine was so matter-of-fact, like it was public knowledge. "Are you sure?"

"I'm not one to be slandering a man's name. I was able to read a sealed deposition from one of his former victims." Charmaine shook his head. "Bad stuff."

"He's been vital to me. I don't know what to do."

"Talk to him. If there's any sign he's not getting the message, cut your losses."

"Is he at it right now?"

"I hear he's diddling a married real estate woman with a husband who's a psycho. You don't want a story about your boy being killed as part of a triangle gone bad."

"No, I don't."

Charmaine stood slowly. "Time for my nap," he said. "I'm glad we had this chat. Come back and see me in a couple weeks. I'll have a better handle on whether we're talking Senate or White House by then."

"Thank you, sir."

"You're welcome," Charmaine said, shaking his hand warmly. "I'm sure you'll remember who helped you on the way up when I come a-lobbying."

Driving back to the city, Robinson was swept by wave after wave of powerful emotions. Joy over the possibilities, anger at his errant staff, particularly Dorsey, shame over Charmaine knowing more than he did about his own people, fear that his bright future would be screwed up. By the time he reached his office, he was settled enough to begin taking action.

The mayor gaveled the close of the city council meeting. There had been minimal dissent, a little grandstanding, nothing out of the ordinary. A couple of audits were reviewed and approved, the actual work having been done by staff before the meeting. At least two of the five-member council knew as much about audits as a third-grader would about calculus.

Dorsey gathered the papers. The mayor prided himself on being paper-free, or at least paper-light, and retaining the information in his head. While he had a phenomenal memory, he relied on Dorsey and the rest of his staff to keep track of details and make him look well informed.

As the mayor and his aide walked down the arched hall to the mayor's office, Dorsey could tell that something was bothering his boss.

"I'll start working on that projection of corporate tax adjustment," Dorsey said as they were about to separate.

"I'd like to speak with you for a moment," Mayor Robinson said in a tone that was clearly a command and not a request.

"Sure," Dorsey said amiably, though his mind was already reviewing possible counterpunches for whatever issue Robinson had in mind.

They entered Robinson's office and the mayor said, "Shut the door behind you."

Dorsey did, and Robinson strode to his desk, then sat in his high-backed leather chair. He gestured for Dorsey to sit facing him.

"I've always tolerated your eye for the ladies," Robinson said, playing with a black Montblanc pen from his desk. "You won't insult me by denying it, will you?"

Dorsey met his inquisitive expression, poker-faced.

"This latest one, she's married, isn't she? She was seated with her husband, next to you, at the dinner?"

Dorsey was trying to figure out Robinson's source. Jeanie wouldn't dare, she had too much to lose. The mayor had ears throughout city hall, from janitors to deputy directors, as wired as a Florentine prince. Did

Dorsey's wife know and would she have called? Or maybe the mayor had only heard rumors and was bluffing.

"Tony, you've got a lot of talent. But it wouldn't be the first time a guy threw away a great career because he was letting his dick do the thinking."

Dorsey was silent.

"I need you to promise that you'll stop this," Robinson said. "I've known about your peccadilloes in the past. This isn't the time. I've shown that what we've done here works. Criminals have learned to find a place for themselves other than our city, while good citizens find it safer than ever. If you want to follow me to Washington, you'd better stop immediately."

Dorsey thought quickly, wondering whether docile contrition was the best way to appease his boss. But he found his anger rising. "What I do off-hours is my own business," he snapped.

"If it is off-hours. And not while representing my office in any way, shape, or form."

"Let he who is without sin cast the first stone," Dorsey said softly.

"What?"

"Let he who is without sin cast the first stone," he repeated. "You know what's been going on. You haven't said anything about any of it."

"Meaning?"

"If I go down, don't expect me to do it without a fight. Like you've said, I am seen as representing your office."

"Is that a threat?"

"Mr. Mayor, you know me well enough to know I don't make threats. I've appreciated your support and confidence. I have worked my hardest to make sure they are well deserved. It would upset me greatly if our relationship were to sour."

"You're refusing?"

"I can be more discreet. But if I go down, you know what will happen to your administration. The press would be intrigued by the real secret to your success. And the full story of Tammy LaFleur. I won't go gently into the night."

Robinson fiddled with his pen. The meeting hadn't gone the way he had anticipated.

"If you have no other questions, Mr. Mayor, I'd like to get back to work."

Robinson waved him off.

The door clicked shut behind him as Dorsey exited. Robinson's secretary gave the deputy mayor a questioning glance. Dorsey bobbed his head and strutted away.

With just a few hours' sleep, a headache worse than his worst hangover, and an arm sore from the day before, Hanson insisted on going to work. Jeanie Hanson had called in sick and he'd left her in bed with an undefined malaise.

"You look awful," Betty Pearlman told him affectionately as he sat in the lunchroom, sipping a microwaved ramen soup.

"Thanks, that's a fine assessment. You ought to consider a career in behavioral health care."

"I would but the pay's terrible," she said. "Okay, enough witty repartee. There's a cop here who wants to talk to you about Eleanor Malinowski."

He mentally reviewed his current caseload and recently closed cases, but the name didn't seem familiar. "I'll talk with him, but I'd like you there," Hanson said. "To back me up on confidentiality."

The way that the detective hurriedly hunched down into his seat as they entered the office made it obvious he had been peering at papers on Pearlman's desk.

Betty held up the top papers, her application for renewal on her Costco card. "Find anything interesting?" she asked sarcastically.

"My name is Detective Quimby," the detective said. He had a sharp rodent face, with a pointy nose and a thin mustache. It was offset by a smooth smile, elegant manners, and expensive clothing. Blue blazer, red classically patterned silk tie, pearl tie tack, Norm Thompson chinos, and shiny brown Ferragamo shoes with tassels.

"Tell me about Eleanor Malinowski," Quimby said.

"I'm fairly restricted in what I can say," Hanson said as Pearlman nodded support. "Even when someone dies, her confidentiality privilege survives her."

"That's if she's a client. I've checked OHP billing records. There's no evidence of her attending this or any other county clinic."

"I would have thought that information would be restricted," Pearlman said.

"Ma'am, this is a homicide investigation."

Hanson suddenly knew who Eleanor Malinowski was. "Did she go by another name?" the counselor asked.

"She had a couple of different trick names. Which did she use with you?"

"Trixie."

Quimby bared a cynical smile that showed Crest-strip-brightened teeth. "That was her S and M name. Also for girl-on-girl stuff. She had another name for the young-girl act, you know, ponytails and short skirts with no underwear. Or maybe that isn't your scene?"

"Questions for Mr. Hanson should be done with our attorney present," Betty interrupted.

"It's okay," Hanson said. "He's doing what he has to."

"Are you two going to do a good-cop-bad-cop routine with me?" Quimby sneered.

"Am I a suspect?" Hanson asked.

"At this point, everyone is. If I start reading you your Mirandas, you'll know you're in trouble," he said.

"I gave a full statement to the FBI. There was an agent at the crime scene who also saw her killer. Neither one of us got much to identify him with. Any leads on who killed her?" Hanson asked.

Quimby turned to Pearlman. "Is it unusual to have a counselor connected with two hookers and both turn up dead?"

"I don't like your insinuation, Detective Quimby. This interview is finished," Pearlman said. "Any allegations about Mr. Hanson's reputation reflect on my clinic."

"We'll stay in touch." Quimby rose slowly, as if he had decided to end the interview. "I'll find my way out."

He was barely out the door before Pearlman was muttering curses. "Slimy little ferret."

"I don't think I've ever seen you this angry."

"Now you know my dirty little secret. I don't like cops. Particularly power-mad jerks."

Hanson was about to say something, when she interrupted. "I'm a child of the sixties. While you were off making like G.I. Joe, I was chanting 'Peace now!' and wishing I looked like Jane Fonda. I never talked about it with you, not sure how you'd take it."

"There was a time when I wanted to kill Jane Fonda and those hippie demonstrators as much as I wanted to kill VC. Then I wanted to kill LBJ, Nixon, McNamara, myself. It was a messed-up time all around."

"Agreed."

He nodded.

"I can get the agency attorney to represent you, but if there's a serious chance of charges, you should get a criminal attorney. I'll see about getting a few recommendations."

"You think I did it?"

"No way. But that doesn't mean you won't get charged with it."

"I—I've always appreciated your support. But never more than now."

"Don't go mushy on me, big guy. You're a pleasure to work with. I look forward to our supervision times."

He stood, trying to think of an eloquent way to express his appreciation. "Thanks."

"You're welcome," she said, and returned her attention to her paperwork.

CHAPTER NINETEEN

Quimby held his classic black leather cop's notepad in front of him and recited what he had learned. Chief Forester sat stiffly behind his desk, staring at the embroidered Nativity scene that his wife had given him.

". . . both dead women were prostitutes, had done tricks together, which gives numerous common associates."

"The wages of sin," Forester mused. "Serial killer?"

"Doubtful. No signs of ritual or sexual assault. The first victim, the former chief's daughter, has the look of a hit or a crime of passion. The second victim, overdose."

"No chance it's suicide?"

Quimby shook his head. "A possible perp is this counselor, Brian Hanson. A strong suspect, if you ask me."

"How come?"

"The deputy mayor is diddling this guy's wife."

"Dorsey?"

"Who else? It's not the first time his willy is a-wandering."

"I know that."

"Hanson's wife was seen leaving Dorsey's office after hours, looking like she'd been rode hard and put away wet."

"Where are you as far as actually making a case against Hanson?"

"It's not going to be today or tomorrow but should be nailed down within a week. The lead detective says the case is moving forward. He's talked with the DA about search-warrant possibilities. Got witnesses that can place Hanson in the area, acting weird, after the first victim. An FBI agent can place him there right around the time of the second death."

"Motive?"

"The guy's a Vietnam vet who came back a violent addict. Appeared to have straightened up until his wife starts getting porked by our city hall Casanova. Then a gear slips and he starts taking it out on women. One of whom, by the way, had been a client of his."

Forester believed all crimes, particularly those that violated the Ten Commandments, were a moral affront, an insult to the God who created the universe. His faith reassured him that the wicked would be punished. He knew that pleasure at others' suffering was un-Christian. But Tony Dorsey was going to get his comeuppance, and he felt a deep and guilty joy.

There were seven people in Hanson's process group, and four of them were crying. One young woman who had been in a domestic-violence relationship had, with the support of the group, at last moved into a shelter. The session ended with a powerful discussion of the risks it took to help oneself.

Brian had the afterglow of an athlete achieving a personal best. There was a delicate balance between not taking credit for a client's progress or blame for a client's failures, but being able to appreciate when he had helped someone along in his or her journey. That feeling of being in the presence of healthy change was what kept him in the field.

Back in his office, he scrolled through a dozen e-mails and noticed one marked "Urgent" from Betty. "See me ASAP," it said.

He hurried down the hall, still feeling the post-group therapy buzz. True successes were few and far between; most of the time what he did was damage control. This client seemed to be heading toward breaking the cycle of poverty, abuse, and drug addiction. The power of group, a high-risk, high-gain intervention.

He stuck his head in Betty's office, debating whether to tell Pearlman what had happened. As a supervisor, most often she heard only about the problems and failures. She was on the phone, absorbed, and gestured for him to shut the door. Her somber expression made him wonder if another client had died.

"I'll call back later," she told whomever she was talking to. After hanging up, she took a deep breath. "Brian, this is one of the toughest things I've ever had to do. I need to suspend you pending an investigation."

"What?"

"Allegations of impropriety have been made. Ridiculous! I told the director so. But there's outside pressure."

"Who?"

"I don't know."

"Which client?"

"You know I can't tell you," Pearlman said, blinking back tears of anger as much as sadness. "This is bullshit." The administrative procedural rules were to protect client rights, with no legal right to confront the accuser or presumption of innocence until proven guilty. "I just remembered I have to go talk to Ginger out front for five minutes. And I don't have time to put away the files on my desk." She hurried out and shut the door behind her.

He hesitated momentarily, struggling with all the messages he had gotten over the years about the sanctity of confidentiality, but desperately eager for more information. He grabbed the personnel file with his name on it from the top of her pile.

The client making the allegations, Greg Burkett, alleged that in the third session Hanson threatened to give him an unfavorable legal evaluation unless he provided the counselor with drugs. He said that Brian was in financial trouble and wanted to work out a way to get money for financing a business. They allegedly even discussed dealing to addict clients within the agency. Burkett had gone to his parole officer with the allegations, as well as to the district attorney and the licensing board.

Hanson tried to recall if there was anything in their meetings that could in any way be construed as an attempt at blackmail and/or drug solicitation. He remembered Burkett's superficial sociopathic charm and narcissistic entitlement.

The counselor sat back in the chair with fingers steepled in front of his face. Betty entered slowly, saw that he was away from her desk, and then sat down.

"You know the drill," she said. "I have to ask for your keys and escort you from the site."

"I was hoping to finish the day, leave with minimal disruption," he said, desperately wanting to access the chart of the man who had made the allegations.

"I'll go check with the director. While you're waiting, I'm sure you won't look in my top right-hand drawer."

Moments after she left, he quickly opened the drawer, finding his accuser's chart. He jotted name, address, phone number, and Social Security number on a Post-it and tucked it in his pocket. Usually he searched charts for underlying psychological processes, the clinician's unstated feelings, the key psychological factors. With Burkett he searched for clues, connections, motivation. Burkett was divorced, six kids he never saw, and last worked as a laborer. His diagnoses included alcohol abuse and dysthymia, chronic low-level depression. There were several rule-outs including a Cluster B personality disorder, either narcissism, antisocial, or the combination of the two known as psychopathy or malignant narcissism.

After noisily clearing her throat outside the door, Betty reentered. "I'm afraid we're going to have to stick to procedure. It's nonsense but I can't be open to charges of favoritism."

"I understand."

He took his keys to the outer door, inner door, and chart room and slid them across the desk, feeling like an errant cop handing over his badge and gun. "How long until it's straightened out?" he asked.

"If it happened right now it wouldn't be soon enough."

Back at his house, Hanson debated whether he

should call Jeanie but ultimately decided against it. He was sitting at his desk and staring at the computer's screen saver as if he could find the answer there when the doorbell rang. The mail carrier, a perky woman who was new to the route, had him sign for a registered letter from the licensing board. He sliced it open and read the first line: "This is to inform you that your license is suspended pending investigation." He dropped it down on the small table in the hall and returned to staring at the screen saver.

Brian called Louise Parker, and got her voice mail. "Things are heating up. Give me a call." He trusted that she would recognize his voice and did not leave his name.

He sat, head resting in his hand like Rodin's *Thinker,* unable to move, the chilly fog of depression creeping in. Don't mean nothing, don't mean nothing. What was the point? Dorsey had won. Jeanie had betrayed him, his agency had abandoned him, what did he have left? He thought about times in the far distant past when he'd been suicidal. No, that wasn't an option. But a drink sounded real good. Just one before he headed out. They kept liquor in the basement for his wife's entertaining and as a sign to himself that he could handle temptation.

He was a loser. Always had been, always would be. A thousand-pound weight pinned him in the chair. The only way up would be through anger. At his father, at the war, at the American public on his return, at his addiction, his wife, and Dorsey. Thinking of Dorsey, he could turn up the heat into a white-hot rage.

The phone rang, startling him and providing a burst of energy.

"Hello."

"You know who this is?" He recognized Louise's voice and was about to say her name, then hesitated.

"Yes."

"Did my uncle ever tell you what I liked to do with him as a kid?"

He thought of sessions with Louie, fighting the creeping clouds that would blur his thinking. "He had lots of fond memories."

"You know the one with the tree in its name?"

Oaks Amusement Park. Built as part of the early-twentieth-century promotional schemes, it had been a major trolley attraction on the shores of the Willamette River. Louis had talked about trips there, riding the miniature train with her, watching her on the carousel, teaching her to ice-skate, how much she'd loved the shooting gallery.

"Yes."

"Be there in twenty minutes," she said. Then a click and she was gone.

Dorsey stood by the railing on the east side promenade, gazing at the Willamette River. The walkway had originally been touted as a waste of taxpayers' money but had turned into one of the most popular paths for bicyclists, joggers, Rollerbladers, and strolling lovers. The ambient white noise of the nearby I-5 freeway was a nuisance, but Dorsey and Wolf knew it made audio surveillance nearly impossible.

The deputy mayor imagined himself on the thirty-five-foot powerboat that was tooling by, a gray-haired man in a sailor's uniform content at the wheel, a couple of blondes on the rear deck.

A man on Rollerblades raced up and paused at the railing a few feet away. Dorsey was stunned to see that it was Wolf, hard to recognize, padded up and wearing a helmet, looking like a human bug with plastic exoskeleton.

"I never would have suspected you . . . ," Dorsey began.

"That's exactly why."

"It's about Brian Hanson," Dorsey said without preamble. "I want to take back my order to destroy his reputation and then kill him."

Dorsey found it hard to read Wolf, but it seemed like the killer was relieved.

"Speed up the schedule. I don't care how. Hit and run, fire in his house, fatal mugging. Kill him now."

"You're sure?"

"If you have time to set it up so it looks like a drug deal gone bad, that would be fine. But I want him gone within the next twenty-four hours."

"Rushing makes for sloppy work."

"I've gotten word that he's getting more dangerous. He's being investigated at work, has plans to make a drug deal, kill the witness against him, and flee the jurisdiction."

"If he does that he'll be out of the area anyway."

"He can't get away with that in our city."

"I don't think—"

"That's right, don't think. Just follow orders."

Wolf didn't say anything. He Rollerbladed away gracefully.

CHAPTER TWENTY

Oaks Amusement Park off-season had the eerie atmosphere of a horror movie set. Fallen leaves rustled as they blew about the grounds. Gaudily painted facades looked out on empty fairways. Hanson recalled the smell of generations of cotton candy, hot dogs, and machine oil from the rides he'd enjoyed as a teen. Memories of dates screaming on the roller coaster and snuggling up close in the haunted house. Now the shuttered rides and attractions seemed faded. Although there was little chance of an ambush at a site that had just been chosen, he walked warily down the causeway, head swiveling, ready to duck and dive.

The roller rink was the only open attraction. He heard wheels on polished wood and happy voices, muted by the walls of the building. The door opened as he approached. The sounds grew momentarily crisper as a mom with two preteen girls exited, talking animatedly to one another.

He entered the rink, looking around like a parent

trying to spot a child. A couple dozen skaters circled, ranging from septuagenarians to preschoolers, from artful ballerinas to stumbling oafs. But no Louise Parker.

After a few minutes, he went outside and scanned the surroundings. He saw a lone woman standing at the far side of the park, near the station for the miniature train. As he approached, he could see it was Louise. A couple beats after they had made eye contact and he was walking toward her, she turned and began walking away. He followed, thinking it was a silly precaution. The two of them were conspicuously alone in the area. She walked to the picnic area, past pockmarked wooden tables, on the graveled path. Then she stopped by a wooden lean-to shelter. From where Louise stood, she was visible only to the side open to the river.

"What's going on?" he asked. "Why the cloak-and-dagger rendezvous?"

"I received information about your finances. I wanted to give you a chance to explain yourself."

"What?"

"Your questionable investments. How they've fallen through."

"What?"

"That's what I said. Didn't believe it until I saw the papers. Why the Grand Cayman banking account?"

"What?"

"If you're not going to be truthful with me, Brian, I'm out of here."

"I honestly don't know what you're talking about."

"Suit yourself," she said. "By the way, in case you think you can pressure me into anything, I covered myself. You're registered as a confidential informant. Nothing more, nothing less."

"I thought you trusted me."

"I gave you the benefit of the doubt. Until proven otherwise. This is otherwise." She turned and walked briskly away.

Jeanie had, for as long as he remembered, taken care of their finances. Numbers were not Brian's forte—he'd barely made it through his statistics class in graduate school. For the first few years, they'd gone over the budget together, balancing checkbooks, verifying credit card receipts, deciding where to put their investments. He had agreed with her decisions and as time passed, left it more and more for her to do independently.

He went to the basement and looked in the small fridge where they kept the beer and a few bottles of wine. A drink would be so perfect. He could feel the tingle as it eased down his throat.

One minute at a time. He'd delay his drink until he checked out the papers.

Jeanie had an oak, cubbyholed rolltop desk in a nook off the kitchen that held their financial records. Locked. He pushed against the rolltop and got no response. It took only a butter knife and a few pounds of pressure, and the lock clicked. He felt guilty as the top slid open, but why should their finances be kept from him?

Brian studied the checkbook first, finding that until six months earlier, they had a surplus in checking. Since that date, they'd gone below the two-thousand-dollar minimum most months and had to pay a fee.

He inspected the credit card statements. As of six

months earlier, they owed twenty thousand dollars to Visa and MasterCard. He remembered Jeanie preaching to him that credit card companies were legal loan sharks and they should never accrue credit card debt. But the biggest surprise was that their mutual fund account, which had held more than three hundred thousand dollars six months earlier, was now empty.

Where had their money gone? There was the mortgage, Jeffrey's school payments, the rest of their usual expenses. What had happened six months earlier? Was there really a Grand Cayman account?

The outer door opened and he almost nervously closed the desk. Instead he gritted his teeth and waited for Jeanie to enter.

On the ride home, Jeanie had been considering confessing to Brian. But when she saw him standing at the pried-open desk, looking angry, she thought about her father's advice, "Never play from a defensive position. Attack, attack, attack."

"What're you doing?" she demanded.

"I got curious about our finances."

"You couldn't wait until I got home?"

"I didn't want to."

She inspected the latch and saw that nothing was broken. She roughly took the papers from his hand. "I would've answered any questions you had without the need for a two-bit burglary."

"I don't believe one can be accused of committing a burglary in one's own house."

"Perhaps one can't," she said sarcastically. "How about invading one's partner's privacy?"

"Maybe." His tone was flat, unemotional, his gaze unwavering. "But your privacy involves my savings too."

Jeanie felt a tightness in her throat. She recognized the repressed menace in her husband's expression. Usually when they quarreled he put up his therapist's shield, absorbing her emotions with calm passivity, reflecting back feelings in a way that was annoying but made it difficult to stay overwrought. Now she didn't know what he was going to do.

"How dare you not trust me?" she demanded.

"I did trust you. Until proven otherwise." He thought of Louise Parker's stinging words. "Our savings disappeared about six months ago and we even have credit card debt now. I don't recall major unforeseen expenses. What happened?"

"We became a silent partner in a project," she snapped. "Bought in with a ten-percent share. That's one-tenth of the possibilities."

"I know what ten percent equals," Brian said. "What project?"

"One of the senior partners told me. It was a bonus, an insider's tip. This was going to be our chance to make it big."

"Is doing this illegal?"

She glared at him patronizingly. "No, that's the stock market. The development has to be kept confidential or every dinky landlord in the way drives up his price. And the speculators come in. Once we're past the initial offering and it's public knowledge, then we can cash out."

"You should have told me about this risk you are taking with our money."

"You could have asked me about this at any time

and I would have told you. You never seemed to care. You never cared at all about finances. I wouldn't have had to go out on a limb if you had been making anywhere near a respectable salary all these years."

"My job won't be a problem. I was suspended today."

"What?"

"Pending an investigation. I'm sure what you've done with our finances will only add to the problem."

"Don't try and blame me," she said shrilly. "I know about the strip clubs you've been visiting, your obsession with your dead whore."

"How can you even say something like that!" He took a slow, calming breath that did little to abate his anger. "You still haven't told me where you put *our* money. What about a Grand Cayman account?" He stared at her silently, arms folded across his chest.

"The Grand Cayman account is only a few thousand dollars. One of the partners suggested we have it as a safety net, if money were to flow in that we didn't want to leave a paper trail on," she explained. "The rest is invested in a chance to be in on the city's development, to be rewarded for my hard work. To finally be an insider, not some low-rent loser wannabe."

He turned and strode away, afraid of what he might say or do.

Sitting in his parked car, Wolf watched the scene through Zeiss 8×40 binoculars. Hanson and his wife were quarreling but he had no idea over what. He had a small aerosol spray in his pocket with a lethal dose of cocaine.

The wife was a complication. But Wolf was pleased

as he saw the light go on in the bedroom and her packing with crisp, determined movements. Two large, matching black Skyway suitcases.

She came out the front door with the suitcases, tossed them into her car, and sped off on squealing tires. Wolf waited in his car, parked in the shadow of a towering elm. He sat on the passenger side, an old surveillance trick, so that if someone saw him it looked as if he were waiting for the driver. About an hour later, the light went on in the master bedroom on the second floor. Fifteen minutes later, it went out.

It was close to midnight by the time the neighborhood was quiet. Wolf stretched like a panther getting ready to prowl. He patted the spray and hefted the twelve-ounce blackjack he carried. A lock-pick gun in his right pocket, a Maglite with red cellophane over the bulb end, and a black ski mask rounded out his prowler essentials.

He switched off the dome light and eased out of the car, walking with a quick determination that would convey to anyone watching that he belonged, while also ensuring minimal open-ground exposure.

He had seen no signs of a guard dog at Hanson's. A quick scan of the perimeter showed no alarm tapes on windows, or eave-mounted siren, or alarm company sign. Wolf put the lock-pick gun against the Medeco cylinder, and the projecting probe rose a half inch, stroking the tumblers. He adjusted the thumb wheel and pulled the trigger again. Rewarded with a click, he tugged the door open and slipped in.

He flicked on the red-filtered flashlight, keeping it low. As he played the light around the room, he saw an open bottle of scotch and a glass on the counter. Good, it would make his job easier. He moved quietly toward the stairs.

Hanson lay in his bed, their bed, unable to sleep. Either he could accept and forgive, or let Jeanie's deception be the final reason to take his marriage off life support. Staring at the ceiling, he focused on his breathing, in and out, the moments of his life ticking by. He envied those who could drift off to sleep without pushing painful images to the side.

The sound. At first his conscious mind could not place it. The old house, like an old man, had its own sequence of grunts and groans. The windowpane on the first floor that rattled with the wind, the hum of the oil furnace as it kicked over, the whistle of air in the gaps in the wall. He thought momentarily it might be Jeanie, but after so many years together, he could recognize her tread as quickly as he could spot her cart in a supermarket full of shoppers. This was different. He was instantly awake.

A heavier tread. Slow, nearly silent. An intruder. His hand snaked under the bed to where he kept a Louisville Slugger. Gone. Periodically, Jeanie would vacuum the bedroom, moving the bat to the basement. An annoying quirk that he attributed to her unstated dismissal of his PTSD concerns. But as his hand explored, finding nothing, he saw it as her last act of hostility toward him. Or maybe she had set him up. Could the intruder have been sent by her? Or Dorsey? His mind raced as he lay still in the dark, like a kid hiding from the boogey man. His hand came up from under the bed and crawled around the night table. He grabbed the TV remote and hefted it. Not much of a weapon, but at least it was a hard surface.

He worked on slowing his breathing. He was moving into his zone, the place where the overstimulation of PTSD was a lifesaving reaction.

The stair tread creaked. He knew which one it was, three steps up from the bottom. A few moments of silence, then another creak, higher pitched. One of the stairs right near the top. He feigned sleep, breathing slowly. The fact that the intruder had come directly to the bedroom and not prowled looking for valuables made him more likely a predator than a thief. Most likely armed.

A figure silhouetted in the doorway. Hanson's hand tightened on the remote. Could he kick off the blanket and quickly untangle? Hanson felt strangely calm. Like on a night patrol when it was so dark all you could rely on was sound, smell, and touch. The splash of a water buffalo, the overripe tropical barnyard stench. The soft loam compressed beneath combat boots. The great relief of spotting the glisten on a trip wire before it sprung.

The figure raised his right hand. Hanson hit the button to turn on the TV with the highest volume. At the same time he pitched the remote at the intruder's head and rolled toward him.

He grabbed at the startled intruder's throat. The man let him grab, then seized control of four fingers, and snapped him backward in a hold that sent a jolt down Hanson's arm. Hanson swung a fast right chop at his assailant's neck. The man dodged, but the glancing blow forced him to let up pressure on the fingers. Hanson launched a kick that caught the attacker's shin and heard a pained grunt. He grabbed the attacker's left arm at the elbow and shoulder and slammed him to the ground.

Then the two men grappled on the floor, trying to gouge, grab, or strike. They were of nearly equal expertise, and despite determined efforts, neither could gain control.

"Okay, Brian, get off."

The voice. McFarlane.

Hanson rolled off, hands still in an on-guard position. McFarlane pulled off the ski mask. He had a slight grin, then a flinch as he moved his left arm. "I think you dislocated my shoulder. Not bad."

"What—what the hell are you doing here?" Hanson panted, massaging his fingers and checking that none were broken.

"I came to kill you."

CHAPTER TWENTY-ONE

A stunned Hanson asked, "Who? Why?"

Wincing, McFarlane stood up. "You know Tony Dorsey?"

"Deputy mayor. He's got something going on with Jeanie. I had a run-in with him at a dinner."

McFarlane nodded. "He wants you dead."

"You agreed to do it?" Fists clenched at his side, Hanson stood about three feet from his sponsor. The counselor was in a state of numbed confusion, trying to make sense out of his sponsor's double life.

"I agreed to do it. That doesn't mean I was going to do it. I've done wet work for him."

Hanson stared at McFarlane. "Wet work?"

"Bloody jobs."

"What's going on?"

"This'll be the last time you see me, so I owe you that. I must admit when I saw the liquor bottle and thought you had relapsed, I was thinking about hurting you some. But you didn't smell like a drunk. Or fight like one."

"Jeanie used it. I decided not to touch it."

"Good for you."

They had been shouting over the noise from the TV. Hanson shut it. The room went dark. Wolf headed downstairs and Hanson followed. They sat in the dining room, the lights off, the dim glow from the streetlight outside providing the only illumination.

"A while ago I did a briefing for the mayor on a case I had worked on where the scumbag was going to get off. A serial pedophile. The cop I had inherited the case from had screwed up on a warrant." McFarlane hesitated, like a paratrooper contemplating whether to take the big step. "Tony Dorsey was there. Invited me out to lunch. Said he had heard about me through some Agency people he knew. Asked if I was interested in covert ops work for him. Dorsey told me he had a mandate from city leaders to clean up the town. You ever hear of the Pareto effect?"

"No."

"Holds true for most systems. Twenty percent of the subjects will consume eighty percent of the resources. In this case, twenty percent of the criminals account for eighty percent of the serious crimes. My task was to get rid of that twenty percent. That small percentage spread their misery on the vast majority. Think of all the people who live in fear when a mugger terrorizes a neighborhood. Think of the economic effects when an area gets known as high crime. Think of the dozens, the hundreds, the thousands of victims. Think about their families, friends, neighbors. The FBI did a study of forty serial rapists. They had more than eight hundred victims. Any idea how much of a ripple effect one serious crime can have?"

"You were a contract killer?" Hanson persisted.

"That's kinda harsh. Never for much money. Talk about job satisfaction. Nothing like seeing a scumbag who had beaten the system when he realized his days of getting away with it were over. They were all bad guys. The worst of the worst. No loss to humanity. Dorsey told me he first got the idea when he heard the mayor's campaign slogan, 'One person can make a difference.' Kind of a double entendre in this case. One creep can make a difference in crime stats and quality of life. One person willing to take out the garbage can make an even bigger difference."

"What about killing Tammy?"

"No way," McFarlane said contemptuously. "Look how clumsy a job it was. Compare that to my work."

"What about Trixie?"

"Amateur hour. Whoever did that screwed up mightily," McFarlane said. "Do you really think you would've survived if I had been intent on killing you?"

Hanson heard the pride in McFarlane's voice, and it chilled him. "Who else did you kill?"

"There's probably fifteen less dirtbags in this town directly attributable to my missions. Another ten or so who were personally scared out of town. I suspect a few dozen more who moved on after getting the word that this is a bad place to be a shithead."

"Vigilante justice."

"Better than no justice at all."

"Dorsey gave you names and you killed them?"

"I'd get background info from him and check them

out, confirm what he had told me. I didn't want to leave a paper trail, so I'd run them through NCIC on someone else's computer or review files at the courthouse. See what I could pick up from on-the-job gossip. I wanted to be sure sure they were mega-scumbags, getting away with real evil." Wolf got a glass of water and sat back down at the table. "The number's been escalating. Dorsey's pushing too hard, too fast. Then he gave me your name with some bogus story. You know what they say about absolute power?" He took a sip of water.

"I'm curious, how were you supposed to kill me?" Hanson asked.

McFarlane pulled a small black aerosol tube labeled "Security Pepper Spray" out of his pocket. "Dorsey gave it to me. CIA surplus, I suspect. Cocaine derivative, causes a heart attack and quickly metabolizes."

"Why'd you come here? Why'd you go as far as you did?"

"I don't know if Dorsey has anyone else working for him. If I passed on this assignment, he'd be liable to farm it out. I didn't haul your sorry ass out of the gutter so many years ago, then watch you grow up into a respectable citizen, just to have a pissant politico with a grudge undo our good work."

McFarlane took a key out of his pocket. "This is to a service door on the southwest side of city hall. It's designed for emergency police access."

Hanson regarded him quizzically. "So?"

"Tony Dorsey is in his second-floor office right now boffing your wife." McFarlane rolled the spray canister toward Hanson. "He wanted me to use this on you."

Hanson held the tube in his hand, unable to speak.

"No one wants this conspiracy revealed." McFarlane handed him the key. "This'll get you in without going past the guard. No security cameras if you follow a direct route."

"How'd you get the key?"

"There are dozens of them in the department. Homeland Security whizbangs got the idea if the big kahunas at city hall were ever taken hostage it would allow SWAT to enter."

"But doesn't having these keys available decrease security?"

"In a way, yeah. But you think a hostage taker would have much trouble overpowering the rent-a-cop at the front desk?" McFarlane stood. "Good-bye, Brian. Wear disposable gloves. And take care of yourself."

"What're you going to do?"

"I'm a survivor," he said with a cheerful wink. "Don't worry about me."

McFarlane had taken a few steps toward the door when Hanson said, "Wait. You said you only killed the worst. Then who killed Tammy?"

"All I know is I didn't kill her," Wolf answered before walking out.

Hanson parked his car a couple of blocks from city hall and walked to the side doorway. Everything was as McFarlane had described it. He stood, hesitating, gazing up at the lit second-floor office. No one in sight on the street, though he had the feeling of being watched.

He slipped on the thin ski glove liners, slid the key in, and opened the door. Part of him didn't really believe he was doing it.

The long narrow corridor was dimly lit, the linoleum shiny, the pale blue walls bare of decoration. He glanced up and down, seeing no security cameras. The spray felt heavy in his pocket. At the end of the hall, he eased open the heavy metal door with his gloved hands. There was the distant sound of a vacuum running. He forced himself to slow his rapid, shallow breathing. This was no combat killing, self-defense, or crime of passion.

Then he was at the door to Dorsey's office. He pressed his ear against the oversize oak door and heard the low murmur of a man's voice. He tried the doorknob. Unlocked. He padded soundlessly across the thick, blue carpet.

There was a blindfolded naked woman, tied spread-eagled across the desk. Hanson recognized his wife's body. Dorsey, without pants, was standing next to the desk.

"You're going to hear greatest hits from the Tony Dorsey collection, sweet cheeks," Dorsey said. He swatted her butt and Jeanie flinched. "Past performers, right from the very spot you're on. Yes indeed, this office is wired for sound. Tricky Dick Nixon did it right." He took out a pair of Koss headphones and slipped them on her head. From a file cabinet drawer, the deputy mayor removed a half-dozen black leather items and several audiocassettes. He set a silver Bose boom box down on his desk and plugged the headphones into it. He popped one of the cassettes in.

Hanson fought the urge to scream his rage as he bounded over. His arm encircled Dorsey's neck. He put his lips near Dorsey's ear and whispered, "Who else besides McFarlane does your dirty work?"

Gasping for air, Dorsey quickly realized who it was. "Just him."

Hanson tightened. Dorsey's erection was gone and his body deflated.

"Just him," Dorsey squeaked. "That's all I could afford. Me and him, that's it."

"Where'd the money come from?"

"Siphoned off a few thousand here and there. He didn't want much. Believed in the cause."

"Which was?"

"Safety for the community." Dorsey had regained his breath and his confidence since Hanson hadn't killed him instantly. "Sorry about your wife, but it's a compliment. A sign of how great she is."

"Tony? What's going on?" Jeanie asked, unable to see or hear.

Hanson ignored her and asked Dorsey, "Why'd you kill Tammy?"

"I didn't. Wolf did."

"McFarlane?"

"Yeah."

Hanson tightened his hold. Dorsey struggled helplessly.

"I don't believe he did it," Hanson said.

"She was into more than you know. Blackmail," Dorsey gasped out in a low whisper.

"She tried to blackmail you?"

"Not *me*. She was greedy." Dorsey sagged, his eyes fluttering.

"I don't believe you." But Hanson let more air into Dorsey. After a few moments, the deputy mayor spoke again. "We can work this out. Your job, the money problems. Just the way I made it bad, I can fix it. Make it even better than before."

"What would you want?"

"Let me go. Take your wife with you. All debts canceled, grudges dropped."

Hanson had uncovered the spray with one hand. He held it, hesitating.

"Tony? Tony? What're you waiting for?" Jeanie asked.

Jeanie Hanson didn't know what was going on. Dorsey was into weirder scenes than she felt comfortable with, and she assumed the delay was deliberate. He had never seriously hurt her and she hoped he wasn't escalating. She thought she heard another male voice and had the feeling someone other than Tony was in the room. How many were there? What was going on?

The tape playing through the headphones was the sound of a woman pleading to be let go, then grunts of pain, and louder pleas. Dorsey's smug, smutty voice was rattling off specific sex acts, and vowing that they would try them all. She had a panicky feeling she had gotten deeper into his perversions than she wanted to be.

Hanson's grip on Dorsey's neck tightened again.

"Don't do it," Dorsey croaked. "You're not a killer. You won't get away with it. I can make life better for you. If you want to be head of your agency, it can happen."

"What about Trixie?"

"I don't know anything about her."

Hanson pressed Dorsey's rib cage where he had kicked the assailant at Trixie's apartment. Dorsey yelped.

"That's right where I got the guy at Trixie's place. You think I'd have a problem with hurting you some more?"

"That was self-defense." Hanson pressed hard on the broken ribs and Dorsey yowled. "Okay, okay. She was a loose cannon. Tammy had told her about the blackmail. She was making noises like she wanted to take it over. It would've killed two birds if you were at her place when she turned up dead. She died happy, I can tell you."

With each passing second, Dorsey was growing more assured that Hanson wouldn't kill him. "Untie your wife, take her home, and we pretend this never happened. I never talk to your wife again. You get a call tomorrow asking you to come back to the agency. Good therapists don't kill people."

From the headphones on his wife's head, a particularly loud scream could be heard. Jeanie responded by struggling against her bonds. "Tony? Stop. Let me loose."

Hanson popped the lid of the steel tube and sprayed up Dorsey's nose, holding his neck with the other hand.

"Wha . . . ," Dorsey said as his body stiffened. Hanson held him momentarily, then dropped him to the floor. He bucked a few times, then was still.

Hanson dragged Dorsey's body near the desk. Dorsey had a little white froth at the corner of his mouth, his sightless eyes wide open. Jeanie continued to buck violently against her bonds.

Brian grabbed Dorsey's tape collection and left the way he had come.

CHAPTER TWENTY-TWO

Jeanie Hanson had sensed that someone had joined Dorsey in the room. She feared being gang-raped but had been left untouched. Was it Tony's idea of a joke to leave her so vulnerable, to be discovered by a late-night cleaning crew or his secretary in the morning? That didn't make sense. He'd be brought down in any scandal. Maybe he was called away on an emergency. The tape had stopped and there'd been nothing but a low audio hiss.

"Tony? Let me go! Tony! Tony!" Was he standing there watching her thrash around?

Her wrists and ankles were bloody from her struggle against the bonds. Her voice had grown progressively louder but she hesitated to call for help, until her fear of uncertainty overcame her fear of humiliation.

"Tony! Dammit, stop this! Help! Help!" Her voice was hoarse from screaming when a janitor finally discovered her.

Moments later fingers removed the headphones,

peeled back the blindfold, and untied her wrists and ankles. She was draped in someone's trench coat.

Jeanie was soon at the center of a buzz of activity—uniform police, paramedics, detectives. She saw the body on the floor under the sheet and leaned woozily against a chair. A detective took her arm firmly and led her into a small, sparsely furnished office in the basement at City Hall.

"My name's Detective Quimby and I need to talk with you," the cop said. She huddled in a rolling secretarial chair. There were no windows and the harsh fluorescent light made her squint.

"How often has this sort of thing happened with you and the deputy mayor?" Quimby asked with no hint of shame or compassion. He stared at her neutrally, which she found more intimidating than if he had been posturing.

"We had been intimate a few times."

"Who else knew about it?" he asked quickly, barely giving her time to finish her sentence.

"No one as far as I know."

"I see from your statement that Brian Hanson is your husband?"

"You know him?"

"We've met. Did he know about the affair?"

"No."

"You answered that question without much thought, as if you anticipated it. You realize in a situation like this your husband is a prime suspect."

"Was Tony murdered?"

"At this point, it looks like a heart attack. Did you hear or see anything unusual?" he asked, continuing his staccato questioning.

"No."

"But of course your ears were covered."

"Correct."

"We didn't find any tapes in his office. There was a fairly elaborate recording set up and clearly he was going to play something for you. What was it?"

"I don't know."

Quimby studied Jeanie with skeptical eyes. "Have you called your husband?"

"No."

"Won't he worry about where you are?"

"Do you do marriage counseling as well as detective work?"

"Not many people could go through a night like you did and still have the juice to mouth off to a homicide investigator."

"If that is a compliment, thanks," she said warily. She glanced at her watch. It was close to 9 a.m. "When can I leave?"

"Will you go to work or go home?"

"Is it any of your business?"

"Until you're clear, we have the right to keep you under surveillance. We also could have a detective periodically stop by the bank and question you and your associates. Notifying us of your whereabouts would probably be enough, however, if you are cooperative."

Jeanie nodded wordlessly.

"This is a small, gossipy town," Quimby warned. "It's in everyone's best interest if the story of exactly what happened last night is not broadcast. No one would benefit. Do you understand?"

"Absolutely."

"Your one-word answers make me think you're someone who has been coached in how to testify."

"I've had a difficult night, detective," she said, with a hint of sarcasm. "What story is being put out?"

"That he was working late, alone, and was claimed by a heart attack. We want to be discrete for the sake of his wife and children, as well as the city in general. That's why I'm talking to you here informally rather than taking a statement at the Justice Center."

"Can I go now?" she asked, and he gestured to the door.

As she stood, Quimby said, "I'd advise you to keep your mouth shut."

"Believe me, detective, the sooner this is ancient history, the better."

When Jeanie entered the house, Brian was waiting for her downstairs, seated in the oversized chair, his face a mask she couldn't read.

"I wondered where you were last night," he said softly.

"What do you think?" she asked.

"With another man?"

"Yes."

"Is it serious?"

"Not anymore." She nearly smiled.

"That's nice." Brian Hanson stood slowly and Jeanie wondered if he was about to give her a comforting hug. He walked away from her without looking back.

Jeanie Hanson sat in the warm chair her husband had just vacated. She knew it was as close to him as she would ever be getting. Her mind shifted to the fall-out from Dorsey's death. Had Dorsey recorded their past encounters or anything from that evening?

Betty invited Brian into the office early the next morning. "The complaint against you has been dropped. I'd like you back as soon as possible."

He nodded. "I miss my clients. But I don't know. One of the PTSD symptoms I never felt was apathy. Until now."

"You want to talk about it?"

"Nah, I don't believe in that therapy crap," he said, with a smile that made it unclear whether he was kidding.

"You've beat up on yourself long enough. I don't think you've ever accepted that we're all flawed, Brian." He looked deep into her sad, wise eyes, and saw himself, accepted for who he was.

"You're really great," he said.

"Maybe," she said.

"Maybe," he responded, and they laughed.

"You never thought I was so wonderful when I was nagging you about paperwork," she said.

"I better go before we get maudlin."

"Scared of your feelings?" she winked.

"No, scared you'll remember a treatment plan I didn't do." As he stood, she came out from behind her desk and gave him a chaste but passionate hug.

Conversations stopped as Jeanie got into the elevator. There were hushed whispers when she entered the lunch room, sideways glances in the hall. Who had told? Dorsey's secretary? A crime scene technician?

One of the investigating officers? What tawdry story was going around? Could it be worse than the truth? She was too humiliated to look people in the eye. All the hours she had spent overtime reviewing deals, building relationships, shepherding difficult projects, would be forgotten.

She expected the summons to Lovejoy's office, the offer that she could resign or be fired. She looked out her office window and could see her reflection in the steel and glass of the Standard Insurance Building across the street. A small face in the big stack of boxes that made up the Wells Fargo low-rise skyscraper.

When the cut would come, they would show no mercy, wanting a swift, uncontested departure. She felt like a little girl, wishing she had her daddy to protect her and tell her what to do next.

Leslie Ford, the only other woman to have risen as high in the bank, knocked at Hanson's door. Jeanie expected her to be gloating over Hanson's imminent departure. Ford shut the door behind her and asked, "What's your secret?"

"What do you mean?"

"The old geezers are whispering to each other, trying to figure the best way to approach you."

"What do you mean?" Jeanie repeated.

"You're known as the woman who *schtupped* Tony Dorsey to death. You're a bigger fantasy item right now than the *Sports Illustrated* swimsuit cover girl."

"You're kidding."

"I'm not." Ford laughed, dropped down into a chair, and shook her long perfectly coiffed blond hair. "Apparently the head honchos have gotten calls from all over town. You're a celebrity, and people are dying to meet you." She chuckled at her own joke. "Major players, you'd know the names. Quite an achievement. I wouldn't mind knowing your secrets myself. I've got a sixty-year-old husband I wouldn't mind trading in for two thirty-year-olds."

"You're wicked," Hanson said with a big smile.

"As if you're one to talk."

Hanson sat on a park bench where he'd once met with McFarlane, looking through *The Oregonian*'s apartments classified ads, trying to decide what neighborhood he could move to. No place seemed appealing, no area desirable. He shifted to the Metro section. The front page had a profile of Tony Dorsey's replacement, a stocky woman with a hard set to her jaw who boasted twenty years of experience in city government. The article included platitudes from her and complimentary remarks from other officials.

He noticed a small article:

HERO COP DISAPPEARS IN PACIFIC
A veteran Portland detective's boat was found abandoned near the mouth of the Columbia River, the Coast Guard said yesterday.

"Robert McFarlane is missing and presumed drowned," said Coast Guard spokesperson Judy Watson. She said that preliminary indications showed no signs of foul play or suicide. "These are treacherous waters. We've had numerous people lean over the side of their boats, fall in, and drown."

There were ten-foot waves yesterday, Watson said, noting that the Coast Guard had a half-

*dozen rescues. "The search will continue today,
although we are not optimistic."*

*McFarlane, 58, was a decorated detective who
had worked homicide, robbery, vice, and several
other demanding assignments during his 25
years with the Portland Police Bureau. He had
shot and killed a bank robber in 1983, and an
alleged rapist who attacked him with a knife in
1997. He had earned three medals for bravery
for those incidents, as well as for a 1979 incident in which he ran into a burning North Portland building to rescue a mother and her child.
His only family is a sister in Ohio who he had
not seen in a dozen years, friends said.*

*Colleagues described him as somewhat of a
loner, and noted that he was active in local 12-
Step communities. Chief Forester described his
disappearance as a "tragic loss for the Bureau
and the city."*

Hanson reread the article twice, muttering, "Sonofabitch, sonofabitch." McFarlane was gone. Was he
really dead, or had he used the cash from Dorsey and
his covert skills to disappear? Hanson held his head in
his hands and stifled a sob. His sponsor. The man who
had saved his life. Hanson wished he could see Mc-
Farlane one more time, to say good-bye.

Hanson returned to his empty house. Jeanie had already begun removing her items. He sat in his favorite chair, brooding. McFarlane was gone and his
original dilemma remained—who had killed Tammy?
What did he know? That the man she went to Vic's
bar with was recognizable, needing to disguise him-

self with a ZZ Top beard. He was wealthy enough to afford the Eagleton condos and, according to what Tammy had told her father, well-connected enough to clear up her legal problems. Dorsey? The deputy mayor seemed to have little problem with confessing to killing Trixie. With his arrogant narcissism and fear for his life, he probably would have admitted Tammy's murder if he'd done it. A rich attorney? But easily recognizable?

Hanson dug out the box of three dozen tapes from Dorsey's office. He slipped one into the Panasonic cassette deck in the entertainment center. He listened to interminable hours of municipal business. Several of the tapes were recordings of Dorsey's sessions with women, including a couple with Jeanie. He fast-forwarded through them.

After fourteen hours of nearly nonstop listening, he found what he wanted.

Mayor Robinson's receptionist relayed word that a Brian Hanson wanted to talk with him. She expected the mayor to tell her to have him write a letter or arrange for Hanson to meet with a low-level functionary to see if there was a rudimentary constituent service that could appease him.

"I'll see him," Robinson said, pacing the room. "Send him in."

As Hanson entered, Robinson extended his hand warmly. Hanson ignored the gesture. The mayor knew something was desperately wrong. Normal citizens were eager for the handshake, the contact with the leader. Preserved in countless photographs.

"You know my wife was with your deputy mayor when he died."

The mayor nodded. "Very sad. Embarrassing for this whole administration, as well as your wife and his family. I'm sorry for any grief it caused." He was casually perched on the edge of his desk, friendly but appropriately somber.

"Thanks," Brian said flatly.

"I hate to rush you after all you've been through, but I must make this brief. I've got a midcounty community meeting in less than a half hour." There was a tiny bead of sweat on his upper lip.

"I know about Tammy," Hanson said bluntly.

The mayor was about to say "Tammy, who?" then sighed deeply, walked to his chair, and sagged like he'd just finished running a marathon. "I thought of what I was going to say if this moment came." Another sigh. "But I'm too tired. I've had nightmares every night."

"Tell me what happened." Hanson had instinctively shifted into a supportive therapy voice.

"I had an affair with her. Stupid, but that sort of thing happens. I was introduced to her by Tony at a one-hundred-dollar-a-plate dinner. He said she was a big admirer. In thinking back, I believe he was setting me up. I knew about Tony's problem with women. Had talked with him about it. I think he was trying to point out my own vulnerability." The mayor sighed again. "The affair lasted only a few weeks. I did stupid things, going out to bars with her, wearing a disguise. The risk was exciting. God, I was such an idiot. Then she began pressuring me for favors, money. After the first few thousand I saw where it was going. A never-ending bleed."

"Tell me more about what happened," Hanson encouraged.

"I decided I could scare her off, wave the gun around, show her I was serious. I should have known she was tougher than me. She grabbed the gun and it went off." He slumped lower in his chair. "One person can make a difference," he said with a snort. "My wife keeps asking what's wrong. I tell her to leave me alone. She's a fine woman, deserves better than a scandal. With a few pounds of pressure on that trigger, I undid a life's worth of good. I don't know if you've ever had that kind of moment, where you've inexplicably, inexcusably, irrevocably fucked up and know your life will never be the same." The mayor didn't wait for an answer. "I called Tony for help. The cover-up was successful, though Tony got more controlling.

"I'm telling you this because you're a counselor, can keep things confidential. My administration is helping people live better lives. I won't let my personal indiscretion undo the benefits of what we have done. You can't tell anyone. If you do, I will deny it. And use the full force of my position to make your life miserable."

Hanson took out a cassette. "Did you know Tony had his office wired for sound? Do you recall when you told him to take care of it, any way he had to?"

"That's out of context. She was a blackmailer." The mayor could feel his career imploding. "How did you get the tape?"

Hanson shrugged. "Not important."

"Your wife's reputation will be ruined. You'll be subpoenaed, investigated."

"My wife's reputation?" Hanson snorted. "Why would you think I give a damn about that? As far as my being investigated, you are aware of his taping system? You having a sex freak as your ranking aide won't help your case."

"What do you want?"

"Call the DA and say you're feeling guilty. Confess, and let a jury decide how much responsibility you have for waving a loaded gun around and what your intentions were. The tape of you and Dorsey talking about Tammy's death is never made public."

"You'll destroy it?"

"Maybe."

For several days, Hanson had been going to the Vietnam Veteran's Living Memorial, tucked into a natural amphitheater in the hillside at Hoyt Arboretum. The low black marble walls, dated from 1959 to 1972, showed the steady increase, and then final decrease, in names of the dead. He spent hours reading the nearly eight hundred names and the recitation of concurrent events that had been going on as young soldiers were dying.

He was only vaguely aware of the people who came and went as he followed the circuitous, sloping route, looking for and finding names that he knew, and the tens of thousands that he didn't. A few other visitors tried to engage him—he was polite but perfunctory in his response.

"Hey, Mister."

The kid, a scruffy freckled preteen on a skateboard, rolled up and demanded attention. Hanson figured him for a panhandler and was set to shoo him away.

"A guy told me to give you this."

"What guy?"

The kid turned to point, then said, "He was over there. Gave me ten bucks, so here it is." He handed Hanson a folded sheet of lined notebook paper with neat handwriting on it:

"Saw the news about the mayor's confession and suspect you had a hand in it, you persistent sonofabitch. You never did know when to stand down. Remember there's no problem that a drink or a drug can't make worse. And the next time you sit on the park bench, have a popcorn and think of me.'"

"Who was he? What did he look like?" Hanson asked urgently, scanning the park for a familiar face. But the kid was already on his skateboard and speeding down the hill.

McFarlane. He had survived, was still watching. The connection had not been broken. They shared a destiny. He was a survivor too.

Hanson walked to the memorial entrance and stared at the marble block with the words, "So long as we are not forgotten we do not die. And thus this garden is a place of life." He felt like saluting the stone but decided that was too corny. He bobbed his head and walked out into the park. A few dozen yards from the memorial, he took out his cell phone, and dialed Louise Parker.

"Uh, I guess I won't be seeing you any more," he said awkwardly.

"I guess so."

He tried to assess what her subdued tone meant. Was she too busy to talk? Sad that he was bothering her? Or did he dare hope she didn't want it to be the end of their relationship. "I've separated from my wife."

"Sorry to hear that."

"Really?"

"Well, sorry for you," she said.

"Don't be, it's for the best. A long time overdue. Uh, I was wondering, maybe, would you like to have dinner some time?"

"I'd like that."

He bounced on the balls of his feet, glad she couldn't see. A passerby looked at him and he grinned. "Friday, around 7 p.m.?"

They agreed to meet at Jake's restaurant. But before he called there for a reservation, he dialed a familiar number. He got voice mail.

"Hey, Betty, it's Brian. I'm ready to come back now."

THE WHITE TOWER

DOROTHY JOHNSTON

It's a mother's nightmare come true. Moira Howley's son, Niall, has been found dead at the base of a communications tower. While the authorities are content to consider it a suicide, Moira won't accept that. She knows only another mother could understand....

Crime consultant Sandra Mahoney is Moira's only hope. While juggling her own daughter, a lover, and an annoying ex-husband, Sandra will travel halfway around the world in search of the truth—a truth hidden by a web of deceit, manipulation...and murder.

ISBN 10: 0-8439-5936-3
ISBN 13: 978-0-8439-5936-9 $6.99 US/$8.99 CAN

To order a book or to request a catalog call:
1-800-481-9191
This book is also available at your local bookstore, or you can check out our Web site **www.dorchesterpub.com** where you can look up your favorite authors, read excerpts, or glance at our discussion forum to see what people have to say about your favorite books.

SWEETIE'S DIAMONDS

RAYMOND BENSON

Diane Boston is a suburban mom with a secret. As her son discovered when he found an unmarked videotape, Diane had a former life as Lucy Luv, star of hardcore adult films. Somehow word of Diane's past has hit the streets, and now all hell has broken loose. Sure, the high school where Diane teaches is upset, but that's the least of her worries. It seems that when Lucy Luv mysteriously disappeared, she took a cache of stolen diamonds with her. And a West Coast porn czar with strong mob ties wants them back. With interest.

ISBN 10: 0-8439-5859-6
ISBN 13: 978-0-8439-5859-1 $6.99 US/$8.99 CAN